BERW

D1135620

___

___

Tic
This
stam
If
pr

A View of the Island

That the dead might become part of the debris left behind in a devastated world, and continue to exist visibly and audibly with the living, was one of the embarrassing contingencies not foreseen either by the scientists or by the members of Roderick Fernay's house-party in the Western Highlands. That well-known television personality had decided, in the event of an atomic war, that if he could not survive he would spend his last days with a group of congenial friends, and die in as civilised a manner as possible. Circumstances conspire to prevent this.

In this post-atomic fairy-tale Jean Ross has departed from her usual vein. Under a gay façade she handles all the deeper implications of the situation, particularly the religious factions, with subtlety and compassion.

A VIEW
OF THE ISLAND

A Post-Atomic Fairy Tale

— 888 —

Jean Ross

HUTCHINSON OF LONDON

HUTCHINSON & CO (*Publishers*) LTD
178–202 Great Portland Street, London, W.1

London Melbourne Sydney
Auckland Bombay Toronto
Johannesburg New York

★

First published 1965

With grateful thanks to Mr Donald MacAulay
of Aboyne for his help with the Gaelic

I

RODERICK FERNAY, the well-known television personality and writer, had made plans, in the event of a third world war, to retreat with a select group of friends to his house in a remote part of the Western Highlands. He did not feel he would be saved, but he wished his death to be quiet and decent.

When, therefore, a small atomic bomb was exploded (by mistake it was believed) close to the Zeeland Islands, and Europe was in a ferment, he was not unprepared.

No sooner did they hear that Roderick was leaving London, than a number of persons, who could not in the strictest sense have any claim on him, began to pester him with requests to be allowed to come with him.

The Government's final instructions (before retiring to prearranged deep shelters in the country) had been of such a contrary nature that few knew what to do for the best, and the whole population was on the move. The trouble seemed to be that no place could be counted safer than any other—even the deserts of Alaska and Mongolia were not remote from the dangers of radiation. The plane that dropped the bomb was never identified; it was as easy to say that it was sent from France or the U.S.A. as that Russia was responsible.

Nobody trusted their allies, and hideous rumours were about.

The idea was current that, although it was never safe in any circumstances to remain at home, one would be best off in the house of a friend; especially if that friend were based four or five hundred miles away, in an isolated situation.

On this particular July morning, Roderick and his secretary Dick Bolton were standing in the midst of their belongings in

Mr Fernay's flat near Victoria. For two years Roderick had been denuding his home, in secrecy, in anticipation of just such an event. Little of any value was now left. A last pantechnicon had taken a few remaining items to Achnabasalt six months before, on the advice of his favourite clairvoyante, Mrs Mottie, who was also his charwoman.

'Thank heaven we shall be a community of kindred souls,' Roderick reflected, pouring whisky into two plastic mugs. He was a large man, of an optimistic, yet occasionally belligerent disposition; he expected much of his friends. 'The great thing, at a time like this, is to have made one's plans well in advance, and to choose one's companions carefully. If one is to be in close contact with people, perhaps for weeks at a time, with death in the offing, one must avoid irritating personalities like the plague. The women are the risk—they are so personal and emotional. I wish we could have done without them. If it were not that I am so devoted to Julia, I would never have consented to her coming for one instant; and if I had realised that she would refuse to be parted from her aunt!—— Please help me not to think of the wretched Mrs Dolman!'

'Maggie Dolman was one of the most famous actresses of her time,' Dick Bolton reminded his employer. He was a small man with large, sorrowful eyes and an anxious expression.

'That has little to do with her suitability for inclusion in a journey to doom,' Roderick pointed out. 'She has religious mania; she recites and reads aloud; it will send me out of my mind!'

'You know that the doctor said you were not to upset yourself,' Dick admonished him. 'You had better take one of your tablets.'

'Where are my tablets? Don't say you have lost them!'

'They are in your coat pocket, where you put them after breakfast.'

Roderick found them, took one, and swallowed it. 'If there is any coffee left, please make some,' he requested in a quieter tone, sitting down and covering his face with his hands, in a moment of weakness which his public would have found astonishing. 'You are a good fellow, Dick, I don't know what in God's name I would do without you! When I think how you kept all those dreadful people at bay, when they kept ringing up, writing and calling at all hours, with requests for help——'

'It is all over now. Do not think of it any more!' Dick called from the kitchen, where he was heating the coffee over a feeble flicker of gas. 'We shall be gone in half an hour, and nobody will trouble you again.'

He brought in the coffee; there was silence as they drank, then: 'I am not a hard-hearted person, am I?' Mr Fernay demanded.

'Certainly not.'

'It worries me a great deal not to be able to help all my friends. You will not believe that!'

'Indeed I do.'

'What is the time?'

'A quarter past two.'

'We ought to have left here half an hour ago!' exclaimed Mr Fernay, in the greatest displeasure. 'We shall be late for our appointment with Julia—why didn't you tell me it was so late?'

'I didn't know, chum, that is why.'

'I don't like it when you call me chum; it is not a good sign, is it?'

'No, it is not,' replied Dick, in a high and trembling voice.

'The tension of this past week, and having to keep a cheerful face before the cameras, has been frightful,' Roderick confessed, 'I will tell you now—I could not have gone on a day longer! All these riots in the city, and that dreadful Dan Bellerophon and his Fascist mob overrunning everywhere, and defeating the police, has quite unnerved me!'

He did not get the sympathetic response he had learned to expect; a look at his secretary confirmed his fears; one of Dick Bolton's nerve-storms was imminent, and he could not have chosen a worse moment. The strain of coping with modern life, quite without atomic bombs, had defeated poor Dick some years before—— After two breakdowns, and a course of psycho-analysis, he had emerged, as from a mangle; only the Catholic Church and Roderick Fernay had saved his reason.

'All London is at a standstill!' he announced, in a voice of terror. 'The prevailing winds have blown the fall-out over us already—— We are contaminated! Nothing now can save us!'

'We are leaving this flat at once!' Roderick told him. 'And you are going to help take the luggage down! We must find a taxi!'

Mr Bolton began to cry. 'There are no taxis!'

7

'Nonsense! I saw several this morning, laden with luggage and making for one of the Northern termini! I am sick of this nonsense! We must have missed half a dozen while you have been carrying on like a lunatic!'

The sound of his friend's voice, raised in such justified indignation, had the effect of galvanising Dick into a frenzy of activity. He loaded himself with three bags, and staggered down the stairs, leaving Mr Fernay to lock the flat and follow him. At the door he hesitated, for since the disappearance of the police the pavements had become the hunting ground of desperate people of all kinds, who set upon everyone in decent clothing, robbing them and leaving them practically naked. A roar from his employer drove him forward.

Victoria Street was deserted, all offices closed. The pavement, Roderick noticed in disgust, was filthy; all cleansing systems had broken down. An ancient bi-plane passed overhead, a Tiger Moth from a forgotten era. It passed slowly across a parchment sky, trailing a banner with the scarlet words: 'FORSAKE THE CITIES OF THE PLAIN.' Someone touched Dick's elbow. He cried out; the knife's thrust would come now. He covered his face, hoping it would be swiftly and efficiently accomplished.

'I beg you to help me!'

Dick lowered his hands. The individual who had spoken was of so frail and wretched an appearance that it was certain he must fail in anything he set out to do, even if murder was his intention.

He told them, in a faint voice, that his name was the Reverend Hector Beek, and that he had been the victim of a savage attack, whilst returning from a visit of mercy to a dying parishioner. His clothes had been taken; he was left in his woollen underwear, over which he had wrapped a bath-towel like a sarong, for the sake of decency.

It was a plausible and ingenious story, Roderick considered, but to call himself a clergyman was too obvious an embellishment.

'We had quite given up expecting you,' Julia Miles told them, in her rapid slurred voice. She was a tall woman with a long neck and a quantity of ash-grey hair. She had been a beauty, Roderick told everyone, and retained her hold on him by her admiration of him, her air of helplessness, and her large, swimming eyes.

'We kept trying to telephone, but the line was quite, quite dead,' Mrs Dolman announced. She had a commanding, opulent presence, and wore a black wig, slightly aslant. 'They are looking utter-ly ex-hausted,' she continued, in her voice of tragedy. 'They must have a drink at once, even before they embark on the history of the adventures which have delayed them—— But who is this I see? It cannot be—— It is Mr Beek! Dear, dear Mr Beek, what has happened to you? Oh, he has fainted! Help him!'

In the confusion which followed, during which Mr Beek was assisted into a back room, attended by Julia, Roderick was heard to say: 'So the fellow is really a clergyman, and that is his name?'

'That is so,' Mrs Dolman sighed. 'I have known him for a number of years. He is the priest in charge of a church on the unfashionable side of Pimlico. He has been a sad trial to his Bishop, for he has completely lost faith in the thirty-nine articles and the Divinity of Christ. He goes about telling people that Jesus died in vain, for the world is more corrupt than it ever was. Whilst one sympathises deeply—nobody has had more Doubts than I—one can see it would never do for a Parish Priest, even if it were in the diocese of Woolwich.'

Mrs Dolman had insisted on serving tea, for without it neither of the ladies would have felt able to begin their journey; the meal had, for Roderick, a sharp unreality—to drink the best Lapsang Soo-Chong out of Dresden cups, poured from the spout of a Queen Anne silver tea-pot; to eat lacy slices of bread, and faintly rancid butter, in a blue and white drawing-room, surrounded by Buhl cabinets, Persian rugs, and paintings by Fragonard, seemed to him a very unlikely introduction to the hazards of the journey they were about to begin.

The traverse of London had been bad enough.

'You must tell us *everything*!' Julia ordered him, holding the copper kettle over the open fire, to bring it once more to the boil.

She presented a pastoral picture in a blue dress, frilled at the neck and sleeves, which displayed her graceful arms and her white skin to advantage. 'Oh what a peaceful person you are, Julia!' cried Dick, flinging himself down on the hearthrug

9

beside her. 'How thankful I am to be here! I wish we need never go a step further—how can you bear to leave all your wonderful treasures, knowing they may be looted, or turned to dust!'

'They mean nothing any more!' cried Julia, in the airy fashion of someone who, having been the mistress of a very rich man for a number of years, and inheriting all his possessions, cannot cling to what she has never truly appreciated. 'But you have one of your bad headaches, poor boy, I can see that!'

She took his cup from him.

'Lie down on the sofa, and, as soon as I have filled the tea-pot, I will stroke your head,' she ordered.

'There is no time for that!' Roderick told her. 'None of you seem to realise how far we have to go, and how late it is, in every sense! I am exceedingly tired and wrought-up myself, *but I do not give in to it!*'

'So you took lifts in three cars,' Mrs Dolman distracted him, holding out her cup to be refilled. 'Were there no taxis?'

'None whatsoever,' Dick assured her. 'The first lift was in a hearse.' He lay down on an Empire sofa, and closed his eyes.

'The last—as I was beginning to tell you—was a dust cart, returning to the depôt,' Roderick interrupted. It was, after all, his story.

Mrs Dolman raised the decanter. As in a ritual, she laced each cup with spirits. Then she sat back, listening with apparent devotion to Roderick's adventures, caressing the jade amulet she wore on a silver chain at her bosom. At the first pause, however, she leaned forward: 'Roderick, dear, I have a great favour to ask of you——'

'No, Maggie; positively not!' Roderick cut her short, with decision. 'I know what you are about to ask—that we take your Mr Beek with us. But it is impossible—there is no room in the car—— It will be crowded, as it is, with four of us and the luggage. Besides, I have had to refuse old friends, and he is practically a stranger!' The burden of guilt she laid upon him in forcing him to this necessary refusal overcame him. 'He practically forced himself upon us!' he reminded her.

'He is old and ill,' Maggie Dolman replied inexorably. 'Spiritually he is a Great Soul, who has gone through Much Tribulation. If nobody cares for him, he will perish, and that would be a Loss, especially at this Time.'

The habit Mrs Dolman had of seeming to speak in capital letters increased Roderick's irritation. 'If, as you say, he is so exceptional I am sure the Almighty will look after him.'

'How can you be so flippant?' demanded Mrs Dolman. 'You cannot surely be prepared to Dump him as we go?'

'A-aah!' cried Mr Fernay in a rage.

'—When he has been Divinely led to us——'

'Hush, do!' the lovely Julia interceded. 'There is no need to upset yourselves. I have arranged everything. When Mr Beek is rested, he is to go to our dear Mrs Mottie; she will bring him with her. I have given him money for the journey, a few biscuits, and a suit of Jack's. It is a little large, but made of the finest material.'

This having been arranged (although not to Mr Fernay's satisfaction) Dick was ordered to fetch Julia's car to the door. On the appearance of the silver Rolls-Royce, with the wickerwork sedan body, everyone rushed to pile their luggage into the boot at once.

'What is this!' cried Roderick, who had appointed himself leader of the expedition. 'You cannot possibly take all these boxes with you, ladies! One suitcase each—that is all I can allow! We must leave room for the extra cans of petrol!'

'How can I choose *one*?' demanded Mrs Dolman, in the accents of Clytemnestra. 'I forget what I have put in any of them!'

'We can waste no more time!' Roderick told her severely. He seized two cases at random from the towering pile in the door-way, and tossed them into the car. At last everyone was stowed inside in the tonneau; as the great car drew away from the gate, Mr Beek could be seen waving, the borrowed suit over his arm. Great golden streaks of evening light striped them as they passed under the plane trees of the Hampstead avenues, and emerged into the Finchley Road.

'To the North!' Roderick ordered, and northwards they glided.

2

RODERICK had given Mrs Mottie, his mediumistic charlady, her fare to Scotland; this was wasted, as no more trains were running.

Julia and Dick Bolton had been careful to keep this news from Roderick, who would have been in a frenzy had he known. In secret they had made other, last-minute arrangements.

An esoteric body, calling themselves the Heavenly Brethren, had chartered a bus to take some of them to Scotland. It was to start at a certain hour from a side street not far from Euston Station. This vehicle was heavily reserved for the elect; at the last moment, however, owing to illness, or frailty, three members had been unable to make the journey. Through the influence of Mrs Dolman, who was well known to the Brethren, these places were taken by Mrs Mottie, and two protégés without whom she refused to travel.

It was Maggie Dolman's suggestion that the old Hydro Hotel at Strumph, three miles from Roderick's home in Wester Ross, would be an ideal refuge for the Chosen Few. Most of the remote and more beautiful parts of Britain had been bespoken well in advance for just such an eventuality, by those religious minorities who knew, without doubt, that they were the Remnant, spoken of in Matthew, Chapter twenty-four, who were to inherit the earth. These arrangements had been made without consulting Roderick.

'He can be so prejudiced,' Mrs Dolman said.

She had given strict instructions to Mrs Mottie. She must walk to Euston from Victoria by the most shadowy byways, avoiding notice.

These precautions were most necessary; Mrs Mottie's companions were coloured people, a father and son, who had been her lodgers. Dan Bellerophon had vowed that only the pure white Aryan races should survive.

And now they were further hampered by Mr Beek's frailty, which slowed their progress. They had had some narrow escapes (crossing Tottenham Court Road, it was necessary to hide Odysseus Jackson under a newspaper, and smother his son Nyeri in a coat), but at last they arrived in the cul-de-sac. Here, as though by a miracle, the bus awaited them; they were the first arrivals, not even the driver was present. They bestowed themselves and their cardboard boxes; Mrs Mottie removed her shoes from her aching feet, and Mr Beek took out his pocket bible, searching endlessly for truth.

'You won't find God in the Bible, dear,' Mrs Mottie told him.

'You will not find God,' Odysseus said. His wife had been killed in the riots a week before; he had given up Christianity.

'God will find you, though,' Mrs Mottie told them, giving the boy a sugared almond. Outside it had begun to rain, the cobbles in the yard shone, and the child fell asleep against her shoulder.

The news that the Heavenly Brethren had taken over the Hydro at Strumph disgusted two guests of Roderick's who had arrived at Achnabasalt in advance of their host.

These were Doctor Sydney Monro, a self-confessed alcoholic, and his friend and patient, the Honourable Nigel Fidgeon. Nigel had been a wealthy invalid since, at the age of twenty-three, an attack of polio had robbed him of the movement of his legs. At forty-five it was his tragedy to appear twice as attractive as before. Women found his condition romantic and his riches irresistible. They pursued him remorselessly.

Sydney, who was averse to effort, was thankful to have accepted the rôle of personal physician and companion to his friend. He had not been a success as a National Health Practitioner. Not only was he seldom sober, but in his search for perfection he made advances to most of his women patients.

He was secretly disappointed that there were to be no young girls in the house-party. He dreamed of finding a maiden in distress on the beach, and bringing her to the house, as though by accident.

'We cannot expect the Brethren to bring any life to the place,' he complained. 'From all I hear, the youngest is about fifty; they wear hand-woven djibbahs, and live on raw cauliflower.'

'I have a shrewd suspicion that Mrs Dolman has engineered this without telling Roderick; he would never have approved,' Mr Fidgeon agreed. 'I said to him from the first it was a mistake to let her come; she will be holding prayer meetings after breakfast, and readings in the garden. I warned him not to invite any women besides Mrs Mottie.'

'Perhaps we should make plans to move on,' he continued, after a pause, 'before any unpleasantness happens.'

'People are unable to move from place to place any longer. There is no more petrol,' the doctor pointed out. The thought of being confined under such disagreeable circumstances made the Honourable Nigel's back feel more than usually painful; he asked to have his wheelchair adjusted until he was lying almost supine.

In order to distract him, the doctor began to tell him of some gossip he had heard while down in the village. A number of mysterious craft had been noticed in the lee of the island of Ebora, which had been deserted for thirty years.

'They say that for months building has been going on, but nobody is allowed to land there. They are turned away by the Navy,' the doctor said. They discussed this phenomenon for a little, then, as Nigel continued in his depression, the doctor helped him to his room, and to bed.

As soon as he had left his patient, Sydney felt younger and more vital. He helped himself to a large glass of Roderick's whisky, then decided to take a walk on the shore.

It was a warm, delightful evening, the sun had not yet set. He ran quickly across the lawn from the white-harled house, and down the rocky steps to the scimitar-shaped bay of white sand. He could see the mysterious green island, veiled in the liquid evening air, deserted of the least movement, and divided from the shore by the blue water, spotted with black rocks.

'I suppose things must get worse,' he said aloud, although in his present state of euphoria he found it hard to believe. He began to sing an aria from *La Bohème*.

He was a large, loosely framed man in his late thirties; a skin complaint prevented his shaving regularly and gave him a rakish look. He had a reddish colouring and walked with a swing to his arms.

The beach was private property; the bay next to it had been declared (on the doctor's recommendation) to be a contaminated area because of some doubtful, radio-active wreckage which had been washed ashore—it had formerly been a camping ground. Sydney Monro was therefore very surprised to see two girls, arm in arm, walking through the gentle, salty foam at the water's edge, almost as though his thoughts had conjured them. They were dressed alike in cotton trousers and fishermen's jerseys.

He became pleasantly excited; he hurried quickly towards them. 'This is private property, you know,' he addressed them in a challenging yet admiring tone.

The dark girl replied in a strong Glasgow accent. 'There is no more private property. All such nonsense has been swept away.'

The thin fair girl stood with her face turned to the sea, and would not let him see her face.

'That's rubbish, you know.' Sydney stood over the girls with a devouring look, his hands in his pockets. 'The fact that an atomic bomb has fallen in Europe doesn't make for anarchy in Britain.'

'What do you call the present state of affairs, then?' the dark girl demanded, her eyes flashing. She entered into a loud argument in which the words government and polis entered; he concentrated his will on making the fair girl turn round.

'We have parked our caravan over there, and there we intend to remain, until someone turns us out by force! And let me tell you, mister—we are just the advance party. Is that not so, Sylvia?'

He was relieved that the nymph-like girl had so sensible and pretty a name. He had been afraid she might have answered to Sandra, Moira, or Shirley. He waited for her to answer so that he might reassure himself that she was as attractive as he expected.

'The advance guard of what?' he asked absently.

'Och—just you wait!' the dark girl threatened.

'I told you you shouldn't, Beattie,' the fair Sylvia spoke at last, without bothering to turn her head. 'I told you it would mean trouble. Miles and miles—hundreds of miles we've come—and every time we've stopped, it's been "Move on! Move on!" "You can't stop here!" And now at last we've come to the ocean——— I suppose you want us to move into the ocean?' she demanded, turning on the doctor. 'Right into the sea until we drown ourselves?'

She spoke with a faintly cockney—perhaps a Kentish—intonation. Her face was even more striking than at the first glance—her large eyes, of a willow-pattern blue, full of tears, were on a level with his waistcoat, her pale, trembling lips were turned down at the corners. It was obvious to his professional instincts that the poor girl was on the verge of hysteria. He laid a hand on her shoulder, speaking in a soothing tone:

'Now, now—no need to get upset, honey. Let me advise you——'

He had been about to suggest that the girls moved their encampment to the rough ground at the rear of the house; he was prepared to explain their presence to Roderick later. He was interrupted by a wail from Sylvia, rocked in the arms of her companion: 'Ooh, it's all very well for *you* to advise; you who have a hole to creep into, with hot and cold laid on!'

'You bet he has,' the girl called Beattie encouraged her. 'He's pals with the Laird, he is! They have a deep, bomb-proof shelter under there, like the Government, and the rest of the high-ups. They can creep into it and be safe the minute the radiation gets here. The upper crust will survive—the working class, as always, will perish!'

'Come now, girls; dear, sweet girls!' Sydney besought them. 'There is no deep shelter anywhere near Achnabasalt House, I assure you! Honestly! Cross my heart, and hope to die—as we all shall, sooner or later; no favours to us more than you!'

Beattie paid no attention to these blandishing words, if she heard them. 'We can drown, darling, for all the Laird and his pals care,' she crooned to Sylvia in a tone of the utmost tenderness. 'But never you mind, Sylvie, hen. Wait or the club gets here!'

'What club?'

'The Burniebank Cycling and Recreational.'

'Are they coming here?'

'Certainly they are! They are well on their way from Glasgow, all twenty-four of them.'

Sydney digested this unpalatable information. 'They can't stay here, of course, you realise that,' he told the girls, who paid no attention. 'Now, as I was about to suggest—had you been on your own, I might have persuaded the Laird to——'

'We want none of your charity!' Beattie interrupted him harshly.

'Ow, why did you say that, Beat? He might have found us a nice place, out of this horrid old wind——'

'We're not to be beholden to any capitalist!' her friend assured her. 'We're staying right here; and so's the rest of us, when they arrive!'

It had turned colder. A slight, driving drizzle had begun.

'You are making a big mistake,' Sydney called to the girls, as they walked away, back to their caravan. 'It's not a joke, you know, about that radio-active waste on the beach. You run a serious risk. What a pity you won't listen to me! We have some nice warm fires, and hot baths up at the house, you know, if you change your minds.'

Sylvia turned back once, with an uncertain and hopeful look, but her companion dragged at her arm, and she was forced to go with her.

It was lunch-time on the following day when at last the Rolls-Royce arrived with Roderick Fernay, Dick Bolton and the two ladies.

'But where is Mary Mottie?' was the first question.

The confession about the train had to be made, the story of the brown bus told. The anxiety was now the greater.

'I should have been told. Anything might have happened, as it did to us! Nobody here has any idea what things are like Out There!'

Had he known where to find the Heavenly Brethren and their Conveyance, he would have set out to meet them then and there, but exhaustion forbade it.

Their adventures were hinted at, but the story was not to be told at that juncture. Decisions had to be taken as to the allocation of rooms, the unpacking of needed possessions.

'I notice that Doctor Monro has appropriated the two best downstairs rooms for himself and Nigel,' Roderick remarked to Dick. 'And has had fires lit.'

He was not pleased.

3

MAGGIE DOLMAN, lying on her brass bed in the room she shared with Julia, exclaimed: 'We have reached our haven at last! As soon as I stepped into that dingy hall, peace came to me! How wonderful to feel I shall soon see the Brethren again!' She sat up on her elbow, and looked across to the other bed, saying earnestly: 'I am sure, dearest Julia, that when you know them as well as I do, all your doubts and hesitations about joining them, will vanish!'

'If you feel so strongly about it, would you not be better to stay at Strumph Hydro?' asked Julia absently. She was not even thinking particularly about what her aunt was saying; she was half in a dream. She was exceedingly susceptible to romantic situations, and quite helpless before them. The sight of Nigel Fidgeon, so handsome and so destroyed in his paralysis, had touched her deeply. She was ready and willing to be in love with him, and half-way towards such a feeling. The more full of potentialities for frustration and disappointment a relationship seemed, the more she threw herself upon it, as on spears.

'I could never live at the Hydro. One has to share a dormitory with several others; at my time of life I need the utmost privacy —it is even a trial to have to share a room with you, my nearest and dearest. One can be of the Brethren without living neck to neck with them,' Mrs Dolman explained. Yet she did not seem disappointed at her niece's lack of enthusiasm; her mind, as always, had darted to another quarter at once.

'I do not know what we are to wear for dinner!' she complained. The thought had occupied her mind increasingly since the first night of their journey, when in the hotel at Chesterfield it was discovered that the suitcase, which Roderick had thrown so impatiently into the car, contained nothing but underwear.

'It was bearable while we were travelling; but now I simply must change into something cooler. I feel that these garments will grow upon me if I wear them an instant longer; I must bath, and I must change. You do not help me; you say nothing!'

'Wear one of your night-dresses,' her exhausted niece advised her, in a voice slurred with sleep.

'You cannot be serious!'

With a great effort, Julia opened both eyes; the matter must be settled at once, or she would have no peace all afternoon. 'Indeed I am, Aunt Maggie dear! You have such glorious nighties that no one will know they are not dinner-gowns.'

'Do you really think so? Perhaps you are right. Some of these négligées date from nineteen-ten, but I could never be parted from them,' the actress declared, lifting the silken frills and letting them fall from her fingers. 'This one reminds me so of dear Arthur and our honeymoon at Menton.'

'You will look like a duchess!'

'I believe you have solved the problem,' Mrs Dolman conceded with courageous resolution. 'You have given me such reassurance, dear child. Yet on one thing I must insist—you must promise to keep me company. I could not venture alone.'

As Julia had laid in a stock of Grecian night-dresses, and flowing dressing-gowns, not knowing what might be expected of her in the event of total war, she agreed after hesitation.

After a sleep, the two ladies rose at last, and spent some time in dressing, although it was still not six o'clock, and the bath water was cold.

The result, they felt, was worth while.

'I think we should go down without waiting any longer,' Maggie Dolman declared, 'if only to prevent Roderick from boring the others with the story of how he syphoned the petrol from that lorry at Bingley——'

'—Or how I drove backwards through the Fascist rabble at Kirby Lonsdale——'

Their entrance caused quite a sensation in the drawing-room.

'You look fabulous!' cried Roderick, kissing Julia's hands.

'Marvellous!' cried the susceptible doctor, who, in this indecisive light, found it difficult to believe that Julia was over forty.

Only Dick Bolton realised that the ladies were in their night-dresses.

Even Nigel Fidgeon was soothed by the decorative effect which Julia presented as she leaned over him humbly at the dinner-table, asking if she might cut up his chicken for him.

'Thank you, but I still have the full use of my hands,' was the reply, yet given in a tone which did not preclude the granting of other favours. He studied her as he might some exotic insect. She was wearing the more exciting of two evening wigs, and had sprayed herself with *Arpege*. She could enchant him after a tiring day; he was, unfortunately, incapable of any stronger reaction.

As for Julia, shining beneath her silver curls, she felt as though her body were on fire; her hand, holding her fork, visibly trembled.

The Mackenzies, the couple who were Roderick's servants at Achnabasalt, had made a special effort to provide a good meal on the night of the Laird's arrival; everyone enjoyed their food more than they had done for weeks. Sydney Monro felt that this was no time to announce to his host that the Burniebank Bicyclists were about to take over the camping site on the shore.

Perhaps, after all, they would never find the road to Achnabasalt. It was well away from any main thoroughfare, down a grass-grown track, and the local inhabitants had torn down all the signposts giving directions to it. They were plagued enough by their own relations from Glasgow, and had never cared for strangers.

As he finished his red-currant fool, the doctor could not help recalling the conversation he had overheard in Macalister the Merchant's shop in the village that morning. Three fishermen had come in and begun to talk about the activities on the island.

'We do not want any more strangers here, *and we shall know what to do with any who come*,' Mr Macalister had said. All four men had bent a concerted stare of such animosity upon the doctor that he had been quite glad to get out into the open air and leave them to their Gaelic imprecations.

The cyclists would be in danger if they did come.

Much cheered by this reflection, the doctor helped himself to another glass of hock, and smiled over the table at Julia.

· · · · · ·

The next day was sunny, the weather was quite warm, and Roderick, accompanied by Dick Bolton, bathed in his private cove before breakfast. Neither of the ladies rose early, an air of holiday pervaded the house; it was possible to forget the tragedy which had brought them all together. The only sadness clouding Roderick's mind was the non-arrival of Mrs Mottie. He went down to the Post Office, after lunch, even although he knew that there had been no mail for a week, and no telephone was working, just to enquire if any message had reached the post-mistress concerning his charwoman.

As he came out of the shop an alarming summons arrested him. There was a chiming of bicycle bells and a chorus of voices. He was pinned against the wall while a concourse of young people on brightly coloured machines, some tandems, some with side-cars, all heavily laden, thundered past him in the narrow street. He gazed after them in stupefaction; it was only too plain that they were making for the forbidden bay.

The doctor, who emerged from the MacOrrery Arms at that very moment, was forced to tell Mr Fernay about the Burnie-bank Club.

'I will not have these impossible people creating a disturbance on my land when we have come all this way to find a little peace to die in!' Roderick cried, in the greatest displeasure. 'I will go down to the Police Station and tell Sergeant Macrae to turn them away at once!'

'You will not find him. He was struck on the head by a bottle last night, while attempting to subdue some of the Glasgow Highlanders.'

'Then you must come with me, and help me yourself, Doctor! They must not be allowed to erect a single tent!'

'They are younger and stronger than I am, and they are desperate people.'

'You mean to stand aside, then, and do nothing?' cried Roderick.

'I don't think you need worry yourself. A very powerful team of persuaders will do the work for you, and the cyclists will be gone before twenty-four hours are up, I promise you,' the doctor told him.

'And who is to do this persuading?'

'Your own villagers of Achnabasalt.'

The doctor went on to give his view that the local people were planning a vendetta against all strangers, which they would presently put into effect.

Roderick became most silent and uneasy at this intelligence. He drew the doctor up the street, until they were clear of the houses. 'One must be very careful what one says hereabouts,' he whispered. 'One does not know how much is overheard and repeated.'

'I don't see why my remarks about the villagers upset you so.' Sydney remarked. He wondered if he might make some excuse and return to the hotel.

Yet Roderick kept a firm grip on his arm, and said no further word until they had reached a sandy tor. 'I am here on sufferance,' he confessed. 'I myself am a stranger; you had better know it.'

'You surprise me. I had supposed your family to have owned the land hereabouts for generations, and that you were the Laird.'

'My mother, it is true, was a MacOrrery of these parts,' Roderick said, in a low tone. 'But my father was a Sassenach from Stockton-on-Tees. I have never admitted this, but it has become known. They do not accept me as the father of the people, as a Laird should be. After all, I can hardly blame them; apart from two visits, as a small child to my grandparents, I was never near the place until last year, when it occurred to me what a splendid hide-out this would make.'

The seriousness of the position was now apparent to Doctor Monro; yet he felt the necessity to put the best face possible upon it.

'Surely the Heavenly Brethren will be next after the cyclists on the list of those who are to be sacrificed?' he asked mildly. 'The Reverend Murdo Macalpine announced last Sunday in his sermon that they were the spawn of the Devil.'

'They are far too superstitious to interfere with the Devil's own. They would fear reprisal from Auld Horny. No, no; the Brethren will be left in peace; it is my household who are in imminent danger.'

The doctor excused himself and returned to the refuge of the inn; Roderick continued on his way back to the house. From the highest point of the road, before he turned in at his own gate, he paused to look down on the camp. Small tents, like conical white fungii were rising already on the green machair round the single caravan; a stiff breeze threatened to blow them down as fast as they were erected. A little child ran out from one of them, stumbled and fell over a guy-rope. Roderick was appalled to realise there were children amongst the campers; he began to worry because there would be no fresh milk for them, and to plan how to steal a canful from his own dairy after dark and leave it where it might be found.

At evening, all of a sudden, the wind dropped; a strange calm settled on the coast. The air was heavily scented; it had an incense-bearing, tropical langour. A sunset of brilliance began to show itself about half past nine—the sky was rayed like the flag of old Imperial Japan.

'It is a sign of the end!' exclaimed Maggie Dolman.

Everyone came out into the garden to watch. Down in the bay groups of villagers stood about.

'The colours are taking an unnatural time to fade,' Nigel remarked. He had ordered his chair to be pushed to the cliff edge. He was not at all supine, and wore a chestnut velvet jacket.

'It is changing!' cried Julia breathlessly. 'It was too theatrical to last—— Look how clear and pale the sky is now—— It is like the window of some great cathedral, with the light shining through!'

'Heaven is behind that window,' Maggie announced in her sonorous voice, spreading wide her arms. In her purple peignoir she appeared an angel with wings.

Julia made no extravagant gestures before Nigel; a new shyness invested her. Even with the thickness of three frilled petticoats beneath her apricot chiffon night-dress, she felt strangely immodest. The light, however, was so golden that it disguised her completely, sponging out any signs of age in her face and neck. Nigel was captivated still more, as with a delightful painting by a master.

Maggie Dolman's cry of ecstasy, however, had attracted an unwelcome attention. The Reverend Murdo Macalpine and his wife, and several of his elders, had come out to take an evening stroll on the cliffs with their families. The women gazed in horror at Mrs Dolman. The word *'night-dress'* was heard, and from another '*whoor of Babylon*'. The actress was most upset, and her niece hurried her into the house.

'If they knew how kind she is to animals!' exclaimed Dick in distress.

Roderick cried out in anger: 'How dare you judge someone of whom you know nothing! Look first at the motes in your own eyes!'

The affronted elders and the minister withdrew, taking their ladies with them, but the evening was quite spoiled. Even the sight of some beautiful, pearl-like discs, flying swiftly from south to north, and which were hailed by Dick as Flying Saucers, failed to distract the house-party, who, by common consent, turned to go indoors almost immediately.

Mrs Dolman had stopped crying; Dick lent her his beautiful Indian silk handkerchief, and she blew her nose gently.

'I beg you not to upset yourself. These people are not worth it,' Roderick urged her. The conduct of the elders and their wives had turned his sympathies towards her for the time being. 'They are nothing but ignorant, narrow-minded bigots.' Yet he was more than a little unquiet. 'This will be another nail in my coffin,' he confided in Dick.

The doctor absented himself for a while. On Mrs Dolman's plea he had gone to a wash-house in the rear of the building where all the stray and petted dogs and cats of the neighbourhood had been shut up on her orders. He was provided with stout gloves and a bottle of chloroform; his duty was to despatch them all before they died of starvation, or were eaten. This was the cause of Dick's earlier remarks about Mrs Dolman's fondness for animals.

4

DICK, upon a borrowed bicycle, returned from a seven-mile ride to Mass, on Sunday morning, to find most of the household still in bed. He helped himself to a half-cold breakfast, and only as he finished it did Roderick appear. Fresh coffee was rung for, and as they prolonged their pleasant confidences on the events of the previous day, they were reminded peremptorily of the Sabbath, by the tinny clamour of the bell on the roof of the Free Kirk, summoning the parish to morning service.

'As the Laird I suppose I should put in an appearance,' Roderick said. They walked out into the garden from which they had a clear view of the village. Everyone appeared to be on the way to church. From all the airts, horse-drawn carts, and horses harnessed to motor-vehicles, brought elderly people from distant clachans; others arrived by boat from across the bay.

'So many people are staying now with their relations in the neighbourhood that the population must be as great or greater than it was at the time of the clearances a century ago,' Roderick remarked, gazing at the crowd through his field-glasses. 'Indeed, if the roofs were on all the ruined houses they would scarcely contain these great-grandchildren of former inhabitants.'

'The kirk cannot. They are sitting on the tombstones and walls of the churchyard,' Dick noticed. 'How fortunate it is so warm!'

They began to walk down to the beach.

'I did so want to bathe! Still, I have a responsibility it would be dangerous to neglect in the circumstances.' Mr Fernay sighed.

'The church is full. As they did not know you intended coming I don't suppose they have kept a seat for you,' Dick pointed out. 'You could go this evening.'

'I suppose I could do that,' Roderick decided, feeling at once lighter in spirits. He took off his shoes and socks in order to paddle in his private sea. 'The water is warm,' he called. 'You should follow my example, Dick.'

Dick was looking through his friend's Zeiss glasses, and declared he could see someone moving about on the island.

Roderick was not impressed. 'It was a sheep, I expect.'

'It was not, it was a man. I can see him now with my naked eyes.'

'Where? Where do you mean? I see nothing!' declared Mr Fernay.

'It is part of the mysterious preparations which I have told you are going on upon Ebora!' Dick said in excitement. 'You would not believe me. They have been digging in the ground; the island is guarded on all sides; nobody is allowed to land, the Navy forbid it! All this has happened within the last six months, since the islands were bought from the Duke of Kintyre by an unknown purchaser.'

'I am not interested in rumours; I don't wish to hear them! I have told you this before, but you will not listen.'

Roderick strode away towards the rocks at the furthermost part of the bay, deciding whether to bathe before lunch. Dick continued his scrutiny of the island; but now he could see only a few black-faced sheep, cropping the grass on the hillside. He began to believe that Roderick was right. He had desired so much to see a marvel upon Ebora that he had created it from his imagination.

Roderick undressed behind a rock, and put on his bathing trunks. He began to wade into the pellucid water, disgusted with his friend for refusing to follow. He ducked, splashed, turned on his back, and paddled his great arms like fins. Suddenly, glancing up, to his astonishment he saw two young men and a girl, looking down on him calmly from a rock. He stood, waist-high in water, and shouted: 'Are you aware that you are trespassing?'

Dick hurried up. He could see, from his employer's frantic gestures, that he had lost his temper and was having the worst of the argument; even although from the distance where he was, he could not hear what was said.

'Very well! There is no food for you here; if you stay you will starve!' Roderick was shouting, as he plunged to the shore. 'It is not my responsibility!'

Dick offered him a bath-towel; it was snatched with the utmost celerity, and draped about the famous torso.

'Food will give out soon everywhere,' said the young man with the beard, as though it could not concern him. 'As we have to live in the same neighbourhood until the end comes, it will be better to do so without exhausting our energies unnecessarily in senseless argument and commotion.'

'Aaah!'

'Roderick! Remember what the doctor said!'

'Aaa-ah!'

'It's the pore little kids like Roy and Valerie I'm sorry for,' the girl said. 'They can't understand getting no dinner, and having to die.'

'Long before a week is up you will be driven from here,' Dick interrupted. 'It is only fair to warn you of this. The villagers will make you go, at gun-point.'

'And what do you intend to do about that, pray?' Sylvia (for it was she) demanded. 'Are you going to sit up in that house, close the doors and windows and put up the shutters? I suppose you'll plug your ears so you don't hear the little children crying, just as your ancestors did when they burned the houses here and turned everyone out.'

Dick was about to protest that they had been no ancestors of his, when a cry went up: 'A ship—— Look, a yacht, sailing round the island!'

They were all distracted from their argument. A white yacht, slim as a tern, was sailing silently into the bay. It was man-oeuvring to cast anchor at the island's jetty. Everyone but Dick and Sylvia ran down to the water's edge.

The girl burst into tears, and he put an arm about her to comfort her; she buried her face in his shoulder.

'I wish I never come away and left Mum and Dad,' she sobbed. 'Goodness knows what's happened to them, and Ethel and the boys. I expect that radio-active stuff's got them! Barry, he's my boy friend, he told me to come up here, see, only he's never turned up. I expect Bellerophon's boys got him. And I do hate camping,' she sniffed. 'I always hated it. There's no privacy, you know.'

'You poor little thing! Cheer up!'

'—No privacy for *anything*,' she confided. 'If I've got to

27

die, I'd like to do it decently, in a house with a *real* bath-room.'

'Let me take you up to Achnabasalt for a wash and a tidy. I'm sure, after that, you'll feel much *much* better!' Dick suggested. It seemed the only polite thing to do. 'At least our plumbing works *some* of the time.'

As they climbed the rocky path together, Dick saw that the congregation were coming out of the kirk at last. It had been a special Communion Service, ordered by the Presbytery, because of the calamity. In the sunshine the top-hats of the men glistened like the shards of so many beetles. They processed down the street in an orderly fashion that was full of menace. Dick ushered Sylvia through the wicket gate into the garden. Julia was standing by the summer house in her travelling dress.

'A yacht has come to the island!' she called to them in excitement.

'Yes, we know.'

Dick hurriedly introduced Sylvia to her, and explained the reason he had brought her to the house. Then he left them together, and hastened back to Roderick whom he had neglected for the past ten minutes.

It appealed to Julia's unsatisfied motherly instincts to have to look after this forlorn and pretty girl, as Dick had known it would. She led her inside the house. At the door they met Doctor Monro, who was delighted to see that Sylvia was to be accepted socially without his connivance. Sylvia, however, avoided his gaze, and had nothing to say to him. She clung to Julia on the way to the bathroom, and afterwards, in Julia's room, opened her heart to her.

When Mrs Dolman came in, a quarter of an hour afterwards, in her outdoor clothes, she found them both sitting on Julia's bed. It was characteristic of her aunt, Julia reflected, that after the first introduction she should ignore the little bicyclist completely; not out of malice, or condescension, but in the fervour of the news she had to reveal.

Mrs Dolman took the centre of the room, every movement full of import. Slowly she removed her Inverness cape, and folded it upon the bed; with infinite deliberation she peeled off her gloves, one by one, and raised her hat from her head, placing it slowly upon the dressing-table.

'I have had a shattering experience,' she announced, weighing each syllable.

Only then did she sit down in the armchair, half turned from the window so that she faced her audience, one hand at her bosom, clasping her amulet, one foot a little in advance.

'What has happened, Aunt Maggie?'

'I have been to a service, given by the Heavenly Brethren at Strumph Hydro,' Mrs Dolman told her niece. 'I had no intention of going. I walked over, meaning to ask for news of the brown bus and the missing stragglers—— I wanted to see my dear Laetitia Tompkins—— I was asked to join in the worship. I felt so overjoyed—so humble—— I expected Bread—— I was given—— *A stone!*'

'But you had been to services before, in London; you had found them spiritually highly satisfying, hadn't you?' Julia asked in bewilderment. 'You believe them to be the Elect, who are to be saved when the rest of us perish?'

'Oh, it is certain they imagine themselves to be so.' Mrs Dolman brushed some powder from her cardigan with a flip of her wash-leather glove. 'It is true I have attended a few little gatherings in London, at Laetitia's house, but those were intimate meetings of an entirely different character. If you ask me, these people are completely bogus.'

Having said this, she sat down, with her back to the room, and began to comb her hair as she spoke. 'Laetitia is a nice creature, but *completely deceived*; she imagined I would be impressed. I was prepared to be—indeed I *longed* to be! I still long to find the answer!' she turned round to say, waving her silver-backed hairbrush. 'But I will not find the truth up at Strumph Hydro, amongst the hand-weavers and the grass-eaters!'

She closed her eyes, and let her hands fall into her lap. 'Yet there was Meaning and Purpose in this discovery,' she went on bravely. 'God abhors a vacuum. I shall be shown what to do. I am neither discouraged, nor cast down.'

'What was it that disgusted you?' enquired Julia, who had an appetite for all that concerned her aunt's spiritual adventures. She herself had now forgotten Sylvia completely; the girl sat on the bed, a wet pink with embarrassment.

'I endured the horrific playing of the organ, by a man like a nanny-goat in a red dressing-gown,' Mrs Dolman went on. 'I submitted to the bleating of unknown hymns, the words so distorted as to be hardly sensible. When the book was opened, I prepared to be pierced by Truth, as by a Golden Arrow——' She could not for a moment continue; in order to gain support in her cruel disappointment she leaned forward and clasped her niece's outstretched fingers.

'I opened myself to Illumination,' the actress breathed, in a voice full of the echoes of a cave of deserted hopes. 'For is that not what we stand most in need of now? To know—to be certain at last?'

Nobody spoke; the silence of expectation was prolonged almost past bearing. 'And what did I get?' Mrs Dolman spoke at last. 'I got a to-tally in-com-pre-hensible discourse, couched in such obscure and flowery terms that I could not understand one single word of it! Nor do I believe it was any clearer, for all their appearance of ecstasy, to any of the Brethren present.'

'You could have asked for an explanation, surely?'

'My dear, that is exactly what I did. I sought out one who appeared to be a Leader; I put my question to him, saying how puzzled, how distressed I was. And I was reprimanded. Oh yes; I was set very firmly in my place. I was told that the language had to be veiled so that those who were incapable of perceiving the truth would be prevented from misusing it, yet if one were a Brother, it would be immediately apparent!'

'Christ veiled His truth also in parables,' Julie felt bound to point out.

'Christ spoke in simple straightforward terms,' Mrs Dolman said roundly. 'In words of two syllables, without embellishment.' A gong rang downstairs. 'I am quite worn out. Bring me a little something on a tray,' Julia was ordered. 'I shall rest the whole afternoon; I shall not come down until supper-time.'

Sylvia, who had felt increasingly humiliated by her situation, decided to creep unnoticed from the room. It was not very nice to discuss Jesus Christ like that, and how very rude the old lady had been, talking through her like that, without a word. Still, I can come back and go to the toilet any time I like, she reflected, with satisfaction, as she skipped down the stairs. A rich smell of roast lamb and mint sauce rose from the kitchen, and she wished she had been asked to stay for lunch; she determined that next time she would arrange this.

She stood for an instant in the porch, and heard from the window above: 'Jesus was simple and good, He had no use for the Spiritually Superior.'

In the drive leading to the back gate she almost collided with an odd couple of people whom she took to be tramps—an elderly white-haired man, and a little old woman like a gypsy. She hurried away before they could beg off her, or steal the gold cross which hung at her throat.

5

'**M**RS MOTTIE!'
'Mr Beek!'
'My dear Mrs Mottie, how glad I am!'
'How thankful we are to see you both!'

These and similar cries greeted the stained and weary travellers. They were forbidden to tell of their adventures until they had bathed and changed out of their gypsy garments; then they must join the dinner-table. Only when they had eaten, and were a little restored, were they encouraged to tell their story.

'We were led by the Spirit People throughout,' Mrs Mottie declared. 'If it had not been for my Guide, we should not be 'ere.'

Their tale was told in such an intermittent, spasmodic fashion delayed by a hundred questions, and tossed from one to the other, that nobody could come at an exact idea of the events recounted.

There was a clear picture of the departure of the bus, however. A Mr Bernard Boonyard had led the Brethren. The driver had failed to arrive, and an intrepid woman member, a Miss Minim, had undertaken the task, aided by Odysseus Jackson, the Jamaican.

'Where is Odysseus?' Mrs Dolman interrupted to ask. 'And where is little Nyeri?'

'Aow, don't ask, Mrs Dolman dear!' The question upset Mrs Mottie; she was about to enter into explanations, but:

'Go on with your story!' Roderick ordered. 'We will come to that!'

'Where we should of been if it 'adn't been for Odysseus, God only knows,' Mrs Mottie continued, with the greatest cheerfulness. She had, she told them, little opinion of Miss Minim's driving, and less of the characters of the other Brethren. Yet they had been kind to the Jamaican and his child, because they were of the Younger Races. The boy, especially, had delighted the elderly spinsters of both sexes.

The bus had not been overcrowded; several more had been expected—age, or frailty had prevented their arrival. The main party of the Brethren had gone ahead to Strumph Hydro, these were the last of the pilgrims.

So they had set off, finding the roads out of London almost empty of traffic: there was no more petrol, and those who wished to travel had done so a week before. The weather continued fine. That this could not last was accepted by the Brethren who had Higher Knowledge of What was To Come (but not through anything so degrading as Mediumship). Indeed as soon as they became aware of Mrs Mottie's profession, so strongly did they feel that it was a Prostitution of the Spirit, that she had found herself in quarantine, and relegated to a back seat; especially when she took a *meat* pie out of her bag.

It had pleased Mary Mottie quite well, so she told them, to be left to herself. She had no anxieties; her Guides had brought her here, she was in their hands. She sat on the uncomfortable seat above the wheels, amused the boy, and looked out at the fields of ripening corn which would never be harvested, the deserted towns and silent factories. Once or twice, desperate people had stepped into the road, trying to stop the bus, but 'Drive on!' Bernard Boonyard had ordered, with an inflexible purpose; for the Brethren knew for certain that they were the Remnant who were to Inherit. It was destined that they must preserve themselves at all cost.

The younger of the lady members (those between forty-five and sixty) were quite gay when they thought of their Divine Destiny. They made little jokes amongst themselves which Odysseus could not understand. When not driving he had sat by himself in gloomy silence.

'Man is a mistake,' he had said to Mrs Mottie. 'All possibilities of survival of the soul are legends. These people are a little crazy, for the soul itself is a legend.'

There were only two male Brethren, Mr Boonyard and Mr Beveridge, who was a pale, fat man ceaselessly concerned with his diet. 'I have given up dairy foods altogether now,' Mr Beek heard him say. 'It has been of great benefit to my colon.'

On went the bus, north to Baldock, through the byways of green and leafy England under a heavy summer sky seeded with radiation.

'But Mr Beek was ill,' Mrs Mottie told them. 'You were ever so poorly, weren't you, Mr Beek?' Receiving no answer from the clergyman, she went on: ' 'E was exhausted, that's what it was, and my Guides told me if 'e didn't get a rest 'e'd never come to the journey's end. The Chief told me, you know.' Mrs Mottie's head control, as they all knew, was an African chieftain called Bubandu. 'So I told the Brethren. They didn't want to stop, but in the end we did.'

The bus had been halted on the north side of Cambridge. 'Near Spalding it was, or some such place. We 'eard there was none of the Colts this side of Bedford.'

The Colts were Bellerophon's men, a sinister army.

Mrs Mottie accepted a cup of tea. 'Thanks, dear. You still get fresh milk up 'ere? Coo, dead lucky you are!'

They had paused at a little Fen village, not far from the Wash, where the sea air, and the quiet in the deep fields, had revived the clergyman for the time being. The power to sleep had returned to him; he had slept nearly all the ensuing journey, like a child.

'One of That Lot said she was a Healer,' Mrs Mottie said. 'She made 'im lay down on the grass, and she sniffed deep and put 'er two 'ands on 'is 'ead.'

'Did she heal you?' asked Nigel, with the first interest he had shown.

Mrs Mottie answered for him. 'Oh she may 'ave done. The others were all 'olding 'im in their thoughts, and there's a lot in prayer. But all it was reely, 'e was wore out and needed 'is sleep.'

They had stayed the night in that place, and when the sun came up, she had gone down to the sea and waded. Suddenly she had seen Odysseus and his boy 'running across the sands without a stitch on'. They had bathed. 'I don't blame them. Very nice and refreshing it was, I'm sure.'

Mrs Mackenzie came in to clear the table, and was introduced to the new-comers, whom she treated with reserve. Dick offered to do the washing-up for her, and was refused.

'I do not think the Mackenzies like us,' he said to Roderick afterwards, when Julia was attending Mr Beek and Mrs Mottie to their rooms.

'They are hostile, and it makes me uneasy,' Roderick agreed.

'Perhaps they disapproved of the ragged state of our newest visitors.'

Mrs Dolman appeared downstairs, and demanded to know what had happened.

'So I have missed the entire story!' she lamented.

'Not altogether. Mrs Mottie has promised us a further instalment after her rest,' Dick consoled her. 'It is only half told.'

'Oh yes,' Julia, returning, chimed in. 'We are to hear of dreadful dealings in Edinburgh, murder and arson; of unheard-of privations on the high seas.'

'Yes, yes, but if you tell it all now, you will spoil the element of surprise!' Roderick chided her.

They walked into the garden.

'It is too cold for you to stay here,' the doctor was telling Nigel. 'You'd be better indoors.'

He wheeled his patient away, and Julia paled with regret; she had hoped to spend the entire afternoon with Mr Fidgeon. 'I shall go for a walk,' she announced.

'I am sorry I don't feel able to accompany you,' her aunt said.

'I walked enough this morning. A book and a rug in the summer house is what I look forward to. Yet I don't think you should go alone; it is not safe in these troubled times. Dick, be a dear soul and go with her. I shall rest easier in my mind!'

Dick hesitated; although he was fond of Julia he felt a certain constraint in her company.

'Dick is tired,' Julia said. 'He bicycled fourteen miles before breakfast, to Mass and back, and then dealt with a scene on the beach. He should rest, while you read aloud to him.'

'You are wrong! I feel a walk is just what I need!' the secretary assured her with the greatest untruthfulness.

Julia received the news with ingratitude; she wished to be alone. She set off at such a pace that Dick had difficulty in keeping up with her.

It was to be (although none of them knew it) the last normal day. There was no forewarning of the change to come, other than the lowering temperature, and the haze on the horizon.

No cloud, as yet, appeared in the pale green sky, even where it met the sullen hills. Only the outline of Stack Herne, a pustule, a thimble of volcanic mud, lifted itself like a dark omen, a finger of warning, to the south.

'How desolate this beauty is!' panted Dick, coming level at last with Julia, who stood upon a rock, gazing out to sea. 'See that abeline bay below; white and ermine sand with tails of rock!' He memorised his precious phrase for a poem to be written later. Julia was silent; she had planned a water-colour sketch, now he had spoiled it all.

Dick sensed her antagonism. Only the knowledge that Roderick would say: 'I told you to keep an eye on Julia while she was here—you should have gone with her!' acted upon him like a goad and kept him at her side.

'Go back and rest, Dick. I shall be perfectly all right!'

Julia forced herself to make a sweet smile; she bent down to pick some harebells and scabious. Dick took the opportunity of reviving himself with a mouthful of brandy from the flask he kept in his hip pocket; sometimes he was sure his heart was failing.

'I am not tired at all now!' he cried gaily. He did a dance like a jester on a flat-topped rock, in order to disarm her; she was forced to laugh, and feel warmly towards him again.

'I wish there were not so many people in the house,' she complained, thrusting her arm through his. 'I do so long to get away by myself at times. I am happy—then all of a sudden I am desperately miserable!'

'Don't be upset!' Dick begged her. 'Please! I cannot bear it!'

Few people were about in the village as they passed, yet they felt themselves observed through the drawn curtains of the closed windows.

'Are they annoyed because we have been picking flowers on the Sabbath?' Julia giggled nervously.

'It is wicked even to take a walk on Sunday!'

They ran up the hill, past the remaining cottages; the further they left the houses behind, the more light-hearted they became; yet Julia could not, in decency, forget her all-absorbing preoccupation.

'I am so unhappy,' she sighed, without meaning it particularly. 'It has been my fate, all my life, to be desperately fond of someone who does not care in the least for me!'

Julia is for ever falling in love with the impossible Roderick
had told Dick, before he introduced them for the first time. For
years, evidently, she had cherished a passion for a Cabinet
Minister; then she had become enamoured of an earl, who saw
at once that she must be dropped, as she could not be kept in
decorous obscurity. Finally she had lived quite happily for
several years with a company director, of whom she had been
moderately fond, who had worshipped her and left her his
entire fortune when he died.

'Darling, please do not be unhappy, for we all love you!' Dick
besought her. 'Roderick cannot bear you to be miserable. He
brought you here to cheer him up.'

The road, little more than a grassy track, had taken them to
the summit of the headland between Achnabasalt and Strumph.
Before them lay an undulating stretch of bare, unrewarding
moor, waterlogged in its hollows and scruffy on its heights. Here
they passed a last monstrosity of a building—a bungalow, with
scarlet paint on doors and windows; from it came the noise of
drunken singing.

They hurried until they had hidden it behind them in a fold
of land; then Dick seized her arm, and they stood still.

'Listen!' he commanded.

'I hear nothing.'

'That's the trouble!' His eyes had become like globes. 'In late
summer, when one takes a walk in the country, there is always
a background of noise. Flies buzz, birds twitter, bees bumble in
the heather——'

'Not if a wind is blowing!'

'Think! Have you seen a bird today?'

'I should not notice. I am not susceptible to birds.'

'I have not seen a gull, even. Look! Usually there are hundreds
on these cliffs, of every sort. Now not one is to be seen!'

They began to compare notes on the strange absence of life,
and even Julia was impressed into a nervous quivering.

'What can have happened?' she began, but these were the last
words spoken before the insects were upon them. Out of nowhere a thickly packed cloud felled them to the ground, covering them so completely that they were invisible to one another.
They flailed with their arms; they could not shout, because if
they opened their mouths they swallowed flies. Then, without

stinging, still in a compact tornado shape, as swiftly as they had come, the cloud flew out to sea. Dick and Julia lay gasping on the grass, watching them go, a trailing black kite of living particles, until they were lost in the haze. Only the ground was covered in dead and crawling flies; and for several minutes they stood, brushing them out of one another's clothes and hair.

'Let us go back at once!' Julia cried.

They were frightened; they felt unclean from their contact with the insects; nothing but a bath would rid them of a feeling of contamination, which was more than physical. They turned, and ran down the hill.

'There's a West Indian girl down in the camp; she has this sickness and di-reer too,' Sylvia told the doctor, as they sat in the summer house which Mrs Dolman had vacated. 'She's ever so ill. It's going right through the camp, you know. I even have a touch of it myself.'

'You should boil all the water.'

'Oh we do, it's not that. Calum says it may be the radiation sickness. Do you think it's the radiation sickness?'

'How should I know, darling?' asked the doctor, never taking his eyes from her, as she sat nervously tapping the ash from her cigarette.

'I mean, you're a doctor, you *should* know, shouldn't you?' Sylvia continued. 'And I thought you could give us something —you know—to stop it. I mean, it makes it very unpleasant, doesn't it, with no sanitation and that.'

'I have no drugs, nothing but simple things like iodine and aspirin,' lied the doctor. He had in reserve a few phials of cyanide, in case of emergency. 'Keep off all fruit and green vegetables,' he advised. He wondered idly if a typhoid epidemic were beginning; in these conditions it would spread like a heath fire, and there was nothing to be done.

'This coloured girl,' Sylvia went on, allowing the arm about her shoulder, but discouraging further explorations. 'She's ever so nice. I mean, I don't take to darkies, not as a rule. I mean they can be, well, you know, funny. Especially after those Notting Hill larks, I steer clear of them. But Glory (that's her name— pretty, isn't it?), Glory, she's different somehow. I feel ever so sorry for her.'

'Did anyone ever tell you that you have eyes like deep wells?' Sydney asked.

'Oh go on!' Sylvia retorted. 'I was telling you about this girl, see—Glory.'

'I'd rather you told me about this other girl, sitting beside me.'

'Listen. Can't you come down and see her? After all, you are a doctor!'

'The only girl I want to see anything of, is you,' Sydney Monro replied, trying to seize Sylvia's hand and pull her towards him.

She eluded him, with skilled practice, and stood, pulling down her jersey. 'You men are all the same,' she said. 'There's only one thing you're interested in, even now. I'd think a lot more of you if you helped Glory.'

'I am tired of the very name of Glory!'

He put a mental curse upon the wretched girl.

He knew he would have no rest, and that, in order to regain Sylvia's approval, he would have to go down to the camp.

6

THESE were the last birds, the last insects, that they were to see, and an inherited, intuitive panic struck the people from Glasgow simultaneously, as dusk fell that night.

Many of them had been drinking indoors, since their midday meal; the combination of a strong, immature and unblended malt spirit, to which they were unused, and the fire of the Reverend Murdo Macalpine's sermon on damnation (some having avoided church since baptism) had affected them very adversely.

No one would say afterwards how the idea had arisen that the only safety lay in escape to the Outer Hebrides. In spite of argument with their native relations, who knew better, a party went down to the shore, and took possession (after a fight) of two fishing boats. The owners put up a good resistance, but were outnumbered and overpowered by the visitors. It was said that the event which had tipped the balance in favour of flight had been the sight of a large army of rats, leaping and scurrying through the street at twilight. Like a concourse of lemmings, these had cast themselves without hesitation into the sea, swimming steadily out into the bay until they could no longer be seen.

The people crowded to their doors to witness the sight, which opened their souls to terror. As dusk fell, the cattle also became uneasy; they kept up an incessant lowing. A bull, belonging to Alisdair Mackenzie's brother James, burst from his stall, made down the rocks, and was drowned instantly in the swirling tide.

None of these portents, nor the events which followed, were reported to the Laird of Achnabasalt; and although the house-party confessed to a feeling of restlessness they were not particularly alarmed.

'Since poor Mrs Mottie is too tired to tell us the rest of her story, and has retired to bed, we look to you to enlighten us,' Mrs Dolman told Mr Beek after dinner.

Mr Beek was reluctant to speak of the horrors they had endured. Yet when Roderick returned from barricading the house (whether against villagers or bicyclists he did not say) and joined his petition to Mrs Dolman's, the clergyman felt obliged to give an account of himself, however faltering.

The Brethren and their bus had, he said, reached Edinburgh without radical trouble. There was a rumour that Bellerophon's troops were in occupation of the city, but they saw nothing of them until they were passing the western suburb of Corstorphine; here they were suddenly attacked and surrounded.

'There was so much confusion that I cannot remember the order of events with any clarity,' the old man admitted. 'But the bus was confiscated at once, and driven away. Our poor Jamaican friend Odysseus was singled out for a most brutal beating; he was left for dead at the roadside, and dear Miss Minim rendered first-aid.'

Odysseus had, however, broken from her ministrations. Like a hunted wounded animal he had rushed across the road, and through the gates of the Zoological Gardens opposite (which happened to be open to admit a vehicle), with three Colts in pursuit.

'It was the last we saw of him.'

Mr Beek paused to allow the exclamations of concern and indignation to subside, and continued his story.

Edinburgh, they learned, had not been evacuated, as many towns in the South had been. The citizens had continued their normal existence, paying little attention, either to the atom bomb or to the desertion of a government which had shown a scanty interest in Scottish affairs. At the time of the arrival of the brown bus, however, it was in a state of siege.

It was Mrs Mottie who discovered that the little boy, Nyeri, was missing also. He must have tried to run after his father in the confusion. In spite of the urgent need to withdraw into shelter, several brave souls had run up and down the roads in search of him; only as night fell did they give in.

Mrs Mottie had then withdrawn to a toolshed to consult her Guides, but the conditions were not propitious for psychic communications.

'We were all so worn-out and shocked by our experiences that we retreated into the garden of a nearby house. The inhabitants, two elderly ladies, were awaiting the return of their brother, a town councillor, who had gone into the city, and who had forbidden them, under any circumstances, to admit strangers to the house. But they were most kind, and bade us sit on the lawn and rest; they even handed cups of tea through the windows.'

Presently, Mr Beek said, as they became more confident that they would take no harm from their visitors, they had allowed them to sit on a garden seat, and to make use of their outside lavatory; yet they had been adamant in their refusal to allow anyone across the threshold; even old Miss Bunch, who had suffered a slight heart attack.

'Pick any flowers you like,' they had offered. 'Take some roses; there's plenty.'

They had spent an uneasy night. Towards morning, Leonora Bunch had had another heart attack, and died quietly, without the least fuss. However, they had found an open drainage trench in a lane to the rear of the house, most convenient for her burial. Then they had set out on foot, and were Divinely Led to the encampment of some tinkers, near Queensferry, who, in exchange for some of their clothes, had agreed to take them in their caravans as far as Fort William. Yet, at Oban, they had been abandoned once more, and had it not been for the kindness of the owner of a trawler, who had landed them at Ullapool, and a farmer, who had lifted them the remaining score of miles in his gig, they must never have come to their destination, even in the piteous state in which they had arrived.

'I cannot deny that we were Overshadowed,' he concluded. 'Some purpose must have been behind our miraculous preservation.'

So saying, Mr Beek appeared overcome once more by exhaustion, and was helped to his room. A sense of anticlimax prevailed; the house-party felt they had been cheated of the extremes of sensation promised. Too tame and even a course of events had supervened upon the promise of horror that began the tale.

'Now, what are we to do?' Roderick exclaimed. 'It is only half past eight!'

'We could play some music on the gramophone,' Nigel suggested.

'I for one am not in the mood for music,' declared Mrs Dolman. 'Nobody is fonder of great music, in its proper place, than I am; yet I should be dishonest if I failed to admit that I find one cantata of Johann Sebastian Bach enough of a feast for an evening.'

She had taken up *The Lays of the Scottish Minstrels* from a bookcase; now she threw the book down. 'I suggest that like the people in Boccaccio's *Decameron*, who fled from Florence to escape the plague, we should each tell a story.'

Nobody was enthusiastic, but she sat down, smoothed her rose satin bed-gown, and folded her hands. 'If you like, I will begin.'

'Make it a short tale, then.' Roderick commanded. 'You can see that none of us is in the mood to listen for long.'

He might have put a direct veto on the telling, except that he wished to follow the discourse with one of his own.

Dick put a couple of birch logs on the fire, and the rest of the party composed themselves as best they could.

'There was once a man, who, late in life, fell in love with an attractive widow, many years younger than himself,' Mrs Dolman began, in a soothing voice. 'Yet when it came to marrying her, he was full of doubts as to the wisdom of entering into such an indissoluble bond. The widow, who was a sensible woman, saw his hesitation, and rather than lose him for ever, made him an excellent suggestion. This was that after marriage she should continue to live in her own little cottage, which was in a secluded and not too isolated spot, and that he should merely visit her from time to time. Thus he would have all the joy of marriage, and none of its ties and responsibilities, and the relationship would not grow stale with familiarity.'

She paused, but nobody said anything.

'The man, whose name was Joseph, agreed very readily to Fanny's suggestion——'

'Ugh! Fanny isn't a nice name at all!' the doctor protested.

'Be quiet, and let Maggie get on with it!'

'——And for a time the scheme answered very well. Every weekend, Joseph set off for Fanny's cottage, where he was given a most loving welcome, and cosseted as much as a man of his age and position has a right to expect. Yet one Sunday, Fanny came to Joseph and said: "Joseph, I am very lonely on my own from Monday until Friday, would you mind if I had a dear friend of my own to stay with me during the week? She would go away at the week-end, while you are here. Her name is Elisabeth Box, and I have known her since we were at school together."

'Joseph, who had a jealous and suspicious nature, like all men who have made a success in business, but none in love, could see no objection to this scheme, whichever way he looked at it, and so——'

'I would like to finish this story!' interrupted Roderick suddenly. 'I can see just how it should end!—— You don't mind, do you?' he asked Mrs Dolman, in a pleading tone.

Everyone looked at him in astonishment, as he stood, enormous in the lamplight in his purple smoking-jacket.

'*Will* you let me finish it?' he begged.

Maggie spread out her hands in a gesture of amused resignation. Yet a few seconds later, while the doctor mixed a round of drinks, both ladies slipped from the room, and hurried into the vast, deserted kitchen.

'Roderick is absolutely insufferable at times!' Mrs Dolman declared. 'If I had stayed another minute in the room with him I should have Spoken Out, whether he is my host or no! He is so overbearing. His rudeness to me was unpardonable just now; it was, after all, my story.'

'I agree,' Julia's voice came from the larder where she was searching for milk. 'He made it impossible for you to go on. He was quite childish about it.'

She carried a blue and white jug of milk into the kitchen.

'Would you like some?' she asked.

'Thank you, no. Milk is the food more likely than any other to become radio-active, is it not?—— I would have adored a whisky and hot water, but I was not offered one. It was sweet of you, Julia, to walk out in sympathy with me.'

'I am afraid I did not walk out because Roderick had appropriated your story,' Julia confessed, pouring milk into a glass. 'I left the room because I foresaw (from my knowledge of Roderick, and from the condition all the men were in) exactly how the story would develop; I should have found it far from amusing.'

She carried the milk jug back into the larder, and returned ready to take up her candle. 'I am afraid we ourselves are to blame, Aunt Maggie, for if we had not lowered our standards by appearing in our night-dresses like this, every evening, Roderick would never have dreamed of attempting to tell such a story in front of us, no matter how much the worse for drink he might be!'

'If Roderick had dared to tell a *risqué* story before me, I should have told him exactly what I thought of him!' her aunt retorted. 'And as for being ashamed of our appearance, far from being humiliated, I am proud! Never once have we lowered our moral standards, my dear child, indeed we have been far more decent than many in modern evening dress.'

She paused to allow the manifest common sense of her words to penetrate to her niece's understanding; she was about to elaborate on her theme when——

'Listen!' Julia exclaimed. 'I heard voices outside. Don't unlock the back door—remember what Roderick said!'

Mrs Dolman was not to be intimidated. 'Who is there?' she demanded in a bell-like boom. 'What do you want?'

They soon recognised the voice of Mackenzie, the house-man, and it was not long before he persuaded them to admit him and his two companions.

In the drawing-room Roderick came to the climax of his story: 'I should have known from the first, Fanny, where your *real* interests lay.'

He paused for the laughter and applause to subside; yet all further comment was prevented by a resounding knocking which came almost immediately upon the drawing-room door. This was opened to admit Mackenzie, and two fishermen from the village, in a great state of agitation.

7

RODERICK FERNAY listened without any surprise to the extraordinary story which Mackenzie, and his son and Sheumas Macrae, now had to tell them; he did not doubt a word of it.

The mist, they said, had descended suddenly and completely; their relations from Glasgow had set off, in spite of warnings, and without a pilot, to make for the island of Lewis. That they had taken the two fishing smacks which provided a livelihood for most of the village, was forgotten almost immediately in the realisation of the danger they would meet; for the whole area was teethed with rocks; no lighthouse operated, all buoys were out of position.

In their extremity, Mackenzie said, the leaders of the community had decided to seek help from the Navy, for they knew there was a naval station of some strength upon the island. In spite of the severe discouragement they had received in the past when attempting to land, six of them had set out, just after nightfall, in a small, unwieldy coble, and had rowed out to Ebora.

It had seemed to the men, rowing with a furious urgency of purpose, that the water was of such a viscid character that it had impeded their oars; however hard they worked they seemed to make little progress. Then suddenly the darkness was cut by a strong beam of light, and at the same time a disembodied voice came through a loud hailer, saying: 'Make no attempt to land! Turn back immediately, or you will be shot down!'

These instructions were repeated in the Gaelic, and heard with alarm and suspicion by those in the boat.

'I warn you men! Do you understand me?' came the voice

again, in educated, authoritative accents. 'You have two minutes from now to alter course; if not, we fire!'

'We need help!' Mackenzie had shouted, through cupped hands. 'All we want is your help; there are boats in danger!'

The mist muffled and distorted all sound; he could not be sure he had been understood.

'Let us turn back,' Macrae had urged. 'We shall be shot like dogs!'

A metallic noise had come from the loudspeaker, and after a brief interval a different voice, one with a mysteriously familiar timbre, spoke to them, demanding: 'Who are you? What help do you need?'

They had revealed their identity, and told their story, of the predicament of the two vessels, *Isle of Arran* and *Island Flower*, and their unlucky passengers. There was a short conference upon the yacht, from which they now realised the voices came, then: 'Stay where you are, and we will come alongside,' the first voice had ordered.

('This is extremely sinister,' Roderick remarked in a low voice, as the tale proceeded, 'I have a pretty shrewd idea what is coming—— Go on, go on!')

There had been the noise of a fast motor launch coming towards them out of the mist; a strong light shone into the boat as it came abreast (but not too close) and they could see that the crew were naval personnel. Sitting in the stern was a muffled figure, in a sou'wester, drawn low over his brow, who kept his face averted, but whose voice they all recognised beyond doubt, having heard it so many times over the radio. This individual asked further questions, and gave orders to the crew.

'Your friends will be rescued—never fear!' he had announced, as one whose pronouncements, like those of a tribal god, had to be believed. He held a whispered consultation with a senior lieutenant, from which only the phrase '. . . gunboat. No, no—the one with the Merlin apparatus, you understand me,' was to be distinguished.

'Go back ashore, and tell them that—ah—their relatives will be taken care of,' the man in the sou'wester had instructed them in ringing, confident tones. 'The Navy has the matter well in hand. But tell them also that, mmmm, *on pain of death*, there must be no more snooping round this or any other island in the vicinity. I cannot, mmm, too strongly stress the importance of this order.'

The launch had made away into the darkness towards the yacht from which a strong red light was visible, even through the mist.

'So it was the Prime Minister!' Roderick could wait no longer to announce. 'I knew it! I have known all along that Ebora was a centre of the Highest Security, the Topmost secrecy. The Government's sudden and cowardly desertion of Britain is now explained—how right I was! How right!' Given the slightest encouragement, Mr Fernay would now have mounted a favourite hobby-horse, and his audience would have been treated, then and there, to his dissertation upon the corruption of Cabinet Ministers, and his belief that the real rulers and directors of policy were a posse of Big Business Men and Armament Kings.

Yet the words 'Do not trust these people!' had hardly been uttered, when a dull, muffled boom shook the room. This was closely followed by another; and then, as they flung wide the windows, by a universal moan, as though the ocean herself had spoken.

They looked at one another.

'God have mercy on their souls!' exclaimed Roderick.

The news of the terrible disaster which had overtaken the two boats lay like a pall, thicker than the sea mist (which still persisted), over Achnabasalt on the Monday morning.

It was given out that the boats must have holed upon one of the two giant pinnacles of rock which guarded the approaches to the channel between the islands and the mainland. The likelihood was that the first boat had struck *A Cailleach*, the Rock of the Old Woman, and the other, following close in the wake, had collided with her before it was realised what had happened.

Both vessels had sunk without trace; so far as was known, there were no survivors. A bulletin to this effect was handed in by a junior naval lieutenant, who came across in a pinnace, and left the message under a stone on the jetty, without speaking to anyone. The notice contained the additional warning that nobody must attempt to approach the island again. 'As you are all contaminated by radio-activity, and as it is most necessary that those on the island (who are of the first importance for the

48

continued safety and well-being of Britain) should keep free of this, much as we should regret it, we should be forced to fire upon anyone disobeying these instructions.'

Roderick went down with Dick to read this bulletin, which had been pasted to the inside of the Post Office window.

'It is dastardly,' was his comment. 'Yet it is typical. *They only are fit to survive*, do you see? Here we have yet another self-constituted Remnant. We have Bellerophon and his racially pure Aryans; we have the Spiritually Superior Heavenly Brethren, and now we have the Monstrous Regiment of Plutocracy, for that is all it amounts to.'

The villagers stood waiting for the bodies to be washed up by the incoming tide.

'I am deeply sorry for what has happened—if there is anything I can do——' Roderick said, but they stared, as though he spoke in an unknown tongue. So many corpses were coming home, as it were, upon the small waves, amongst the flotsam of the wrecks, that Roderick felt it imperative that the ladies of Achnabasalt be prevented from coming down to the beach.

Mr Beek offered his service to the minister. 'I could at least help with the burials,' he suggested, but Mr Macalpine refused to be associated with a Papist and unbeliever.

As he walked sadly from the shore, Mr Beek was accosted by a tall negro.

They fell into one another's arms, with every appearance of joy, then retreated to a sheltered spot and sat down. When delight had subsided, the clergyman was anxious to hear at once of Odysseus Jackson's adventures since they had parted in Corstorphine.

Odysseus tried to speak; he was unmanned. He could only ask: 'Has my boy been found?' and when answered in the negative, could not control himself sufficiently to be able to speak until some minutes had passed.

'I can tell you quite categorically sir,' he confessed at last, 'that my experiences have caused my rational self to leave me, perhaps for good! I have returned to the primitive behaviour of my forbears. I have no longer a belief in God.'

'You must not blame yourself for what happened!'

'I have never for one minute ceased to blame myself!' cried the distracted Jamaican, clasping his head. 'If I had the courage,

I should throw myself from this cliff! Only the hope that my boy may still be alive somewhere, somehow, prevents me.'

Mr Beek attempted consolation, the black man interrupted: 'I gave way to blind, instinctive panic. I could not realise your desire, all of you, to help and protect me, I forgot my own son! All I knew was that they wanted to kill me—I had to run away at once and hide!'

He had not realised at first that he was in the Zoological Gardens, he said, until he saw the sea-lions, yet he had not paused for an instant in his flight uphill.

'The Colts were close behind me,' he said. 'They were armed.'

Since the city was under siege, orders had gone out that all dangerous animals were to be shot, and this was now being done. Two men with guns had just entered the tigers' cage when Odysseus, closely followed by his enemies, burst in upon them. The door had been left open, and before the keepers could act, one of the enormous cats had sprung, and the first of the Colts suffered a speedy end. Seizing the gun from the surprised official, Odysseus had turned it upon his remaining pursuers, who fled with two other tigers behind them.

Seeing this, Odysseus, still holding his weapon to cover his retreat, had made uphill through the protecting shrubbery as through a jungle, and out of a revolving exit on to Corstorphine Hill.

Here he had lain concealed until dusk. The air was full of shouting, and the cries of dying animals. Towards Edinburgh the sky was red, as Bellerophon sacked the city with systematic thoroughness.

As darkness came, he had ventured down to the road, and, finding no trace of the Heavenly Brethren, had stolen a bicycle, and made for the North, riding it night and day until it buckled beneath him and he could ride no more. Every band of refugees had been asked if they had seen 'a lot of ladies and gentlemen in cloaks, and a little coloured boy', but there was no trace of Nyeri.

Beyond Stirling he had been given a lift in one of the last army lorries, and had made up for his cowardice in Edinburgh by his bravery in assisting some men of the Scots Greys in a skirmish with Bellerophon's army in the foothills of Ben Lui. Together with a single survivor as his companion he had taken to the hills to cross into Glen Orchy, where a crofter had succoured them, and lent them a couple of shelties to ride on. The story of his further adventures and wanderings, by night and alone, through the wild moors of Inverness and Wester Ross, until at last he came to the address given him by Mrs Mottie, were now, mercifully, a dim jumble of events in his mind, which he could not have recounted even had he wished to do so.

'Who am I to blame you?' cried Mr Beek, when Odysseus could say no more. 'I who am so lamentably without faith or direction! I have been blown where the wind blows, until I was miraculously preserved and brought here, for what reason I cannot think!'

He began to tell the Jamaican of their own adventures, and of Mrs Mottie's search for Nyeri, and their prayers for the child's safety.

'Bless her for her kindness!' cried the negro, weeping afresh. 'If only I could see her and thank her!'

'She is here!' Mr Beek was glad to tell him. 'Mrs Mottie is here, at Achnabasalt House! She will be rejoiced to see you, and by means of her heavenly ministers, she can help to find your boy.'

'I must say you and your aunt behaved badly last night, Julia,' Roderick told her in a hurt voice. 'You are my guest; I invited you because I am extremely fond of you. You were my friend before you met any of the others; yet since your arrival I have hardly seen anything of you. You left the room without a word of excuse, during the story-telling; yet you do nothing but trail after Nigel Fidgeon—much good may it do you.'

'You were very rude to my aunt,' Julia retorted. 'You would not let her finish her story.' She became red and flustered; argument always defeated her, and she was afraid of Mr Fernay.

'Your aunt agreed to let me tell her story.'

'You forced her to do so! And—well, I could see what you were going to make of it, and I had no wish to hear it. I think I had every right to leave the room!'

'And what was I going to make of it, pray?'

'Oh, well, something disgusting no doubt. You were drunk, all of you!'

'In what way disgusting? How do you know, since you were not present?'

'Oh I saw a certain expression on your face, and——'

'What right have you to object to an improper story?' Roderick demanded. 'You, whose whole life has been the height of impropriety? How dare you pretend a virtue or demand a respect you have forfeited by years of immorality? The very fact that you and your aunt have slopped about in your night-clothes, since your arrival, has made us accept you at your own estimation.'

'How dare you speak to me like that!' Tears spouted from Miss Miles's splendid eyes. 'Oh, oh! I knew this would happen! I said so to Aunt Maggie! And whose fault is it that we have nothing better to wear? Who was it said on the first night how wonderful we looked? But I will pack immediately, and go to Strumph Hydro, if necessary!'

'That would hardly be your *métier*!'

'Aaa-aoh!' Uttering a cry like a cat whose neck is being wrung, Julia ran from the room.

Roderick was sorry at once that he had let his temper get the better of him, and sought out Dick Bolton in the morning-room, begging him to intercede for him with Julia. 'The old lady can do as she likes,' he added.

Dick was silent.

'I have been so upset over this horrible business, and what we saw on the shore this morning, that I hardly know what I am saying or doing. To be a Laird is a great responsibility, and now they are turning to me at last in their difficulties—— Yet I should not have allowed myself to quarrel with Julia. Her trivial attitude, at a time like this, irritated me. But I am fond of her. She has many good qualities.'

'You are in love with her, although you don't know it,' Dick said. 'Don't shout at me! It is not physical love. I don't know that I would call it mental affinity either, for she is not on the same intellectual plane as you, not by a long chalk. I would rather say you are obsessed by the idea of Julia.'

'What a ridiculous thing to say!'

'Oh it is quite true; I have known it for months. What do you suppose your little story last night was about, if not about her?'

'There is not a word of truth in what you say. You are behaving just as in the bad old days before your illness, Dick. Be careful! You are letting things get twisted in your mind!'

Dick covered his face with his hands. When at last he bared his face he was pale but calm. 'I apologise,' he said. 'I too was a little upset by what happened to the boats. We seem to have been living in a dream, and believing nothing of the kind could happen to us; but now I feel as though some dreadful fate were approaching, and nothing could stop it!'

Roderick said nothing, merely waiting abstractedly until Dick should have finished speaking.

'I am not going to speak to Julia on your behalf, however,' Dick went on, in a different, firmer voice. 'You can do your own dirty work.'

'Have you taken a dislike to Julia?' Roderick enquired.

Dick left the room.

'And how are your patients in the camp?' asked Mrs Dolman, walking beside Doctor Monro, as he pushed Nigel's chair along the road. 'I hope there is not to be an epidemic?'

'Oh I should not think so. Of course, there is very little I can do without proper medication.'

'Just what is happening?'

'Oh, some form of gastro-enteritis,' Sydney told her.

'I hear it is very bad, especially amongst the children.'

'What are you talking about?' Nigel demanded.

Doctor Monro was compelled to give a guarded, colourless account to his patient.

'If it is infectious, it is your duty to keep away. Can't the village doctor deal with it?'

As he was paying Sydney a large retaining fee to be his personal physician, he felt he had the right to demand this precaution.

'There is no doctor here. The nearest one lives twenty miles off.'

'Sydney should not ignore the Call of Suffering, wherever it is found,' Mrs Dolman announced. 'Even if he feels there is little he can do, he can at least give them the benefit of his knowledge, and his Moral Support.'

'On the contrary, it is his duty to keep infection away from us,' Nigel insisted. 'It may be typhoid, or cholera; how can you tell? There is nothing he can do, as he says, to prevent these people dying like flies; and much as one may sympathise, I venture to believe that the lives of some, at least, at Achnabasalt House are more worth preserving than a collection of brash young bi-cyclists. For my useless self, I am indifferent to death, but would have wished it to be speedy and as pleasant as possible.'

'Who are you to be the judge of the value of a Life?' cried Maggie Dolman, barring the way, resplendent in her Paisley shawl. 'Who are you to say who is too worthy to survive? If you forbid the doctor to go amongst these unfortunates, and if he is too great a coward to disobey you, then I shall attempt it! I may be ignorant of modern scientific methods, but I was a V.A.D. in 1917. And I shall take One with me who will be of more use to them than any doctor, with all the degrees of Paris, New York or Edinburgh behind him!'

'If you go, it is entirely at your own risk,' Sydney warned her, returning her shawl which had dropped to the ground.

'And who is this healer amongst us?' enquired Nigel, as the chair went forward once more. 'A member of the sacred and exclusive Brethren, I suppose?'

'It cannot concern you, feeling as you do about humanity,' Mrs Dolman rebuffed him. 'It is a Humble Channel, that is all I am prepared to say.'

She marched ahead, her shawl, like a Roman toga, wrapped about her. As they approached the house, Mary Mottie ran out.

'Oo ever d'you think 'as turned up?' she demanded gleefully. 'My friend Odysseus Jackson oo I thought was dead! Ooh, am I glad to see 'im! Come and meet all the friends, Odysseus!' she called, leading the enormous negro by the hand.

8

M R BEEK was studying Psalm seventy-nine: '*The dead
bodies of thy servants have they given to be meat unto the fowls of the
heaven, the flesh of thy saints unto the beasts of the earth.*

'*Their blood have they shed like water round about Jerusalem, and there was
non to bury them.*

'*We are become a reproach to our neighbours, a scorn and derision to them that
are round about us.*'

There was a knock at his bedroom door. He opened it. Mrs
Mottie and Mrs Dolman were waiting without.

'You 'ave work to do, Mr Beek dear,' Mrs Mottie told him.

'What work?' he asked in alarm.

'The Lord 'as chosen you,' Mrs Mottie said simply.

His legs felt weak beneath him; she sat down on a nearby
chair. 'Chosen me for what?' he asked, in a trembling tone.

'My Guide told me this morning that you are the Chosen
One,' Mrs Mottie informed him. ' "*He is the instrument of the Lord*,"
the Chief said to me. Six o'clock this morning it was. I open my
eyes and there 'e stood, plain as plain, in 'is ceremonious robes.
'E don't often come to me like that, on'y when it's something
important. "All in your paint you are," I said to 'im; "something's up, then." 'Course 'e don't mind me. 'E laughed! Beautiful white teeth 'e's got. And I said to 'im: "I know why you 'ave
come, Chief. You 'ave come in answer to our prayers. You 'ave
come to show me, sure and certain, oo is the Chosen One." '

She paused so that her hearers might realise to the full the
significance of the conversation. ' 'E nodded 'is 'ead at me,' she
told them, doing the same. ' "And 'ow shall I know the Lord's
Chosen One?" I ask 'im. And do you know what Chief Bubandu
done then?'

Mr Beek shook his head.

' 'E pointed aht the window!' cried Mrs Mottie. 'So over I goes, and peeks aht—— And there you were!' she finished in triumph.

'I could not sleep for thinking of the tragedy,' Mr Beek admitted. 'About five o'clock I rose, dressed and went into the garden. I walked up and down——'

'You were praying!' asserted Mrs Mottie.

'No, no! How could I pray to a God who allowed such a terrible disaster to overtake the innocent?'

'You were praying!' Mrs Mottie insisted. 'I saw your lips moving! You were praying for a sign, just as I did, and this is your answer, Mr Beek dear. This is wot you were saved for; so now you 'ave to come with us, down to the camp.'

'It is not the answer!' cried the distracted priest. 'How can I be the Chosen of the Lord when I have denied Him, and broken my vows?'

'Oh but you have been chosen, my dear Mr Beek, whether you like it or not,' Mrs Dolman told him equably. 'There is nothing you can do about it. There never is anything the Chosen of the Lord have been able to do about it, from Elisha onwards. It is no use waiting until one feels worthy, or nothing would ever get done.'

She appealed to her niece, who appeared, looking a little sulky, for she had been persuaded, against her will, to stay on at Achnabasalt.

'Don't ask me!' Julia declared, a little hysterically. 'I betray myself in every contact I have with another!'

'Never mind about that, dear,' her aunt cut her short. 'Now listen, kind, good Mr Beek. There is nothing any of us can do now for those poor drowned people from Glasgow, but much we may still accomplish for the living sufferers at the camp in Rona Bay. The mortal sickness is spreading amongst them; a message, just after luncheon, told the doctor that two have died already.'

'But I am not a doctor; what can I do?' cried the wretched clergyman. 'I am old and ill myself!'

'Remember Jonah! It is no use fleeing from the Lord and going unto Tarshish!' Mrs Dolman reminded him. 'You will have to go to Nineveh in the end; it might as well be now. It is your duty to lay your hands on the heads of the sick and heal them in the name of Christ,' she told him briskly. 'As you are an ordained priest, the power is vested in you whether you believe in it, or whether you don't. Besides, the Lord has chosen you. Let us waste no more time. Put on your cassock——'

'I haven't got one!'

'—Take up your prayer book, and come!' was the summons, and each lady seized him by an arm and urged him forward.

'I see a way to save you all,' Odysseus told the leaders of the camp. 'It is an old way. It was taught me by my grandmother who came from Haiti. First, you must get me a cock.'

'It's worth trying. Anything is worth trying,' Calum said. They sat or lay in attitudes of apathy under their flimsy canvas shelters. They had no strength any more.

'Man, we must not give in to this!' cried Odysseus. 'We are young. The young must live, to inherit a new world.'

He did not know why he said it; he had been in an abyss of despair. Now an almost light-headed feeling possessed him. He had fallen in love with the girl from Trinidad, the girl Gloria, who reminded him of his wife; he determined to use any means to save her.

Roderick returned to the house in the late afternoon, after an exhausting session in the village.

A lone survivor from the fishing boats had managed to swim ashore with disquieting news, which had excited and upset him: not even Dick could calm him. 'Although I had known, deep down in my being, that this is what had happened, now I have it confirmed I can scarcely believe such calumny could exist!' he exclaimed, striding up and down the dining-room.

The doctor, who had just returned from the camp, had to hear the story.

The survivor, a relation of Ellie Macrae at the Post Office, had declared that the boats were fired on by 'a sort of torpedo' from a small naval craft, which had immediately made off. The vessels blew up on the instant; everyone else was killed, and only a lucky chance, and the fact that he was a strong swimmer, had saved him.

'I cannot believe that our own navy would fire on British boats!' the doctor argued. 'It would be madness!'

'Ah, but although these appear to be members of Her Majesty's Forces, *they are nothing of the kind*,' Roderick confided, in a low tone. 'These are puppets of a corrupt government, and tools of the Big Business and Armament Kings, who are the real rulers of the world.'

'Frankly I don't believe a word you are saying.'

'It is the sober truth,' Roderick reiterated. 'I am in a position to know it, and Dick will tell you that for a long time I have been increasingly horrified at what I have found out. We have the government the country deserves.'

'If you will forgive me, I think you are talking utter nonsense,' the doctor said.

'For some time we have been heading towards an authoritarian type of government, that you will admit,' Roderick went on, in a reasoning tone. 'The advances of science have dictated it. We have left the Parliamentary Democracy of the nineteenth century a long way behind. We have had to embrace a form of government able to cope with the hegemony of financial and military power, in its enormous and sinister concentrations, which is the pattern today. The people have less and less voice in their own destiny, although they are not aware of it. So it is only natural that Mr Mannifold, our Prime Minister, and his masters, should decide that, if they are threatened by contamination, or even with discovery by a handful of Glasgow keelies in two small fishing boats, they have the right to destroy them, in the interests of the survival of the fittest.'

His dreadful words had the effect of reducing even the doctor to silence.

'However, they may have reckoned without our Highlanders,' Mrs Fernay went on.

'You don't mean they would think of revenge!' cried Dick. 'Why they will be mown in pieces! They must be prevented!'

'I am all for a little Highland bloodshed,' the doctor contradicted him. 'I'd gladly join them.'

'But where is everybody?' Roderick demanded. 'Where are the ladies—where's Julia?'

'I met them in procession, on their way down to the camp with Mr Beek,' the doctor told them.

'They will catch the infection! You should have forbidden them to go!'

'My dear chap, have you ever forbidden Mrs Dolman to do anything?' asked the doctor.

'I myself must fetch her back. Perhaps it is not too late!' So saying, Roderick strode out of the house; yet in a few minutes he was seen returning at a run.

'They have gone completely mad down there!' he announced. 'They are singing and dancing. Come and see!'

As they rushed into the air they could hear a sound of distant chanting, and the thundering of feet.

'Bring the sick out here! Lay them by the fire!' the Jamaican ordered.

After their first surprise at such a wild, painted figure as Odysseus now presented, the campers obeyed him.

'Play the drums!' he commanded. 'Go on, man; play those drums!' He knelt, muttering to himself, tracing patterns in the ashes. Then he stood, throwing something on to the flames which he took from a leather bag, hung from his neck. There was a burst of fire; the smoke curled, writhing into the air. The drums beat louder.

'Aaaaeee-ah!' shouted Odysseus in a loud, terrible voice.

'Aaaa-eee-aah!' answered the campers in unison.

The Jamaican leapt; he exploded into the air in a bound; he sprang, he danced upon the sand, sending up a fine cloud of dust.

'Ooo-lulla-lulla-lulla!' beat the rhythm of the chanting with the banging and the beating of the bongo drums, the twanging of the guitars, as Odysseus danced in his frenzy, as the cyclists, in their madness, danced with him.

Of themselves, in their sickness, they had no strength; yet under this fevered possession they shot three feet into the air.

Into the midst of this uproar, Maggie Dolman was about to lead Mr Beek; but they were arrested on the perimeter of the circle by the extraordinary sight before them.

The sick had arisen from their pallets; they were joining in the dance.

'Come! Let us go back to the house,' Mrs Dolman commanded. 'There is no need for us to remain an instant longer.'

    ·   ·   ·   ·   ·

'What do you make of it?' Roderick enquired of the doctor later in the evening.

'Well, of course, when the ground is prepared by a fervent mass hysteria, such as we saw this afternoon, anything may happen,' was the reply. 'It is the right climate for an instantaneous, and apparently miraculous, healing. I shall be surprised if the effect is lasting.'

Roderick hardly listened to his reply. 'Julia—speak to me!' he begged. 'You are not still angry?'

Instead of replying, Miss Miles crossed to where the doctor stood, the usual glass in his hand. 'Go down and see what you can do to improve the lot of these wretched people!' she besought him, almost in tears.

The experience of the healing had been a great deal too much for her. It had been too dramatic, too vulgar and ostentatious for her sensitive nature to endure. It had smelt in her nostrils, far worse than the stench from the foetid latrines.

9

IN SPITE of Doctor Monro's pessimism, there were no relapses amongst the campers on the following day, and he was able to recruit an enthusiastic labour squad to dig trenches for new latrines, to disinfect and fill in old ones, to burn rubbish and infected clothing.

Only Mr Beek remained in a state of bewilderment, retiring to a lonely place to meditate. Mrs Dolman went in search of him, however, for it was her opinion that too much solitude was bad for him. She took him a little luncheon in a hand-woven basket; some nourishing broth and chicken sandwiches. To please her he drank a mouthful of soup, and ate a bite or two; yet after a minute he waved the food away.

'You must not give way, nor continue to let the events of yesterday upset you,' she counselled him.

'I cannot get it out of my mind—— That power was not Divine—it was evil! No good can come of it!'

'It cannot concern you, Mr Beek, nor divert you from your purpose. Your strength must be in the Lord. Another little sandwich?'

He shook his head, and she continued: 'Your work is not begun yet, Mr Beek. It will be shown you. *You have been chosen* and nothing can change it!'

The mist had lifted, and concentrated itself into one black and lowering cloud, which seemed to hang directly over the Island of Ebora. As Mrs Dolman assisted the clergyman down the precipitous path they met no living thing save a sickly sheep, staggering drunkenly between the rocks. She paused absently, to bless the animal, which, almost as soon as she had passed, fell over and died; then, trotting as briskly as possible down the rutted track, she attempted to distract Mr Beek's attention by enquiring how he imagined Mr Mannifold and the Cabinet must pass their time on the island; did he think they played cards, or perhaps attempted a few shots at golf on the far side of Ebora.

'What a pity they did not think of bringing the Queen up here with them!' she remarked. 'She is so fond of the Highland air; yet I heard a rumour Prince Philip had flown her to Australia which is not too hot at this time of year, and free from radiation, unless, of course, China has decided to do a little bombing of its own in the Southern Hemisphere.'

She bent down to pick a spray of wild thyme, which smelt delicious. The poisonous conditions had not evidently affected the flowers as yet.

'Nobody will be able to shoot any birds this season, thank heavens,' she noted with satisfaction, carrying on her monologue to which Mr Beek had long since ceased to make any reply. 'But, of course, there are no birds to shoot.'

So, urging the old man homewards, with a gentle pressure on his arm, and an inconsequential flow of useless information, Mrs Dolman came at last to the gate of Achnabasalt.

'Mr Mannifold's money was all made in armaments,' Roderick told Dick Bolton. 'And there is your answer. War is big business to him.'

Dick gazed at his employer with a look Mr Fernay could not interpret, but which left him uneasy.

'It is no use looking like Little Owl, and attempting to distract me,' Roderick went on. 'I have My Own People to think of now. They look to me for leadership and protection. However, I see it is useless for me to discuss this further with you. You do not believe me, any more than Sydney does. If anything, you think me mad.'

'Since I am mad myself, it makes not the slightest difference,' Dick replied. 'I don't happen to be interested in politics.'

'Everyone must interest themselves in politics. They are a part of living,' Roderick retorted.

They were interrupted by Julia, who approached, a finger on her lips. 'Please do not talk so loudly! Mr Beek is giving Nigel healing!' she told them. 'We must pray for him; we must give it Every Chance.'

Mrs Dolman approached Laetitia Tomkins like an angelic messenger, wrapped in her cape; Laetitia and Miss Minim awaited her coming.

They could not be unaware of the atmosphere of portent she brought with her.

Mrs Dolman spoke first. 'I hoped to find you,' she began, using the hushed, reverent tone suitable to the occasion, and to the news she brought. She turned, and walked with them towards the Hydro. A seat in a sheltered spot attracted the ladies; they sat down.

'There has been a revelation of Power,' Mrs Dolman told them. 'Yet it is not of the Divine. There has been a Mass Healing, but it makes me uneasy.'

She told the story of Odysseus and the campers in the simplest, most direct way, and awaited their comments. 'We need your help,' she concluded.

A look passed between the two other ladies. They had thin, reserved faces, and hair drawn into knots on their necks. Laetitia wore a velvet band at her throat.

'One has to be very careful to be guarded at a time like this,' she said at last. 'Especially those of us who are preparing ourselves for revelation.'

'You mean you will not come over and help us to exorcise this spirit of evil?' demanded Mrs Dolman.

Miss Minim jumped up, but was restrained by Laetitia's thin, transparent hand. 'We will pray for you very especially,' Miss Tompkins promised. 'Go back and rest, dearest Maggie.'

'Rest!' exclaimed Mrs Dolman. 'I never felt less like resting! There is work to be done, and I must do it!'

She pulled her wig and her hat straight. 'I came here against my better judgement, because of the seriousness of the situation at Achnabasalt,' she told the two Brethren. 'I wish I had not troubled to take the fatiguing walk. I might have guessed what your answer would be!'

Indeed, in face of her disappointment, the homeward way was exhausting to the elderly actress, nor was she much encouraged on her arrival at Achnabasalt to be told: 'Mr Beek's healing has made absolutely no difference to Nigel; in fact he is more depressed than before.'

.   .   .   .   .

As the Mackenzies had announced that because of the tragedy in the village they could no longer attend in the capacity of servants, Julia offered to cook the dinner that evening.

'For God's sake give us no more salmon-trout!' had been the plea; so she had found and opened a number of tins and packets. She boiled potatoes but they turned black—they had to be thrown away.

Nigel, after the failure to heal him, had retired to bed; Mr Beek, ashamed, had also excused himself.

'I should never have allowed this hocus-pocus,' Sydney Monro said to Julia, as he came into the kitchen to fetch a tray for his patient.

'Make him eat,' Julia begged in a tragic voice. 'I have saved some breast of chicken for him!'

The doctor made no reply. He opened a bottle of champagne.

'Not bad,' he remarked, sampling the wine.

'I suppose that means he is dying!' Julia trembled with emotion.

'We are all dying, my dear lady, and the quicker the better,' said the heartless doctor, draining his glass, and taking the tray from her before she dropped it. He was thinking of Sylvia, whom he had arranged to meet as soon as dinner was over. Her pretty face, with its appearance of inane innocence, had inflamed him as no other woman's could do.

As soon as he had gone, Julia burst into tears, and wept into the soup. She helped herself to a glass of champagne, just as the doctor returned to take the bottle; but he made no remark.

'Is dinner ready?' asked Roderick, putting his head round the door. 'Is there anything I can do? Mrs Mottie has decided to hold a séance afterwards, so the sooner we get this meal over and done with, the better.'

He helped to carry the dishes into the dining-room.

The soup, which was half cold, was eaten in silence, except for Mrs Mottie, who was unusually talkative.

'You remember when I first come to you, Mr Fernay?' she reminded him. 'I daresay you've forgotten, but I shan't never forget that day; the day I come to your 'ouse in answer to the advert. From that moment,' she told the others, '' e could not 'ave been kinder to me if I'd been 'is own flesh and blood. If it 'adn't of been for 'im, I should never 'ave developed. No, I was afraid of giving in to it; I thought it was a hevil madness, see. But Mr Fernay took me down to that circle in Eccleston Square, and——'

'Yes, yes, Mrs Mottie, there is no need to elaborate upon it,' interrupted her idol.

Mrs Mottie wiped her streaming eyes. Perhaps, thought Dick, she had been drinking; she had had two glasses already of the white Chianti, which was having a strange effect upon everyone, and Julia had told him she kept a supply of milk stout beneath her bed.

Julia felt as though she were floating a little above the table. 'I took infinite pains with this meal, but it is completely tasteless,' she said, speaking in a thick, strange voice. 'What a waste of effort.'

'It is a charming meal,' the doctor told her. 'Allow me to compliment the cook.'

He leaned over and took a rose from the bowl in the centre of the table, and handed it to her with a low bow.

'I must go and fetch——' she began, and hiccuped politely.

He opened the door for her. Holding the rose like a votive candle before her, she swept from the room.

Dick, who, like the Dormouse, had fallen asleep, his head in his plate, now woke up to ask: 'But why hasn't the United States done anything about Britain in her hour of need?'

So great had been the chaos in their minds that nobody had thought of this before.

'Why indeed?' demanded Roderick. 'Yes, why?'

He thumped the table.

'We don't know that they haven't,' Sydney felt bound to say. 'We have no means of knowing what is happening in the world outside our little community.'

'Let yourself go, Mrs Mottie,' the medium quoted from her book of happy memories. 'Let yourself slide over; after the first time it'll be as easy as yawning; that's what this lady told me.'

'They have deserted us! They do not care!' Roderick was working himself into a frenzy, as Dick sped quickly round the table collecting dirty dishes and forks. 'Our most loyal ally (we might have expected it of France, knowing what de Gaulle thinks of us). But America! I have such good friends, all over the

States, who have told me they would give their life's blood for England—you see how little it means!'

The perfidy of the United States almost overwhelmed him. He collapsed in his chair at the thought of it.

'If I could have half an hour on the national networks to talk to them, I would explain how Mannifold has misled them!' he cried.

Dick swept up the crumbs round his host, working with speed to get the room ready for Mrs Mottie and her séance.

10

'MRS MOTTIE is not in a trance at all; she is in a stupor,'
Roderick broke the heavy, carpeted silence in the
darkened room after half an hour.

'Let us put one more hymn on the gramophone!' pleaded
Dick, well knowing the effect of such a disappointment on his
friend. 'What about "Jerusalem the Golden"? It is such a jolly
tune, it always has a good effect on the Chief.'

'No!' Roderick was decided. 'We will waste no more time.
Nothing is likely to happen now. Don't put on the lamp! It
might be dangerous, in her condition. Wake her up gently. I
can't stand her snores any longer.'

'Mottie!' called Dick, in a low, insistent monotone. 'Mrs
Mottie!'

'Wake up, Mrs Mottie!' Roderick ordered her.

'A-aarch! Oooh,' groaned the medium, twitching in her seat.

In a minute, however, she opened her eyes and asked, in a
normal voice: 'Everything all right, then?'

Instead of answering her, Dick enquired how she felt.

'I've been ever so far off. Yes.'

'You have been snoring,' Roderick told her sourly, rising to
put a match to the paraffin lamp. As the light flowered, everyone
appeared stripped of personality for an instant, like a row of
effigies.

'So it wasn't no good,' Mrs Mottie realised, gazing from one
to another, and wiping her face with her hands. 'I thought that,
you know, before ever we started. The conditions were bad
tonight, like a weight, pressing me down. I've ever such a
'eadache with it. Ffff!'

She drank water, sip by sip, touched her lips with a

handkerchief, looking round as though she saw strangers. 'There's a child here tonight,' she told them. 'A little girl; a lovely little soul, ever so bright with curls all over. Gives a name like Olive.'

Everyone was unanimous in rejecting Olive, so cross were they at the failure of the séance; especially Odysseus, who, in spite of a professed rationalism, had cried: 'But what of my son? What of Nyeri?'

'It's no use, dear: I can't get through to the Chief tonight. It's the conditions. Oh dear, oh dear; something very bad is 'appening, I sense it!' She belched a little, politely covering her mouth. 'Pardon me! Oh dear, my 'ead! I think I'll go and 'ave a lay down, if you'll excuse me, Mr Fernay.'

'Do that, Mrs Mottie! Go to bed and sleep it off!' Roderick commanded her briskly, eager to tidy the effect of her personality out of the room.

In truth, as Dick could tell, Mr Fernay had not been in as calm a state, nor in as receptive a mood as might have been helpful; a condition for which he, Dick, had been responsible with his demand: '*And what of the United States?*' The more Roderick dwelt upon the challenge, the more frustrated he felt. That he, the international television personality, with contacts in the innermost circle of the Pentagon, should be so ignorant of the state of the world, was wormwood to him.

'After all, it is no worse than a number of other mysteries which we have dismissed quite easily,' Sydney Monro attempted to console him. 'Such as why no general mobilisation was ordered; and why the Army was so depleted by its scattering abroad, in so many theatres of war, that it had no effect upon Bellerophon.'

'How right you are!' Mrs Dolman came to life at the words. 'Where are all those splendid creatures, the Guards? Where are those glorious Grenadiers and Fusiliers: where have the Highland Divisions hidden themselves, they who ought to have sprung to the aid of their own kinsfolk, their kilts swaying and pipes playing?'

The emotion in her beautiful voice brought tears to the eyes of her hearers. The doctor, however, felt bound to point out: 'In modern atomic warfare a hundred thousand fully trained and experienced soldiers could be destroyed in an instant.'

'They could be held in reserve, I suppose.'

'No doubt they have been put into a coma, by modern scientific methods,' Mrs Dolman agreed. 'They could be frozen, and kept in refrigeration, perhaps for months at a time. I can just see it—rows of perfectly dressed troops, equipped for battle, in some underground ice-house, like boxes of lead soldiers, ready to rise when the Hour Strikes and the Trumpet Sounds!'

'That is all very well, but what I wish to know is, what is happening in the world? Or, at the very least, what is happening to Britain? Is it covered by a pall of death? Are the streets strewn with corpses? And, if so, *what is being done?*'

He received no reply. The doctor crossed to the window, where, in the half-light, he could see several boats being rowed, with an appearance of urgency, towards the shore. A rolling mist was rising; it was difficult to identify the rowers.

'How is Nigel now?' Julia took the opportunity of asking Sydney. 'Why, oh why, were those silly cyclists healed, while he, who has so much to give the world, remains untouched?'

'It is in Higher Hands; we may not question it.' Mrs Dolman raised red velvet arms to the ceiling.

'That is pitiful nonsense!' Roderick contradicted her.

Sydney hardly heard the question; his attention was on the boats which now grounded upon the beach. Immediately figures jumped ashore, and ran up the rocks.

'Something has happened!'

With these words Sydney diverted their attention; he told them of the boats, of the figures even now approaching Achnabasalt House with news of a momentous character.

'I was afraid of this,' Roderick said, in a more cheerful voice. 'There must have been a massacre.'

'Do you mean upon the island? You think the V.I.P.s have been murdered?'

'Since it is our people who have returned, I must believe it. I was afraid it might be the other way about. Yet no doubt they were taken by surprise. Mr Mannifold and his associates could hardly have expected such regardless bravery; they do not know our Highlanders.'

'It is the Law of Moses; an eye for an eye and a tooth for a tooth,' Mrs Dolman remarked. 'I am shocked by such a return to barbarism. I dislike Mr Mannifold, but he is sincere, and has acted according to his beliefs. To be knifed under cover of darkness, is the basest treachery.'

'So you do not think it base and treacherous to order those harmless boats to be exploded?'

'There is no proof he ever did so,' replied the actress calmly. 'I have no reason for believing that story to be true.'

There was a pounding upon the front door, and Roderick went at once to answer it. Those in the room could hear his voice raised in excitement.

'I hope he does not intend bringing the murderers into this room, with the fresh blood on their hands,' Mrs Dolman said. 'It is obvious we shall be the next to go. Let us be found standing here,' she suggested, drawing her red velvet dressing-gown about her. She placed an arm round her niece, who tonight wore flowing draperies of dove-grey wool, with heliotrope frills at the neck and wrists.

'I pray that I may remain calm,' Julia was heard to say. 'I hope I shall not be forced to scream.'

'If I am to die, I will do so sitting down,' Dick Bolton announced. 'My legs might give way at the wrong moment.'

'Why don't you go to Roderick's assistance?' asked the doctor. 'If all is as you say, he is in the greatest danger.'

The front door slammed, and Julia screamed in C flat. A minute later Roderick returned to the room. His face was pale, yet he was quite composed. 'I asked them to stop and have a dram,' he told them, 'but in the circumstances they felt they must return home as soon as possible. It was an honour which I greatly appreciate, that they felt they must come to me first with the news. It shows that they are beginning to trust me.'

'What news? What has happened?'

'How many did they butcher?'

'None. None whatsoever.'

Dick felt for his last cigarette, and lit it.

'They crept up to the island, under cover of darkness,' Roderick told his story. 'It had all been most carefully planned. Macrae and Alisdair Mackenzie are Commando-trained—— They shipped their oars, and glided the last hundred yards—— The sea was as calm as a trout pool——'

'Go on!'

'There was nobody on board the yacht!'

He paused for their astonishment.

'At first they thought it was a trick; they looked for mines and booby traps. They searched with the greatest thoroughness. There was not a single soul on board. And the whole ship had been stripped bare!'

'Perhaps they were in hiding!'

'You have not listened to what I said! The ship was *bare*! Not a scrap of food, not a piece of linen, no upholstery! And the reason soon became plain, oh yes! They have gone into hiding all right, but not from us! They are battened down into their deep shelters, but not to escape from the Macraes and the Mackenzies, but to be safe from the rats!'

An exclamation of horror came from the ladies.

'When our men landed upon the island they had to run for their lives back to the boats. Hundreds and thousands of rats were in possession; the very army of rodents which were seen, two nights ago, entering the sea, have occupied Ebora. They have eaten the sheep; they are eating their way through those stores which were left above ground; there are even the skeletons of two or three unfortunates who did not escape to the shelters in time. They are an outsize in rats, as big as coypus; God knows where they have come from!'

'What about the Navy?' the doctor asked. 'Are they going to sit by and see the Government eaten alive or suffocated? It would be quite simple, one would think, to put out a spray of poison gas and finish off the rats.'

Nobody had an answer; each one was silent, thinking of the escape they themselves had had through the simple accident of the rats taking to the water instead of remaining on the mainland. It was so gnawing a fate to contemplate that Julia felt a little faint; it sobered the whole party as little else could have done.

The ladies took up their bedroom candles and made for the staircase; Sydney slipped out of the garden door into the night, and Dick looked in on Nigel, on his way up to bed, to tell the invalid of the evening's adventures, and make sure he had all he required.

'What a pity the rats did not finish us all off,' was Nigel's comment, on hearing the grotesque story.

'I am sorry about your disappointment this afternoon.'

'I did not feel I should be healed. It is a comfort to know however that I shall not be alone in death; it cannot be far away for any of us.'

The calm voice in which this was said made Dick fear the expected. As he hurried from the room, he was certain that the invalid, disappointed in his last hope of cure, meant to take his life that very night.

He tapped upon Julia's door, and, when she opened it, held a whispered consultation with her, telling her of his suspicions.

'I don't want to alarm Roderick,' he said. 'He has enough to worry about. If only Sydney had not gone down to the camp——'

'If Nigel dies, I don't want to live,' hissed Julia. 'I could not bear life without him!'

'What nonsense is this?' came Mrs Dolman's voice, and she appeared, like a votaress, shielding her one candle from the wind. 'How could he kill himself? He has not the means!'

'He has sleeping tablets at his bed side. He could take an overdose!'

'Then why did you not remove them?' Maggie Dolman demanded.

'Oh, I had a presentiment that this would happen!' sighed Julia.

She fled like a great grey moth from the room, gliding down the stairs to her beloved.

Down at the camp a duet was being performed by the doctor and his Sylvia, who were both skilled in the technique of such affairs. She stood combing her hair, outside the caravan, wrapped in a pink plastic mackintosh, and, it is to be imagined, accompanying her diatribe with all the flourishes attendant on rolling a score of ringlets into plastic rollers, and pinning them into position upon her head.

'You needn't bother to come here any more, Syd! A fine doctor you turn out to be; keeping away in case it was catching, and letting all those poor people die!'

Sydney did not feel that this was worth the trouble of an answer, merely tightening his hold on the waist beneath the plastic covering.

'*And* good night!' she finished.

'What do you mean, good night? It is quite early.'

'It's cold, and I'm going in.'

'You can't go yet. I want to talk to you.'

'I don't want to talk to *you*——'

'Sylvie!' called Beattie from within the caravan. 'Come away to bed. I want some kip even if you don't!'

'I despise you, reely I do.' Sylvia stuck the last grip into position, and tied up her head in a flock nylon scarf.

'Your miraculous healing hasn't improved your temper, has it?' Sydney enquired, continuing his fondling.

'I don't want to talk about it,' she returned primly.

'Why not?'

'Well, it wasn't very nice, was it?'

'What wasn't nice about it?'

She nestled shivering into his arms. 'I wonder when they'll let us go back. I do hate this place, honestly I do.'

'Back where?' enquired Sydney absently, exploring the contours of the map of beauty.

'To London, of course!' Sylvia removed his hand and replaced it upon her waist.

'London may not exist any more.'

'Don't talk so silly! You can't finish London! And when all this fuss is over——'

Sydney silenced this foolish chatter in the only way possible. They drew into the shadows until they were part of them, while a few hundred yards away, Odysseus walked with Glory upon the deserted shore. They strolled hand in hand in the deepest thought.

'You were brought to me, Glory,' Odysseus told the girl from Trinidad for the twentieth time.

'The Lord used you to save me, Odysseus.'

'I know nothing about that, girl. I don't want to know. There is no Lord God, or He would find my son Nyeri.'

'There is a Lord in Heaven, and He will find your child, and bring him to you,' Glory insisted. She was a tall girl, still weak from her illness.

'You saved my reason, Glory,' Odysseus told her. 'I had become a senseless, primitive being once again. None of my education, paid for by the sacrifices of my family, helped me. But do not speak again of what happened on the beach. It is shameful to me, and I have no wish to remember it.'

'Ashamed! The Lord used you to heal me and all those other poor people. That is a silly way to talk, Odysseus!' She shivered in her thin coat.

'You do not remember what happened that day, Glory! You were too ill to know.'

'I can remember dancing to the Lord, upon the sand.'

'I acted like a child, like an ignorant, uneducated person. I gave in to evil!' Odysseus covered his face with his hands.

'Are you too proud to admit the Lord used you? Are you so superior, with your university education, that you can't become humble as a little baby?'

'For pity's sake do not keep talking of the Lord, Glory! He had nothing to do with that day, as I keep telling you!'

The girl put an arm about his shoulder, yet even the warmth of this human contact did not release Mr Jackson from his despair. Glory was a Jehovah's Witness; the name of the Lord was on her lips in every sentence; she had converted twelve since the healings, and was intent upon Odysseus' salvation.

About the same time, upon a northerly part of the shore, Mr Beek had been found, wandering in a state of exhaustion, by Bernard Boonyard, and Coryton Beveridge, and taken to the shelter of Strumph Hydro.

Here he was put to bed, and lapsed almost at once into a state of seeming unconsciousness.

'It is providential he was led to us,' Laetitia Tompkins told Ethel Minim as she tiptoed out of the room where the clergyman lay. 'Here is a Sensitive Soul, in a state of Spiritual Awakening and needing the most sympathetic of atmospheres for True Growth, who has instead (one does not like to say it, but one must) been exposed to the Most Unsatisfactory and Perverse Elements. He has been Exploited and Made Use of.'

'Do you mean by the Astral Powers?' enquired Miss Ann Bulb, a very new member, who had overheard.

Miss Tompkins looked at her with gentle reproach. 'That is a question, dear Ann, which you will be able to answer for yourself, if you ask for Guidance.'

Miss Bulb sighed. It was difficult to remember the special

language to use, and the need at all times to be guarded in speech. As she walked down the corridor, with her hands clasped over her solar plexus, a swarthy, squat figure with unhappy eyes, she wished there were more nice men amongst the Brethren, and dismissed the thought as Unworthy.

As one of the newest and youngest of recruits (she was forty-seven) she was not considered very balanced, and knew herself to be ignorant and inferior. People were most kind, and she was jolly lucky to be here, she kept telling herself, and to have a place reserved for her at the last minute, as it were, upon the vessel of salvation.

As she passed a window on the landing, she glanced out, and thought how strange the sunset appeared. All at once the realisation came to her that the sun had set over an hour before, and the strange flickering glow over the island came from something other than a natural cause.

Bernard Boonyard and his wife Stella were coming towards her from the chapel, and Miss Bulb uttered a low cry and seized Mrs Boonyard by the arm.

'Look! Look at the island! It's a fire, or something!'

If she had not been in such a state of excitement she would have remembered the edict that it was strictly forbidden to speak to Those Who Had Come Out of the Silence for at least an hour afterwards, until they had Come Down in Consciousness. The sudden impact of her coarse rough voice on their state of high sensitivity made Mrs Boonyard reel; and Bernard had to take her in his arms to prevent her falling. He did not even glance out of the window as he bore her away. Mr Beveridge, who had been in attendance, and who realised the seriousness of the situation, stepped forward and took Miss Bulb into the custody of a firm grip.

'What is it, Mr Beveridge? Oh what can it be?' jabbered the unfortunate woman, as she was hurried from the scene.

'It is better not to speak of such things,' Coryton Beveridge told her. 'And never again accost *anyone* who is coming from chapel. The consequences might have been extremely serious.'

The doctor, returning to Achnabasalt house at a trot, summoned by Roderick, found his patient drenched to the skin and highly indignant. Nigel had been about to take his sleeping pill when Julia had thrown herself upon him, knocking it out of his hand, and upsetting the glass of water he held. After the pills had been found and re-bottled and the bedclothes changed, everyone went back to bed in a state of exhaustion. Too much drama had packed the evening; they did not have the slightest interest in looking out of the window, where the glow over the island was fading already.

II

T HE sullen, menacing cloud, which had had such an appearance of evil, had lifted by the next morning, and the mist with it; the island, the rocks, the horizon were all visible like a newly discovered country to their sight. Yet no sun shone; a curious darkness painted the landscape, as though the colours of the spectrum had been sponged away, leaving a monochromatic world.

This melancholy outlook had an effect upon the spirits of all, not least on Mr Beek.

He felt that the dispassionate love and attention which were given him at the Hydro, were his under false pretences, and that he could stay no longer. Therefore, in spite of his weakness he insisted upon dressing himself, and walked out upon the terrace after breakfast, while the Brethren were at prayer in the ballroom. He had been invited to attend, but had refused, saying he felt unable to pray.

Now, clinging to the uneven, weather-beaten balustrade, looking out upon that oily, bird-deserted ocean, Mr Beek cried aloud in his wretchedness to his Maker: 'Why has Thou made a sport of Thy servant, humiliating one who is already in the dust!'

A woman, walking with a child on the beach below, looked up, thinking he addressed her. She was wearing filthy yellow trousers, and carried a rusty saucepan in her hand; the little boy was dark-skinned and emaciated, and walked with a limp.

'I beg pardon? Were you speaking to me?'

'No, no—I apologise. I was talking to myself!'

'Mr Beek was talking to God,' the black boy said.

'It's no use talking to God,' the woman told him. 'Do you know this gentleman, then?'

'Of course he does! It is Nyeri, isn't it?' cried Mr Beek, peering short-sightedly down into the shadowed bay. 'Oh how over-joyed your poor father will be that you are safe and sound!'

'Is there fresh water hereabouts?' the woman asked. 'I was told there was a spring round here somewhere.'

'I will help you to find it,' the clergyman offered. With great difficulty he scrambled down the steep and slimy steps to the shore, his weakness a trouble to him at every breath.

'I will take you to your father at once,' Mr Beek told the boy. 'He has been nearly out of his mind with distress. But how did you find this spot? How did you know where to come?'

Nyeri turned back his ragged T-shirt; a label was stitched to the underside; under a coating of dirt, an address was visible written in Mrs Mottie's characteristic script.

'Is the water far from here?' the woman persisted. Her face had a dried-up, ageless appearance, her hair, which was streaked with grey, fell down her back. Mr Beek led them to the spout in the rock; she filled her pan, paying attention only to the need to hold it steady, so that no drop should spill. Then she knelt upon the sand, and offered it to the boy, who drank thirstily.

'You must come with us, and allow us to take care of you in return for all you have done for the child,' Mr Beek urged her, sitting down on the sand beside her. 'It is easy to see you have suffered much, and are at the end of your strength. Let me hold the pan while you drink!'

The woman shook her head, and turned away.

'Rest here, then, and I will go for someone to help you. I will not be gone longer than a few minutes, I assure you!'

Mr Beek left them, and made the best haste he could up the steps, like a black crow in his flapping coat.

'Where's he gone, then?' the woman, whose name was Mrs Joyce Leland, whispered to the child.

'To fetch my father,' Nyeri answered.

'Do you want to see your father?'

'I d'no,' the boy replied indifferently, drinking from the rusty pan.

'Your father ran away and left you, didn't he?' Mrs Leland reminded him. 'He doesn't want you. We'd best be getting on.'

'I don't want to go no further,' Nyeri said. 'My leg hurts.'

Mrs Leland made no answer; she lay down on the sand. The

pan turned over, the last drops ran out, her arms covered her face.

The boy sat with his bad leg stretched before him, drawing patterns in the sand, filling them with shells and round white pebbles, which were abundant above the tidemarks.

So Miss Minim and Laetitia Tompkins found him, when they came down on their mission of rescue to the shore.

'It's no use trying to wake *her*,' he told them. 'She's dead, like her little baby's dead, and her man's dead back along the road.'

Miss Minim had only to make a brief examination in order to prove that the boy was correct. Hurriedly both ladies blessed the conditions and took the child away from the shore; he was as light to carry as though he had been a baby.

'Why is Roderick wearing a kilt this morning?' enquired Mrs Dolman, as they ate a standing picnic breakfast round the kitchen table.

'He has been accepted as the head of his clan at last,' Dick said. 'Now that every other authority has gone, he must take command; we must obey him.'

Dick himself, although he sounded confident, had certain private reservations. 'Roderick found this kilt of his grandfather's in a cedarwood chest in the attics. It has been perfectly preserved, and he looks simply splendid in it. He has become a new person already; like a king, who when crowned becomes at once a greater person than before.'

The enthusiastic tone in which these words were spoken had no effect upon Doctor Monro.

'I for one have no intention of obeying Roderick, nor do I accept his right to dictate to me,' he announced.

It was clear that he had been drinking; he was unshaven, and unsteady on his feet already. He presented a sight from which the ladies retreated in dismay.

'Don't worry! Sydney will be made to toe the line,' Dick re-assured them, following them from the room. 'Roderick has gone down the village to select his bodyguard; the clan is solidly behind him. If the doctor still refuses to do as he is told, he will be locked up.'

'I don't see how that can benefit anybody,' Maggie Dolman protested. 'What will Nigel do, if he is imprisoned? What will all the sick people do? He is the only doctor now for miles around.

This very morning he is to see poor little Nyeri, who may not live without treatment.'

She swept from the room, and urged her niece to come with her to the top of the house, where the trunks and kists in the garret yielded them a rich harvest of tartan shawls, plaids and sashes, with which to drape themselves. A strong tribal feeling now prevailed at Achnabasalt, appropriate to Roderick's new resolution.

'The house must be garrisoned like a fortress,' Dick declared. He was wearing a MacOrrery tie, to which he had no claim.

'That is not necessary. We shall be protected by Providence if it is meant we should be,' Mrs Dolman contradicted him. She flung open a window. The skirl of pipes was heard, and both ladies burst into tears of emotion.

'How glorious this is! I feel as though I were back in another, finer, simpler age!' cried the actress.

'Here they come!' Julia was leaning over her aunt's shoulder. A ragged crowd came into view, led by a standard-bearer holding a faded flag. Two pipers, followed, in diverse regimental tartan, and behind them, leading the rabble, came a gorgeous figure in a bonnet with three eagle's plumes, a velvet jacket and swinging kilt.

The watchers were in ecstasies at the sight.

The marchers halted just inside the gates of Achnabasalt House, and Mrs Mackenzie carried out a great tray of full glasses which were distributed, and a toast drunk, to cries of '*Slainthe*' and the rallying cry of the MacOrrerys '*Gach Ni Air Neoni*', All or Nothing.

Roderick was seen to address his followers; he finished with a pronouncement in the Gaelic; this was followed by a more lengthy reply in the same language by Sergeant Macrae of the County Constabulary.

Then, at long last, Roderick dismissed his army, and consented to come into the house.

Only now was it apparent that the efforts he had made had tired him. He was persuaded to remove his plaid; Mackenzie knelt before him to take off the brogues with the silver buckles. The man, who had appointed himself Roderick's personal body-guard, could hardly be persuaded to leave him; his apathy of a few days before had been replaced by a burning devotion, which was echoed by the dozen men now sitting in the courtyard behind the house.

Roderick addressed his household: 'Everything in the district is now under control. I have taken entire responsibility. They wished it so. It appears we are quite cut off; no strangers have entered the peninsula for the last week—no news has come from outside. We have food to last for a few weeks yet, if we are not invaded; this we must resist to the limit of our strength.'

'Why?' enquired Nigel, but was ignored completely.

'The first step to take, is to find out what is happening on Ebora.' Roderick spoke with calm determination. 'We must discover if the Government are still in their shelters.'

'Take care!' Mrs Dolman warned him. 'They are more powerful than you are!'

'Where is Sydney?' Roderick demanded.

'He has gone down to the village to see the Reverend Murdo Macalpine,' Nigel announced.

'Whatever for?'

'Oh, in order to arrange to be married,' Nigel told them. 'His paramour will not have him without benefit of such a ceremony, so, as time is short, he is willing to go through with it.'

'He must be mad!' exclaimed Roderick in dismay. 'If he marries that Sylvia, she will have to come and live here. She will spoil everything.'

'If Sydney marries, he will have less time to devote to you,' Dick pointed out to the invalid. 'And less interest in doing so.'

'As he has neglected me for some time, it can make very little difference, one way or the other,' Nigel replied. 'In fact, marriage may improve him; he may settle down, and be less of a bore.'

Roderick, who had been listening closely to this argument, now announced: 'You are right. It is the best thing that can happen. In fact, I have a good mind to follow Sydney's example. I know I have always disliked the idea of being tied down, but as Nigel has pointed out, it can only be for a short space of time. In fact, as clan chief of the MacOrrerys, it is my duty to marry. There must be a first lady at Achnabasalt.'

'Now it is you who are mad, chum,' Dick was heard to say, but little attention was paid to his interpolation. Roderick rose, and crossed the room to the lady of his choice.

'Julia, we like and admire one another, and have done so for years. I think you understand me very well. I cannot imagine anyone better suited to be Lady of Achnabasalt and Strumph, and to be nice to the villagers.'

Julia attempted to speak; words choked her. She rushed from the room.

'What have I said to offend her?' asked Roderick, deeply hurt. 'I paid her the greatest compliment a man can do, and she ran from the room.'

'There is nothing more humiliating to a woman than to be proposed to for the wrong reasons,' Mrs Dolman told him. 'Much as Julia likes you, she is not in love with you. Presently when she grows calmer she will appreciate the honour you have done her in asking her to become the figurehead of the MacOrrery clan.'

'I leave her to you, Nigel!' Roderick suggested. 'No doubt she would lavish her entire devotion on *you*! Go on! Marry her! And I wish you joy of her hysteria!'

He marched from the room, followed by his secretary, carrying all the impedimenta of his new office, his plaid, his cromach, and the *skean dhu* which had fallen from his stocking.

'Yes indeed, you could do worse than marry Julia,' Mrs Dolman said to Nigel, beginning the arrangement of a few phlox, tattered sweet williams and large daisies in a Coleport tureen.

'No, no—such a relationship, quite apart from its futility, would be torture to me! I could never bear to be *pawed about*!'

'I *thought* you would say that,' Mrs Dolman replied. 'Life is increasingly unreal, is it not? All this talk of marriage, all these noble sentiments, and bagpipes playing has an unfortunate effect upon our higher natures. Nobody has thought of lunch. The kitchen fire is out; nobody has made an attempt to relight it. It does not seem to matter that there is no food, and no hot water. I find it most strange, do you not?'

Moving as in a dream, she picked up a few stalks and superfluous leaves, gathering them into a silken apron she wore, and, with her curious, swan-like walk, glided from the room.

'I do wish we could go back to the days when Mr Fernay went in and out the house quietly, without a signature tune,' Mrs Mottie complained, putting her hands to her ears to shut out the sound of the bagpipes. ' 'Ere they come again, and a prisoner with them, by the looks of it.'

Julia leaned out of the landing window and looked down. 'Why—it can't be! It is—it's Mr Mannifold!'

The others crowded round; they ran down into the hall in the greatest excitement, hardly believing what they saw.

'I have taken the Prime Minister into custody for his own protection,' Roderick explained. The noble, solitary figure excited the ladies' compassion. His face bore traces of shock; he gazed quite blankly in front of him, his hands tied behind his back.

Yet his captors were most evidently restrained only by Roderick's influence from putting an end to the scoundrel who had ordered the sinking of the *Innis Nam Blath*, and her sister ship, with all on board.

'Mr Mannifold can remember nothing.'

Roderick motioned to the guards to allow the statesman to sit down.

'The rats should have finished him off!' cried Donald Macrae, with which sentiment the rest of the party were in agreement.

'Justice will be done,' Roderick told them. 'In the meantime he is a sick man; your duty is to use him well.'

He motioned to the guard to take the prisoner away.

'And what of the rats? Are they still in possession of Ebora?' was the first enquiry.

Roderick shook his head. 'It is an astounding story,' he began, much as he might have done before the television cameras. The scouts had found the island completely sterile 'As though it had been scorched by lightning.' The bodies of the rats, charred skeletons, were everywhere. The deep shelters stood open to the air and abandoned; yet on the highest, farthest point of rock, like a later Lear with his wits clean gone, they had found this, the last survivor.

The far sea, which his vacant eyes never ceased to search, was empty of any craft; the desertion of his friends was absolute; so the scouts had taken him, without resistance, and delivered him to their chieftain. Roderick had questioned him, but Mr Mannifold had been unable to reply, nor to tell them how he had come to be there alone, nor what disaster had blanched the island. He remained, as now, in a state of apparent catalepsy.

'You see that it is more than ever necessary that I take charge,'

Roderick pointed out, as Mackenzie appeared with yet another service of whisky and glasses. 'We must make plans for a longer siege than I at first thought. Winter may come before rescue. We must organise parties to gather driftwood, we must——'

'Why must we?' interrupted Nigel. 'Why this waste of effort? Already some of us are affected by a heavenly langour. It will be divine to give in to it completely. If we let go there need be no winter for us.'

His words shocked Roderick, who sought out Sydney a little later in the evening, saying: 'Nigel is in a very bad way. Ever since his attempted suicide I have known it. He looks filthy. We must retain certain standards, or our morale will go. He could do with a shave to start with.'

Sydney, who was in a state of euphoria, thinking of his approaching marriage, could only murmur: 'My dear chap, I have nothing to do with his shaving. If he wants to be dirty, that's his affair.'

'He is your responsibility. While you are both guests under my roof, I insist that you keep him sanitary!'

'I don't take orders from you!' Sydney began, but found himself pinned from behind by two retainers, and immediately put up a strong resistance.

'I really can't stand all that fighting going on, Mr Beek dear,' remarked Mrs Mottie to the clergyman, leading him past this distressing sight, up a back staircase to the room where the boy Nyeri was lying. 'All those drunken layabouts, shouting and swearing, and Mr Fernay so unlike himself. All them swords and pistols—it's like something out of a Western. There'll be an accident soon and finish some of them off and good riddance.'

Mr Beek, with a new calmness and strength, which had sustained him since his stay at the Hydro, entered the small bedroom. The power, when it came upon him, was remarkably invigorating, he felt it to be under his control and quite unlike the healing on the beach.

When they rose from their knees, the boy was in a healthy sleep. Odysseus burst into tears of joy, and Gloria sang praises. As they came downstairs, however, he happened to look out of the window.

The cloud had descended once more to clothe the island with a luminous glow.

12

A FEW days, perhaps a week, elapsed. As nobody now took the trouble to wind their clocks or watches (for there seemed little object in doing so), time had ceased to matter. By day and night the cloud hung over Ebora; after dark it had a ruddy luminosity; nobody would approach the island under any inducement.

The weather continued colourless and sultry; a mist obscured the sun, as though the air were filled with a million visible particles of destruction; even breathing was an effort.

Roderick, however, seemed immune from such a weakness; his galvanic energy infected his followers. He made plans to bring the campers into the rooms above the stables before the bad weather set in, and plans for an expedition to the Outside World.

That these schemes, and others like them, trickled, as it were, into a sea of inertia, escaped his present realisation. Dick Bolton had been ordered to break open the despatch case which contained Mr Mannifold's private papers, and to decipher the documents within. They were in a code, but Mr Fernay was not prepared to make allowances for that.

'Once you have found a keyword, the rest will be easy,' he told Dick, who was surrounded by French, German and Esperanto dictionaries. 'The British Intelligence service is of such a limited brain power that only the simplest cryptograms can be used by them without mistake; everyone knows that nowadays.'

'That's all very well; but these despatches may be in a foreign tongue. Mr Mannifold was an expert in Hindustani and Bantu; I do not know a word of either.'

'Do not be such a defeatist, Dick! It would be very simple for any foreign power to decipher a native dialect, however obscure. This is a code! You will find I am right! The key word is probably something elemental; some memory of schooldays which all educated Englishmen have in common.'

'I wish you would let me speak to Mannifold,' Dick sighed.

'No, certainly not!' Roderick replied, with the greatest firmness. 'I have thought for some time that he could speak quite freely, if he chose; he is as wily and astute as a serpent, and you are an innocent child compared to him. Years of dealing with the House, to say nothing of Russia and our allies in Nato, have made him aware of every possible move; like an experienced chess player, he would have you at a disadvantage before you began.' Roderick wagged his finger in his secretary's eyes. 'That one is playing possum, let me tell you! He is doing so, because he knows that the minute he reveals himself, his guards will finish him off. Leave him alone at present, that's my advice; indeed it's an order! He will betray himself, sooner or later.'

Roderick shivered. 'I am going to change into trousers. I think I've caught a chill; I am not used to the kilt—I find it extremely draughty.'

As soon as his employer left him, Dick set himself to his task once more, and gave an appearance of furious activity, his large moon-glasses well down on his nose; turning over papers, annotating this, cross-referencing that, until he ran himself to a standstill. Then, ruffling his hair, until it stood up like feathered ears above his high forehead, and he looked more than ever like a little owl, he cried aloud: 'If I could find a single word, or syntax—a link with any known language!'

His cry was heard by Mrs Mottie, who had wandered into the room, Nyeri at her side.

'Oh dear, Mr Bolton, you do look in a state; whatever is the matter?' she enquired, without much appearance of real interest, sitting down and drawing the boy towards her.

'What should be the matter?' was the answer, given with a wild, desperate stare. 'We are living in a sane, reasonable world, aren't we? There is nothing in the least remarkable about having a deaf-and-dumb Prime Minister as a prisoner in the house! There is nothing odd about not having eaten a proper meal for three days, and having no hunger; nor about being ordered to crack one of the most secret codes in Europe at a minute's notice, with the aid of *Chambers's Pocket Dictionary*!'

'Oh you did eat yesterday, Mr Bolton, you know you did. I scrambled an egg for you myself; or was that Monday?'

'You might ask your Guides to help me, dear Mrs Mottie!'

'Oh no, I couldn't do that, Mr Bolton. That would be using the power for material gains, and the Chief wouldn't like it. He's ever so particular about things like that. If you are meant to find out them secrets, you will; but they don't signify. Oh, you don't need to look at me like that, dear! I daresay it's all very clever, what's in them papers; it's the Government's plans, no doubt; but they've all come to nothing, 'aven't they? So don't worry your 'ead, and don't let Mr Fernay worry 'is. It's not what's in that black leather case, but what's 'appening, and going to 'appen on the island that matters, so me Guides tell me.'

So saying, she took the boy on to her knee, and began, as a monkey does, to examine his head for nits, and, finding them, to crack them between her horny nails, talking to the child in a low, soothing monotone, to which he seemed apathetic.

Dick noticed for the first time how dirty and neglected her appearance had become; her hair was uncombed, her brown dress unstitched at the hem, her shoes unfastened, and caked with mud; she who had been as shining as a burnished apple. And wondering upon this, he happened to glance down at his own fingers. He was horrified to find his nails black and broken, the lines in his palms a map of grime, his shirt cuffs dark with grease. With an exclamation, he rushed to the mirror on the over-mantel. The face of a mad stranger looked down at him, a beard of three days' growth sprouting beneath his cheekbones.

'What has happened to us?' was his cry. 'We are filthy!'

'Mr Bolton, 'ow dare you!'

'Look at yourself, Mrs Mottie; you whose apron used to crackle with starch, you who were the neatest, trimmest char in Pimlico!'

Without waiting for a reply, the distracted secretary ran from the room, finding all about him the evidences of a shameful neglect, the decline of ordinary decent standards which had, up to this minute, and so unaccountably, passed unnoticed by all of them.

To his heightened senses the house not only seemed dirty but had the sweetish odour of a slum. He rushed upstairs to his employer's room, and, almost without knocking, burst in upon him, in order to satisfy himself that Roderick, at least, was free of the general taint.

Yet here was Mr Fernay, half naked, his kilt dropped on the floor beside him, scrambling into a pair of flannel trousers of such spotted dirtiness (his hairy shanks, long pale arms and matted hair all testifying to his condition of deterioration) that Dick was no longer able to deny his involvement in this nightmare.

'Stop this hysteria!' Roderick ordered the trembling man. 'What does a little dirt matter? Other far more important issues are before us.'

'Only a week ago you ordered Nigel to be shaved!'

'There are more vital priorities than washing. You might as well tell a soldier on the field of battle to take a bath! Go back to your work, and do not let me hear from you again until you have solved the secret code!'

'You have changed utterly in a week!'

'I have come a long way since then, thank heavens, and so must you. Let us hear no more of this washing. Anyway, there is no hot water.'

'There is the sea!'

Roderick advanced upon Dick. 'If you wish to bathe in the sea (which is now thoroughly contaminated) that is your business; you have my full permission to do so. But there is to be no more hysterical wailing about it, is that clearly understood?'

'I cannot understand you!'

'Then don't attempt it! I have work to do, even if you have not.'

'What work?' cried Dick. 'Except to lead your ragged rabble up and down the village, with pipes skirling?'

There was no need, Roderick felt, to reply to such a wild and untruthful accusation. His men were downstairs, waiting for him to lead them in a foray to the deer forest of Beann nam Liach, where some stray cattle had been reported, and must be brought in. 'For now we must share everything in common,' he had told them.

'We have to have the ceremony, like you promised,' Beattie said to Odysseus. 'After the wedding.'

'Like before,' the young man with the guitar told him. 'We can't have the dancing without you.'

'I don't want any part in it,' Odysseus protested. 'No sir! I tell you; I've changed my mind, I'll have nothing to do with it!'

'You began it,' the young man said. 'It's your responsibility. Yeah, we were healed; but there has to be the sacrifice, see. You said so. To make it right.'

'It has to be done the proper way,' Beattie reminded him.

'Now look—I made a mistake,' Odysseus told them. 'You misunderstood me. I didn't mean that kind of a sacrifice. Another cock, maybe.'

'You don't have to give us that kid's talk,' Beattie said. 'We're initiated now, remember? We have to complete the healing; tonight, at the feast after the wedding, we'll have the sacrifice.'

'You're mad!' the Jamaican cried. 'I don't remember I ever said that!'

'You said it all right, brother,' the second guitarist insisted. 'When you put on your robes again, you'll remember.'

'I shall not put on my robes! I refuse!—— Why, you are just nice British boys and girls—what's come over you, then?'

'You began it, with the dancing and the healing that day,' Beattie continued in an inexorable voice. 'You'll stay here until they come from the church. Hold him, boys!'

The struggling negro was swiftly overwhelmed; a blow on the head rendered him harmless; he was secured with ropes, and dragged into a tent until his presence should be needed.

The campers went on with their preparations.

Soon the bridal couple appeared, walking from the church.

Sylvia's gown was a clean white sheet, pinned into neat folds and brooched to one shoulder; she wore a veil of grocer's buttermuslin and a pretty crown of shells and sea-thrift, sewn together by her own hands.

Her friend Beattie (who since the death of Calum MacKay, had been appointed Leader of the Camp) was waiting to receive them; close behind her stood the guitarists, known as the Far Out Friars, whose songs and music had become so popular since the healings.

Two deck-chairs had been decorated with clumps of heather, and had rugs thrown over them to form thrones for the bride and groom; here they were expected to hold court.

There was little to eat, and less to drink, although Sydney had appropriated some bottles from Roderick's cellar; but the singing, and the dancing which presently accompanied the refreshments, seemed to intoxicate the campers more thoroughly than any spirits.

A little of this entertainment was enough for the doctor. In his younger days he had spent some time in what was then known as the Gold Coast; the stamping, twisting figures, which processed in an endless circle before him round the fire, began to remind him of some curious ceremonies he had witnessed up country. He was not too surprised therefore when Odysseus Jackson (with dazed and staring eyes) appeared in a robe and horned head-dress, his torso painted in a striped design, and began to dance an intricate solo on his own in the midst of the ring.

Sydney wished to slip away, but was prevented by the press of people about him. The faces and forms of the celebrants (for so they now appeared), bathed in sweat, were reflected in ruddy relief; the ceaseless twanging of the guitars, and the beating of drums, and the cries which accompanied the music, rose to a crescendo. All at once there was a rush forward; before Doctor Monro became aware of what had happened his bride had been lifted from the seat at his side, and passed over the heads of the crowd behind him. Her shrieks, like the whistle of a steam engine, died into silence as she was borne behind the tents.

Shouting her name (yet still with the feeling that this must be a joke in poor taste) her bridegroom pursued her.

The news of the dreadful orgy down at the camp was brought to Mr Beek by running figures in the darkness, who could hardly speak. In his new cassock and surplice (made for him by Mrs Mottie as a thank-offering for his healing of Nyeri) he appeared leaning upon a cromach, as on a bishop's crook. His face was composed, grave and resolute; a new strength had come to him, and the ladies leaned on him for comfort.

'We shall uphold you with our prayers,' Mrs Dolman promised, as he strode into the darkness, a lone, frail figure. 'It is the least we can do, since we have been forbidden to return to the camp.'

Two of Roderick's men, who had been sent to fetch

the priest, accompanied him on his downward journey.

'Hell has opened!' cried Mrs Dolman, watching their departure. 'I can only hope that Mr Beek will be powerfully protected.'

Nigel's bell was heard in a desperate tintinnabulation, and Julia ran to attend the forgotten invalid, and tell him of the fearful events of the evening; in the midst of the excitement the rescued bride was borne in on a litter, and placed on the drawing-room sofa.

'It was a regular disgrace,' Sylvia told the household, between sips of *Courvoisier*. 'I never saw such things in all my life; those girls ought to've been ashamed of themselves. Patsy and Chris even had their bras off; naked to the waist they were, and as for the *men*——'

'But whatever did they do to you, love?' enquired Mrs Mottie.

'You won't believe what they were up to.' Sylvia rubbed her reddened wrists. 'They wanted a sacrifice, see——'

'A human sacrifice? Oh no!'

'It had to be, well—a girl who wasn't really married, if you know what I mean; so they were going to put *me* on the bonfire!'

'It must have been a joke!'

'Joke? You should've seen Odysseus' eyes! He's mad, I tell you —out of his mind, I should say, and as for those others——'

'Odysseus? Little Neeri's daddy? Never!' Mrs Mottie defended the Jamaican stoutly.

'I was frightened, I tell you. I mean, they were ever so rough! What a sauce, tying me up like that! I screamed and screamed, and one of them hit me—it shows, doesn't it?' she enquired, asking for a hand-mirror. (She had been moved, at her own request, to Julia's bed.) 'If Syd had left it a little bit longer, I should've been dead, or worse. I must say he laid about him, and soon got me out of it.'

'Where is the doctor now?' Mrs Dolman demanded, and was answered by Sydney himself, who burst into the room without knocking, filthy, singed and triumphant.

'About time too,' was his bride's comment, as he flung himself down at her side. 'But don't touch me—you're all ashes and stuff, and look at your face, covered in blood!'

The rest of her observations were muffled by her husband's embrace, from which she lifted her face to say: 'A nice wedding night this turns out to be, I must say. You don't know how I was looking forward to a clean bed, with a spring mattress, an eiderdown and all!'

'But you shall have them, love!' promised the doctor. 'My silly conventional Sylvie, who wouldn't let Mr Beek marry us because she said he was loopy, and who couldn't feel properly married unless in a church!'

'Keep away from me!' ordered his bride. 'Don't lay your filthy dirty hands on me!'

'What the devil's the matter with her?' cried Sydney in a rage. 'Have you women been upsetting her?'

'She has every reason to be nervous,' Mrs Dolman pointed out. 'It is not everyone who is sacrificed upon her wedding day, and then confronted by a bleeding bridegroom.'

'You'd better 'ave a wash and a tidy up, Doctor,' Mrs Mottie advised him. 'And let me give your 'ead a bit of a bandage. I 'ope things are settled down at the camp, and Mr Fernay is O.K.?'

The doctor paid no attention to the enquiry. 'No wonder Sylvia feels slighted,' he said. 'None of you has given her a wedding present. I believe it is usual.'

'A wedding present at a time like this, Doctor?' Mrs Mottie had brought a bowl, and was attempting to bathe his forehead, which had received a knife-cut.

'You must all of you have some little things put by, which you could part with.' Sydney winced, as the disinfectant touched the open wound.

The word 'present' had had a magic effect upon Sylvia, who sat up and dried her tears.

Mrs Dolman stepped to her dressing-table across a sea of clothes; for she had been 'going through the boxes' in the house, and had found some new treasures from a distant age; the bedroom was knee-deep in garments of all kinds, which, like a rising tide, had wrapped themselves about bed-posts, spilled out of drawers, and made the beds themselves into flowery catafalques.

Mrs Dolman waited until Mary Mottie had left the room, then she took out a jewel-case. 'After all, we cannot take our treasures with us into Another World, so there seems little point either in giving or retaining them. Still, it may amuse you, child, to choose a trifle for yourself.'

'Ooh, Mrs Dolman, may I? It's ever so kind of you, reely. Ooh, aren't they smashing? I like this one with the rubies; beautiful, isn't it, just like fire! But Beattie says rubies are more for dark colourings like her, and I ought to have more of a blue stone, or a emerald. Of course, a aquamarine's my birth-stone, you know—— But look at those pearls! Beauties, aren't they! I've never seen real ones before, that I know of!'

'These are not real,' Maggie Dolman told the girl briskly, staring at her own shadowed image in the glass, and trying a gold dog-collar against her neck. 'Why should you imagine that I would give you genuine jewels? If this were a real ruby, for instance, it would be worth a fortune. You cannot know the true, inward meaning of precious stones, or your would never have expected it. Their value must be earned by right conduct on Life's Path, or they will never give happiness to their owners! No, no; you must not lose your sense of proportion, my dear. I am offering you one of the trophies of my stage career; each and every piece has a history. Here is the Grecian buckle I wore as Phedre; here the emerald necklace which looked so magnificent in the *Duchess of Malfi*. And here, like a virgin tear, is the pearl I wore upon my forehead when I made a childish début as Juliet, fifty years ago in Manchester!'

'You mean it's nothing but a lot of old cos-tuum jewellery, then?' asked Sylvia in indignation, tearing off the beads.

'Is that all you think of them?' demanded the actress, in a voice which carried through the house. She rose and advanced towards the bed, where the girl shrank before her, and Sydney had tumbled over in a stupor. 'Get up! Get out of my bedroom, both of you! I have no intention of enduring any more of your ignorant impertinence!'

As she hustled them on to the landing, the heavy tread of doomful feet was heard on the gravel; Roderick had returned with news of a tragic character.

13

THE scene, as they approached the camp, had been of such a barbaric beauty that Roderick confessed afterwards he had been momentarily diverted by it.

The flames from the high cone of the fire lit the faces of the naked people, so that it seemed their bodies were made of white-hot metal. They had ceased to dance; they were chanting, and had pressed as close to the fire as possible; their eyes were open, but it was plain they did not interpret what they saw before them.

High on a platform stood Odysseus, his arms raised; even as they watched, a bundle was handed up, and placed on the trestles before him. It was the girl Gloria, trussed for the roasting; even as recognition came to the watchers, an attendant handed Odysseus a knife.

Roderick had roared an order; in an instant the pattern was broken. The Jamaican, seized from behind, in a Commando tackle, disappeared over the platform's edge; the rush forward of the fighting MacOrrerys broke the picture into as many fragments as a mosaic.

Even the fire was scattered by the onslaught; as though the purpose for which it had been ignited now sought a hundred new channels for its work of destruction, the sparks and tongues of yellow flame dispersed to burn wherever they alighted. A tent caught here, another there; soon the whole camp was blazing; the shrieks, the cries of battle, epitomised for Roderick the embodiment of the evil which had been induced that night.

'Release the girl! There must be no more violence!' were his vain cries, as he ran to and fro.

'Glory is dead,' Dick told him. 'The shock must have killed her.'

They searched for the doctor, but he was nowhere to be found.

'Evil had entered even into me,' Roderick told the shocked household at Achnabasalt. 'Something primitive in me was released, and exulted in the bloodshed. I felt, God help me, that our revenge was righteous, and my men the instruments of justice!'

In the midst of these terrible doings, Mr Beek had made his appearance; he approached over the sands, unaccompanied now, his crozier held before him.

'I shouted to him to go back,' Roderick recounted. 'I warned him that I had no more control over my men and that murder was being done!'

This dreadful intelligence had not deterred the clergyman, who was seen to go steadily forward, looking neither to one side nor the other. The fighting, struggling men, in the smoking shadows, gave way before him; his appearance upon the platform caused a sudden pause and a silence.

Mr Beek had held up the cross, which hung from his neck. He had struggled to speak. 'Have mercy upon us!' came from him. 'We have sinned!' He was seen to kneel.

A light drizzle, the first for weeks, began to change to a drumming downpour which helped to extinguish the fires and cool the passions of the people.

Mr Beek remained kneeling, and some knelt with him in the drowning darkness.

The doctor, who had returned to the camp, worked steadily in the shambles, separating the dead from the living. The casualties, some of which were the result of panic, were not as heavy as had been feared at first; even Odysseus, although beaten and unconscious, had a chance of survival.

'This has shaken me,' Roderick finished his story. 'I would never have believed how thin is the veneer of civilisation; how near we can get to primitive savagery.'

'It does not surprise me in the least,' Nigel said. 'The events of the last two wars should have opened your eyes.'

Arrangements were soon made for the drawing-room to be turned into a hospital. The campers who survived were brought up to the house, and moaning bodies lay along the floor. Dick, who had had a training in first-aid, nipped quickly up and down with his tin box of bandages and unguents; Julia and Mrs Dolman, in borrowed kitchen aprons, followed with ineffectual devotion.

Mrs Mottie took up her scrubbing brushes once more; she was to be seen, on her knees, purging the stains from floor and landing; washing away the neglect which had led to such an outrage.

'Oh there was a very hevil atmosphere down on the beach last night, Mr Fernay,' she told him, filling another bucket with quite her old briskness of manner. 'I sensed it direckly after the wedding. There was crowds of devil faces building in that fire. All them campers was possessed of demons.'

'The madness entered into all of us, Mrs Mottie; none were innocent.'

'Oh no, it didn't enter into *me*, Mr Fernay. I was protected. Evil can't get in where there's no opening, you know. By their fruits ye shall know them.'

'What happened to us?' Roderick demanded of the company in general. 'It fills me with terror to think of it! Until Mr Beek came tottering along with his cross——'

'His crozier,' Maggie Dolman corrected him, raising a sufferer to moisten her lips with water.

'He had a cross, hanging round his neck! Why do you interrupt me? And, by the way, where is Mr Beek? He should be here, surely, to assist us with his gift of healing!'

Everyone had forgotten the clergyman. He had been last seen, still kneeling in the downpour, his face turned to heaven; for all they knew he still knelt there, in the midst of the steaming faggots and the bodies of the dead.

A boy arrived on a Highland pony, and handed Mrs Dolman a note.

'There is no answer,' Maggie told him, giving him an apple, and half a sovereign which she had found in her trinket box, and which had the present value of a farthing.

He mounted, and trotted away over the dusty road.

'Tcha!' exclaimed the actress, tearing up the letter, and throwing the fragments into the air.

'What is the matter?' her niece asked.

'I sent word to Laetitia, telling her what had happened. I asked for help from the Brethren in our emergency. It's quite useless, however.'

'What did the note say?'

'She regretted they could not come to our aid,' Mrs Dolman recited. 'We would understand, she said, that after all that happened last night, grieved as the Brethren were to hear of it, it had become more than ever necessary for them to hold themselves Apart in a state of Purity, making ready for the Momentous Days to Come. We have their prayers; these will be very valuable to us.'

'Why should you be either angry or surprised, dear Aunt Maggie?'

'I could beat her with a carpet-whisk!' Mrs Dolman hissed through clenched teeth. 'But you are right. I should not be upset by Laetitia's reply, or the Brethren's reaction to our plight. I was mistaken in appealing to them. Force of habit impelled me to write: so accustomed am I to thinking of Laetitia and her friends as far more spiritually emancipated than I could hope to be, that it is second nature to me to turn to her in a crisis.'

So saying, she banished her niece once again to the kitchen, urging her to light the range so that there might be a supply of hot water for the wounded. Here Roderick found Julia in tears before a heap of clinkers.

'I cannot get this wretched fire to light, in spite of all I do!' she whimpered.

'How is it that you are so incompetent at your age?'

'I have never had to light fires, nor battle with the coarser side of life,' Julia confessed. 'Don't bully me, I beg you—I've been up all night! Surely it is Mackenzie's duty to light fires, or that wife of his could come up and help!'

'Mrs Mackenzie is down in the village. One of her own sons has been mortally wounded,' Roderick replied heavily. 'Several here are dying, and we have not a drop of hot water.'

'What does it matter?' wept Julia, from her humble position amongst the ashes. 'We are all dying, aren't we? It is no use keeping on!'

'What do you mean "*It is no use keeping on*"?' Roderick demanded with the greatest annoyance. He had not felt kindly disposed to Julia since her refusal to marry him. 'Of course we must keep on, as long as we have life! If we give in to despair, it will be all up with us. As a nation we have never given in, even in the most hopeless circumstances; it is the reason why Britain has survived so long.'

'There is no nation now,' Mrs Dolman, having overheard, was quick to remind Roderick. She folded her arms in the kitchen doorway. 'Your men are lying drunk in the yard again. Yet, if keeping on with a lot of little busy-ness of various trivial kinds will save our reason a little longer, by all means let us do so.'

She pinned up a strand of her wig with a pine needle, and adjusted her kerchief.

Roderick pushed her aside with a roar of impatience, and was heard calling to Dick to find him a primus stove.

'It was in the wash-house when last I saw it!' was the answer, bellowed from an upper storey.

Julia at once abandoned her fire-lighting. She rose, yawning and stretching herself. 'Is it still raining?' she asked. There was no reply. Mrs Dolman, tired out with nursing, had fallen asleep across the kitchen table, so Julia crossed to the window to look for herself, murmuring aloud: 'Fancy that Sylvia getting into my bed! What appalling impudence! I wonder where they spent their wedding night in the end?' There was the noise of a continuing argument from the dining-room next door.

'The methylated spirit has been moved! Someone has stolen it!'

'Someone has probably drunk it, Roderick.'

'Of course they haven't drunk it! Are you mad? It was in this cupboard, to which only you and I have the key!'

'You may have drunk it yourself, chum, in a fit of absent-mindedness; that may be the reason you have not been yourself today.'

'*You* yourself have mislaid it, I tell you! Now I can't light the stove, and get hot water, and lives are endangered! *You are completely useless!* Get out!'

'Very well, I shall get out! I shall be glad to go! Now that you are a Highland chieftain, you don't need me any more. I shall go, and I shall never come back!'

'Go! Go, I say! I am not stopping you! I shall find someone who puts first things first, instead of allowing petty jealousy to prevail at a time like this!'

A door banged; Julia saw Dick flying across the garden, his plimsolled feet scarcely touched the grass; the rain had hardly time to wet him.

Some minutes passed, then: 'Dick! Where are you? Dick!' was shouted; another figure ran into the downpour.

Then for a while, except for the groans of the injured and the drunken, there was silence in Achnabasalt House.

As soon as the waves touched his chin, Dick wanted to get out of the sea. The water, which was to have solved all his problems, was in too disgusting a state for him to drown himself. Dead fish floated all around, their white and swollen bellies uppermost; there was an oily film on the surface, which meshed a deal of nastiness. Dick plunged through it with great gasps, floundering ashore at last at the southernmost end of the bay. Here he tore off his jersey and trousers, and cast them from him; then, kneeling at a rock pool, which was drumming with a constant rainbeat, he washed himself, jumped in and soused himself all over with the clear water.

'You are taking sensible precautions,' came a voice from the rocks above him.

Dick looked up to see a tall man with a beard, under a golfing umbrella. He wore an old-fashioned knickerbocker suit of a light-coloured material, and reminded Mr Bolton of George Bernard Shaw.

'Allow me to lend you a coat,' this individual went on, handing down a comfortable gaberdine which he had been carrying over his arm, as though he had expected just such an eventuality. Dick, who had begun to shiver, was pleased to accept the offer. It seemed only natural to walk with his new acquaintance over the rocks to a small cove, where a blue boat was anchored.

'Are you staying hereabouts? I don't remember having seen you before,' Dick made conversation.

'I am at present on the island,' was the surprising reply. 'And if you are doing nothing this morning, perhaps you'd like to come over and have a spot of lunch with me?'

'I am not dressed!'

'I think I can fix you up with some clothes. I should like you to come if you can.'

The stranger moved his large umbrella from one hand to the

other, and Dick noticed that it was furnished not only with a small antenna, like a radio mast, but that the burnished ring on the top rotated at an uneven speed.

He drew his eyes from this fascinating sight, and asked a little diffidently: 'May I know your name?'

'You may call me MacArtney,' was the reply. 'It will do very well.'

'I suppose you are closely connected with the Government?'

'You might say so.' Mr MacArtney seemed amused. They stepped down into the boat, where he slotted the umbrella into a metal tube, where it immediately took up the function of a rotor blade. A humming note drowned all other sounds; the blue boat raised itself above the waves, and skimmed with a delicious motion towards Ebora.

Dick Bolton's disappearance cast a sad blight over Achnabasalt. His clothes were found on the shore; Roderick was not to be comforted.

'I parted from my best friend in anger!' he told them, in the deepest emotion. 'I said things I did not mean; now he has drowned himself!'

'It is not certain he has; in fact it is most unlikely,' the members of his house-party consoled him.

The discovery, on Dick's desk, of careful notes, showing that at last he had managed to decipher Mr Mannifold's secret papers, was a double-edged sword in Roderick's breast. The cipher had been composed from *The Tale of Two Bad Mice*: keywords were *Doll's House, Belinda, Hannah* and *Tongs*.

'It was a code of genius; how right I was in my suspicions,' sighed Roderick. 'Only a man brought up in the best English nursery would have the slightest knowledge of Beatrix Potter's works; no foreigner could have a clue.'

Mr. Fernay's burst of energy had left him; he was a broken man, and could no longer be persuaded to interest himself in the care of the sick, nor in leading Clan MacOrrery.

'You'll 'ave to pull yourself together, Mr Fernay dear,' Mrs Mottie told him. 'We all look to you, you know; especially now Mr Beek 'as left us.'

'Mr Beek? Has he drowned himself too?'

'Oh no, dear! But one of your 'ighlanders was telling me this morning that 'e saw someone fetch 'im away. Down at the camp it was, ever so early, just as it was getting light. This man 'ad gorn back for something 'e'd lorst, and as 'e come over the sands, 'e could see Mr Beek, ever so plain, still kneeling there on the platform. And then 'e saw this man come up, raise 'im to 'is feet, and 'elp 'im away. 'E thought it was the doctor.'

'They all go,' Roderick said, in a fatalistic voice. 'I expect it was one of the Heavenly Brethren; Mr Beek would be better off with them. Nigel is right—why should we struggle any longer? Let us die, dear Mrs Mottie, with what dignity we can.'

'You're not yourself, Mr Fernay dear; what you want is a nice cup of tea.'

'What a remarkable place you have here!' cried Dick in admiration, as he entered the small, dome-like building on the far side of the island. Then he cried out in astonishment: 'Why, Mr Beek, how did you come here? Are you invited to lunch too?' He hardly recognised the old clergyman, so completely was he transformed from his abject exhaustion of the night before. Although his face bore marks of his sufferings, he had regained a measure of his new serenity. He was dressed in a brown woollen cassock with a blue-lined hood, like some sort of mendicant friar, and looked so clean, so unusually tidy, that he seemed to shine.

'Mr MacArtney has been so kind,' Mr Beek told Dick. 'He brought me here, away from the dreadful—— I cannot speak of it!'

'If you will come this way,' Mr MacArtney invited Dick.

He was shown into the neatest of small cabins, furnished with two bunks, one above the other. A siren suit, of the same material as that worn by Mr Beek, lay on the lower bed; it was in a becoming shade of blue.

'There is a shower, with hot and cold water, in the closet here,' Mr MacArtney told his guest. 'There is a razor, and all you need, I hope. When you are ready, come through, and we will have a drink.'

Half an hour later, Dick was accepting a glass of clear, yellow liquid from his host. 'This is like a dream from which I expect to awaken at any moment,' he sighed with pleasure.

'I can assure you it is no dream.'

'This is a most delicious aperitif; I don't recognise it, however.'

'It has a flavour like apricots; but it is not sickly. The astringency is most pleasant,' Mr Beek pondered.

'It gives one a vital warmth,' Dick enthused, hoping he would be offered another glass.

'Let us call it an elixir,' Mr MacArtney suggested, re-corking the bottle. 'It will, I hope, help to revive your energy, and give you an appetite.'

The drink had an immediate effect upon both men.

'I have hardly eaten for days; now I feel positively hungry!' cried Dick.

'It is like liquid sunshine!' Mr Beek agreed. 'It has given me a vitality I did not know I possessed!'

'I am so glad it appeals to you.' Mr MacArtney busied himself at a hatch, through which an enticing fragrance wafted itself.

'I suppose this building was prefabricated?' Dick enquired. 'It must have been, for I have never seen it before; it has risen like a mushroom in the night.'

He wished to ask a thousand questions, as to the real fate of the boats, as to the strange scorching which the surface of Ebora had suffered, and the sudden departure of the Government Leaders. Yet there was no present time for questions; they sat down to a species of *ratatouille* of unfamiliar, but delicious vegetables, served in an excellent sauce. This was followed by a bowl of fruit. There were some globular yellow plums, the size of oranges, with a distinctive sharp taste, which appealed particularly to Dick; he ate two very rapidly.

'I don't seem to recognise the variety; I would have said these might have come from Marienbad, but they are too large and of the wrong colour.'

'We call this fruit pa'pla,' was the courteous reply. Mr MacArtney was an amiable host, but not informative.

'You know we have Mr Mannifold with us?' Dick tested him, putting a gentle regret into his tone.

'Ah yes; poor Willie! I'm afraid the shock of the blast-fire was too much for him. Then, when it was discovered that his wits had gone, the order went out that when the rest of the Cabinet and Chiefs of Staff were evacuated by the Navy, he must be left behind.'

'But that is monstrous!' Dick could not help exclaiming. 'I

hold no brief for Mr Mannifold's party; I abhor their policies, and have often deplored his complacency; yet according to his lights he was sincere. He served them well. To abandon him like that is perfectly heartless! Even if you throw me back into the sea for saying so, I cannot keep silent!'

'I agree! I must say I am astounded!' cried Mr Beek, in a voice of surprising strength.

'Please calm yourselves, and be seated!' their host implored them. 'I assure you, I had nothing to do with the decision. The power behind your government gave the instructions.'

They were silent only long enough for the full implication of his words to soak into their understanding.

'Roderick has been right all along!' Dick announced at last. 'International Big Business is behind all this! When you have monopolists like Cornelius Platt financing party funds, in the most secret and sinister way, what can you expect?'

'No no, you are wrong! The Communists, the Anti-Christs, are solely to blame!' the clergyman protested.

'My dear Mr Beek, you are too unworldly, if you will forgive me saying so, to have the slightest idea of the wickedness in high places in our own country today!' Dick was quick to contradict him. 'The scientists—especially the chemists, who work hand in glove with the armament kings, and whose profits depend on the power gained by destruction—are the true villains! They engineered the dropping of the bomb!'

'It is a matter of opinion.' Mr MacArtney wiped his lips with a fine white napkin. 'Yet one might ask oneself what it is that motivates both Communists and Cornelius Platt; what is the common denominator?'

The air of authority with which he spoke, could not fail to impress them, and now Dick ventured: 'We have been cut off from news of the outside world for so long; you appear to have special knowledge. Can you please tell us what has been happening in the last few weeks? Will you explain some of the mysteries concerning this island, and the fate of the Government; and, most important of all, tell us when we may expect this state of emergency to be over?'

Mr MacArtney pushed himself back from the table, and suggested that they sit upon one of the comfortable couches which lined the walls. Then he swung himself round to face them, looking over the tips of his joined fingers in a judicious, yet rueful manner, as if wondering how best to acquaint his hearers, in their frail state, with the disquieting intelligence he had to give them.

'I regret to say that civilisation, as you call it, is in a bad way,' he admitted. 'The dropping of that first, small atomic bomb, was followed in a short time by several others. Trigger-happy fingers, both in the war room at the Pentagon and in the Kremlin, made the excuse that it was better to be early than late in the struggle for supremacy; yet dressed their actions in the guise of a defence of freedom. Devastation in North America, and parts of Russia, is almost total; what the bombs began, the fall-out is completing. Radio-active dust is drifting over Europe; with the exception of a few isolated pockets, it has already covered Britain.'

'Do you mean that the population is wiped out?' cried Mr Beek in the utmost horror.

'With the exceptions I have already mentioned, this, I am afraid, is the truth.'

Mr MacArtney rose to his feet, and slid back a panel to show a wall-map. 'Here is a plan of Great Britain as it is today. Those small green spots show where a few people survive. The same situation prevails in Europe, and in most of the world. The United Nations, now transferred to the High Sierras, has declared Britain to be a H.C.A.—a Highly Contaminated Area. Britain is therefore out of bounds completely to those who might have helped her.'

'So millions have perished! It is impossible to contemplate! Was there much suffering?'

'Fortunately no. So high was the rate of radio-activity that most fell into a coma and died within a few hours quite painlessly. For the same reason (and the peculiar nature of the fall-out, expressly designed by scientists for this purpose) their bodies were quickly dehydrated; they were subject to a most sanitary and hygienic cremation, which obviated the need for burial; most have completely disintegrated already.'

This appalling statement stunned his hearers; Dick's eyes grew so large they appeared about to leave his skull; Mr Beek bowed his head in his hands.

'And these monsters of wickedness, who now rule the world, what will happen to them?' he faltered.

'I cannot say with certainty at the moment; yet it is inevitable that the forces they have unleashed will rebound eventually upon them to destroy them; it is an irrevocable law. In the meantime it is no use blinking the facts; unless we can prevent them in time the whole world is in danger of combustion.'

'Surely God will intervene to save us?' was Mr Beek's impassioned plea.

'Alas; there is this business of Free Will.'

'Yet if even a few Righteous can be found?'

'Exactly.'

'You do not imagine there are any? Not a hundred and forty-four thousand, as the Bible tells us? Not forty thousand? Four thousand?'

'It is a moot point. I act only on instructions.'

'I must ask it!' Dick trembled, in his bravery. 'Whom do you represent, if not the Government?'

'I suppose you could call me a deputy of a neutral power.'

'Nobody could remain neutral in the face of such monumental suffering!' came from Mr Beek in agony. 'I do not believe you can stand apart! You, who have such superior resources, must have been sent to help us!'

MacArtney paused again before replying. 'I will, of course, do the most that is in my power. Beyond that point, I am forbidden to interfere; that is not part of the plan.'

'Whose plan?' Dick spoke under almost insupportable pressure. 'Whose inhuman, ungodly purpose is it that prevents intervention? Are we to be studied like an ant-hill, which you kick open with your foot? Are you to watch our frantic, feeble efforts to survive, without the slightest pity?'

'I did not kick the ant-hill.'

'Then we must be destroyed?'

'It might depend a lot on you.'

'It must depend on the Mercy of God!' Mr Beek had needed just such a challenge, evidently, to restore his faith completely.

'It might depend on an alliance between God and yourselves,' MacArtney told the angry men. 'In the meantime, I must explain why I asked you to come here. You have been chosen to help me in my special mission.'

Dick sensed a regret in his tone, at a course evidently a little distasteful to him.

'Chosen for what? To spy on, and pass judgement on the others? If so, I tell you now, I'll have no part in it!'

'Please be calm, Mr Bolton! Nothing of the kind is expected of you.' Mr MacArtney piled the dishes upon the hatch, and closed it.

'Let us hear what he has to say. We have no right to judge him,' Mr Beek urged the secretary.

Again Mr MacArtney seemed to have difficulty in deciding how to plead with them; Dick had the opportunity of studying him in his silent reflections. The regularity of the stranger's features, the depth, and piercing glances of his shrewd eyes, beneath shaggy eyebrows, the smoothness and luminosity of his skin, made an uncomfortable impression upon him. He had a growing feeling that this physical resemblance to a great playwright was a mere garment adopted by a being calling himself MacArtney; a disguise chosen by a superior spirit used to quite another dimension of manifestation.

'I have no interest in judging the inhabitants of Achnabasalt, nor in requiring you to report upon them,' MacArtney spoke at last. 'Any judgement is made elsewhere, in a higher court, as it were. I ask only for your co-operation. A direct approach is not allowed to me; you must be my emissaries. Difficult as things have been in the last few weeks, they are likely to become much more so before the end.'

'The end of the world?'

'I hardly think it will be allowed to come to that; merely the end of this civilisation.'

'The millennium?'

'Perhaps.'

'What is to be our task?'

'Great changes are coming to all of you; you must be prepared for them. You will have to help your friends to accept not only these changes, but the fact that you are different from them.'

'In what way, different?'

The question amused Mr MacArtney. 'Quite a constitutional difference; you might say a chemical one. I can say no more.'

'Yet we shall not be parted from them?' Dick implored his interlocutor.

'Not in the meantime. Your mission is to make them accept these changes.'

'Yet, eventually we must part?'

'The difference imposes it.'

'I would rather die than be parted from my friends!'

'Death will not part you, dear boy—rather the contrary.'

'I am so thankful to hear you say that!' Dick wept with relief. 'That means, at least, that we shall die together, even if parted for a time.'

Only Mr Beek remarked the curious expression on Mac-Artney's face. It was gone in an instant, and almost immediately he began to give them their instructions. He gave them a little satchel which contained a special soap, and a bottle each of the elixir ('to be taken, three drops, night and morning, in water'). They were never to be without the clothing they had been given, as it would protect them.

'What about the others?'

'As I have told you; they are differently constituted. It would not benefit them. Just keep them calm and happy as long as possible, until they are sent for.'

'Then there is to be a rescue—an evacuation?' Mr Beek cried. 'Thank God for it.'

'I suppose it will be an air-lift?' Dick brightened at the thought. 'You misled us. We shall not be deserted, after all. May I ask where we shall be taken?'

'Oh each person will go to the destination best suited to his needs.' Mr MacArtney looked at his handsome gold repeater. 'And now, I regret, I have an appointment I must keep, so I will take you ashore. I hope to contact you again before long. Say as little as possible to your friends about this encounter. You will not be believed. Yet let no ridicule shake you, nor make you abandon the routine I have instructed you in.'

As they embarked in the blue boat, Dick looked back to the island. Already a light mist had veiled the white dome of the building. The faster the boat danced away, with its rotor whirling, the thicker the mist became, until Ebora was invisible once more in its hovering cloud.

Like missionaries, upon a savage shore, in the dark ages, Mr Beek and Dick Bolton returned, as it were, from the dead. They climbed the rocks before them, and approached the house.

14

ASTUNNED incredulity was the first reaction at the sight of Mr Bolton and the Reverend Hector Beek at Achnabasalt. A welcome was not immediately forthcoming to those who had been given up, mourned, and consigned in imagination to a better world. Their return, in outlandish guise, must embarrass before delighting their friends. They were made to feel that, like Thomas the Rhymer, they had returned after many years into a different epoch.

Much, they were told, had happened in their absence; the whole situation had deteriorated alarmingly.

'There has been a revolt,' Roderick informed them. 'While I was in a state of collapse, believing you drowned, Sydney Monro betrayed me.'

The doctor had broken into the cellars, taken the entire store of whisky, and distributed enough to the clansmen on guard to make them quite incapable. Then, knowing that the party at Achnabasalt were without defences, he had entered the house at the head of a band of campers, with whom he now associated himself. These had, in two hours, removed most of the hoarded provisions; worse still, the females had fought for the possession of clothes and jewellery belonging to Julia and Mrs Dolman. In spite of Julia's training in judo (which had enabled her to overthrow several of the Burniebankers) the invaders had been so superior in youth and numbers that they had prevailed. The ladies were left with nothing but a few blankets in which to drape themselves.

Doctor Monro, who seemed to have appointed himself chief of the rebels, had then returned and plundered the house in a more systematic fashion, taking away bedding, furniture, lamps and stoves to the rooms above the stables, which, together with other outbuildings, had become his stronghold.

'He must have changed completely since his wedding!' Dick exclaimed. 'He was weak and lazy; I would never have believed him capable of such excesses!'

'His new wife, Sylvia, is behind it,' Mrs Dolman affirmed. 'She is egging him on; he is inflamed by her and by drink.'

'He resented my authority from the beginning,' Roderick reminded them. 'I had to have him restrained; he will not forget or forgive it.'

'Drink and the devilry down on the shore 'as changed 'em all,' Mrs Mottie pronounced. 'Hevil 'as entered into them campers by what they done. Mark my words, they'll be back and try to turn us out of 'ere before long.'

'I believe you are right,' Roderick agreed. 'I can't think why they did not take the house at first.'

'They may have been restrained by the thought of their own wounded, being cared for here.'

'I do not believe it. They are quite inhuman now.' Julia entered the room with a fateful step. 'Two more have died this morning; the three who are left don't look as though they will survive. Will you arrange for a burial-party, Roderick dear?'

'I will go and say a prayer for them,' murmured Mr Beek, stepping out of the room. 'I will keep this afternoon free for the funerals if you wish.'

'We cannot possibly have a burial this afternoon!' Roderick spoke with the utmost irritation. 'There is nobody to dig the graves; all my men are drunk, and likely to remain so for the rest of the day.' He uttered a groan of complete frustration, and fell into a basket chair.

'Things have certainly taken a dreadful turn,' his secretary approached to commiserate with him, 'but, Roderick—there is something very important I must tell you—— We——'

'——If you had not rushed off in that hysterical fit, giving us such a fright, none of this would have happened!' Roderick interrupted his friend, with quite the old severity of manner. 'You are the one who is to blame for the situation! If I had not been so upset, I would have been on guard——'

'So you wish I had remained drowned, and never returned, or so it appears!'

'Oh do not drivel! Of course I am pleased to see you back. Where did you get that nauseating suit? All it needs is a couple of furry ears!'

The injustice of the accusation of blame had quite depressed Dick. He was unable to reply immediately. In the hall, Mrs Mottie could be heard admiring Mr Beek's appearance.

'That's ever such a nice dressing-gown, Mr Beek dear—so sensible for the cold mornings.'

She asked where he had found it, yet did not wait for an answer. Nobody was in the least interested as to where the travellers had been in their absence, or what had happened to them; even Nigel had allowed himself to be involved in the excitements of the rebellion.

'Sydney has persuaded the campers that Roderick is responsible for the bloodshed at the camp,' he told Dick. 'And Roderick feels, naturally, that this is a cynical betrayal of his hospitality.'

'I have a right to feel so!' Roderick drew himself to his full height. He was allowing his beard to grow. In his tattered plaid and the kilt (which he had resumed) he appeared to Dick like an illustration from an early edition of *Rob Roy*. 'I have been kind to that one, let me tell you! I will be honest with you; I never wished him to join our party in the first place. I have nothing in common with him; I find him unsympathetic, and I knew his weakness. It was for your sake, Nigel, that I allowed him to come, and this is how he repays me. He has betrayed your friendship too, let me remind you!'

'I employed him,' Nigel said. 'He was paid to look after me.'

'There was more to it. You were friends.'

'I will admit I was sorry for him. I was fond of him, in a way,' Nigel admitted. 'I must feel responsible now.'

'I sent word to Sydney to come and see me, and talk this over in a civilised way,' Roderick said. 'I wanted to give him a last chance to behave. He has not replied. I wish you would go, Dick, and speak to him.'

'What good will that do?'

'You instantly ask, *what good will that do*? We must try everything! We shall starve in a week; all we have left are a few potatoes, a bag of rotten carrots and three scrawny hens! You can tell him that two more of his people died this morning, and he must arrange to fetch them away immediately, and bury them, as I have no facilities for doing so. If you are afraid, you can carry a white flag!'

'I am not in the least afraid.'

'It is very little to ask of you, Dick, after all the trouble and anxiety you have caused us. Please!'

Dick made up his mind. 'Very well; I shall go in a minute or two. But first there is something of the utmost importance I must tell you——'

'Can't you understand that the most important, most urgent thing, at this moment, is to stop Sydney?' shouted Mr Fernay. 'God knows what he may be plotting! As soon as my men recover from their hang-over, and realise what has happened, I shall be unable to restrain them from further revenge! A state of complete anarchy will prevail! We must act *now*, not in a few minutes' time!'

Dick saw that it was useless to expect Roderick in his present state to listen to what he had to say. The only course open to him was to acquiesce in his demands immediately.

'How right Mr MacArtney was to suppose that our task would be increasingly difficult!' he murmured, stepping over the out-flung bodies of the MacOrrery tribesmen, scattered on the cobbles of the courtyard. So deep was their sleep, that he bent to turn one over to assure himself that the man still breathed.

As he approached the stables, he heard the twanging of guitars. A savage voice was raised in a moan of lust and triumph.

'I *hold* you, yah, yah; I told *you*, yah, yah! I'll nev-er let you go!' was taken up by half a dozen brassy, menacing voices.

Mr Bolton, feeling a little sick, swallowed and hesitated. Only the thought of Roderick's anger and disappointment, if he failed him, made him step to the door and knock.

The singing did not stop, but presently a window above was opened and Sylvia, her head crowned in a paste diadem, and wearing Julia's sea-green velvet bed-gown, looked over the sill.

'Well, what do *you* want?' she asked, in a bored voice.

Mr Beek, like a friar, whom he now closely resembled, with his cassock, bare feet, and silky white hair, moved amongst the sick and the dead in the drawing-room at Achnabasalt. Mrs Mottie followed closely behind him, with Nyeri, an acolyte, bearing a basin of water and a towel.

'I think I will take the name of Brother James,' he told them. 'It seems right to do so, and more in keeping. Do you know, that since I put on this habit, I feel a different person, so much stronger and more courageous! I am no longer afraid to serve God as I know I ought; I do not care what may happen to me, or what people may think of me. Now, my poor child, let me see that arm, will you?'

He passed down the row of neglected sufferers, who felt an immediate benefit; then he turned to console the members of the household who had been so severely shocked by the happenings of the past few days.

'So you accomplished nothing whatsoever?' Roderick accused Dick, who stood in silence before him.

'I have told you; Sydney refused to come and speak to me. He sent word that four of the men would come and fetch the dead away this afternoon, that was all. As I left, he was sitting on the wall, eating an apple, and called out "*Bugs Bunny*" after me. I turned and faced up to him, as I told you, demanding to know what he intended doing, to which he replied: "*You will know all in good time.*" I could hardly hear myself or him for the caterwauling that was going on.'

'I don't like the sound of that. We are completely at his mercy.' Dick had the courage of desperation. 'Roderick, please! The time has come when you must listen to what I have to tell you, or worse may happen than a raid by Doctor Monro and his campers. I have news of the gravest character for you!'

The solemnity of his secretary's tone made an impression on Mr Fernay.

'I suppose I shall get no peace until you have told me; but be brief. I don't feel too well, and have a great deal to see to.'

'I think everyone should be present.'

'You are being dramatic. It is quite unnecessary.'

'It is vital they should all hear what I have to say,' Dick persisted.

'Very well. Fetch them, and be quick about it; I may change my mind.'

At last all the household were gathered in the dining-room, where they sat about the table, like a tribe of Indians, wrapped in their blankets. It came to Dick that they had all changed in a startling way since they left London; that even in twenty-four hours a subtle alteration had taken place in their appearance; an insidious attenuation was transforming them before his eyes. The growing uneasiness which this realisation gave him, almost distracted him from his purpose.

Yet, aided from time to time by a word of encouragement from Mr Beek (or Brother James, as he now called himself) who sat beside him, and quite oblivious of any warning Mr MacArtney may have issued, he told them the full story of their visit to Ebora.

He was heard to the end without interruption, the faces of his hearers reflecting a blankness of disbelief.

'That is an astonishing story,' was the first comment from Mr Fernay.

'We were warned not to expect you to believe us. Yet every word is true, as Mr Be—I mean Brother James—will confirm.'

'It is obvious you were light-headed when you jumped into the sea with all your clothes on. You must have bumped your head on a rock, and suffered a slight concussion,' Roderick went on, as though Dick had not spoken.

'Then Mr Beek must have had the same hallucinations; and he did *not* jump into the sea!' Dick defended himself.

There was a heated discussion. Some, like Mrs Dolman, declared that MacArtney was a Government Spy.

'How right you are! Of course that is the explanation!' Roderick cried in relief. 'For some reason best known to himself, this sinister character takes these two innocents (I beg your pardon, Mr Beek, but it is no less than the truth) to a hide-out on the island, supplies you with these extraordinary rig-outs (I wish you would take yours off, Dick, it gives me the shivers). Then he fills you both with stories of coming calamity and tropical fruits, in order to disguise his real activities!'

'I have told you—he had nothing to do with the Government!'

'My dear Dick, you have only his word for it! As for your tale that you were taken to Ebora in a whirly-gig, I may tell you that I myself went down to the shore a quarter of an hour or so after you had rushed out of the house like a madman. I saw no boat. It was a clear day; if there had been any sort of craft I should have noticed it; certainly one of a bright blue with a rotating parasol and a whirling noise!'

'You are ready, as usual, to reduce everything to absurdity!'

'I wonder why it is that only you and Mr Beek have caught a glimpse of this stranger?' enquired Nigel. 'What is so special about the pair of you that you should be singled out for this honour?'

'Yes, tell us!' came a chorus from the rest, but, instead of replying, Dick took his employer by the arm. 'You have only to row out to the island to prove the truth of what I have been telling you! You will see the domed house—you may even catch a glimpse of MacArtney!'

'I have not time to go on wild-goose chases!' was the irritable reply. 'We have wasted enough time listening to this fairy-tale. Sydney may attack us at any minute. We must place ourselves in a state of seige. The dead must be carried outside the gate, so that he has no excuse to enter!'

'Nobody here has the strength to carry them!'

'It must be managed! We have to be prepared for anything, from now on!'

Mr Beek stood up, with new authority. 'You must be prepared for something more drastic. A great change is coming; the whole district, which has been such a safe haven to us all, may have to be evacuated.'

'Is this some more nonsense from your bogus philosopher and self-styled prophet?'

'It is the truth,' Dick confirmed. In a voice trembling with emotion, hardly able to make himself clear, he hurried to tell them the story of the map with its green spots and heavy brown encroaching scoriations; of the fate which was overtaking the civilised world, and the rescue by air which must affect them.

'Now I know you are mad, my poor friend! Your sufferings have turned your brain!' was Mr Fernay's reaction.

'He is speaking the truth!' Brother James protested.

Nigel interrupted. 'There may be something in what he says. I have been examining the transcript which Dick made of Mr Mannifold's papers. They were not, of course, up to date, but the report they give, as to the probable fate of Europe, is much the same.'

The confirmation, from such a source, of the catastrophe could not fail to dismay.

'I do not understand why there should be some pockets of survival,' Mrs Dolman said. 'Or why some places should be singled out.'

'They may be like bubbles of air in an aquarium; eventually they must burst, or be absorbed. It can only be a question of time.'

'Yet rescue is promised us, before that happens?'

'I was assured of that. But we must experience changes. They are inevitable; they are happening now, and due to radiation of a special nature. We must prepare for them.'

'What changes?' demanded Julia.

Dick, looking into her face, saw already the tincture of the most final of changes. 'Changes of a chemical nature,' he faltered, dismayed at what he read in her. 'Changes in the world's atmosphere which must affect our bodies, yet not frighten us when they arrive.'

'I continue to distrust this man MacArtney,' Roderick was saying. 'He tells you that is not his real name; why should he need to conceal his identity? In spite of his denials, it is obvious to me that he is hand in glove with the late government. Now he makes use of his special knowledge to gain power. He issues instructions which are, in all probability, meant to mislead. I for one shall disregard anything he is purported to say; I advise all of you to do the same.'

'I believe him to be genuine,' Maggie Dolman announced, rising, like the goddess of some primitive tribe, in her red blanket. 'These things seem absurd to us merely because we have never before experienced them. If, sixty years ago, when I was a child, anyone had said to my parents (as dear Mr H. G. Wells tried to say) that man would fly into space in a little capsule; that he would circle the earth, and attempt to land on the moon, they would have declared, as Roderick does now: "*You are mad!*" If these changes are to come, then you must teach us how to bear with them.'

'Yes, dear Dick, tell us how to prepare ourselves!' came from Julia.

'Why should we prepare?' Nigel answered her. 'I do not wish to be evacuated to some strange and desert place, however beautiful, only to be overtaken in the end by the same fate that will reach us here. Let the Heavenly Brethren ascend in their cohorts; it is just their cup of tea. I will retire to bed and await my fate in peace and comfort.'

'No no! You must not say that!' With a rush, Julia swept forward to kneel by his chair. 'You are needed, Nigel, never more so than at this time! Your wonderful qualities of intellect and irony will help us to a sane appraisal of what is happening to us! If you turn your face to the wall, I will die too!'

'You are talking like an idiot,' her aunt informed her.

'While you are all expressing these high-class sentiments, may I remind you that we are in danger of being overwhelmed?' Roderick spoke harshly, recalling them from the empyrean. 'We are outnumbered; half of us are sick. If our physical survival is so necessary, I suggest you send an urgent message, Dick, to your extra-sensory friend, telling him to speed up his rescue, or at least to provide us with the means to exist and defend ourselves meantime.'

'A passive resistance is all that's necessary now that we know we are to be saved!' cried Julia exultantly. 'By adopting a Gandhi-like serenity, in the face of provocation, even if we starve for a little, it cannot matter!'

'We shall starve all right; that's very plain.'

'Exactly,' Mr Beek corroborated. He hurried to the bookcase and retrieved a small prayer book. 'Psalm thirty-seven, verse eleven. *"But the meek-spirited shall possess the earth, and shall be refreshed in the multitude of peace."* '

His look of happiness was not returned.

15

'IT WAS the most extraordinary thing,' Roderick recounted to the ladies the following day. 'The bodies were as light to carry as parcels of paper! The weight had completely gone from them. They were as shells, with no substance internally; one felt that they would crack if roughly handled. It was no trouble in the world to carry them outside the gates; indeed the only worry I had was that if a wind sprang up, it might blow them away. Isn't that so, Dick?'

Dick's reply was the briefest of nods. 'There is no wind,' he said.

'If this is part of the promised chemical change, it is to be welcomed,' Nigel remarked. 'With all these deaths happening hourly, it could not be more convenient. I can think of no pleasanter end than to become a paper parcel.'

'You are very silent, Dick!' Roderick was more cheerful; as time went by and there was no attack from the stables, his spirits rose. His experience with the bodies had done nothing to alarm him, rather the contrary; everything was to be welcomed which eased the burdens of present existence.

'To lose weight without any effort, as we must all be doing, is quite delightful,' Julia laughed. 'Yet we do not appear to have shrunken up; my skin is as smooth as it was ten years ago—— Will nobody tell me how young I look?'

'We have eaten the air, promise-crammed,' her aunt quoted. 'Yet I cannot truthfully say we look younger.'

'You look different,' Roderick said to Julia, in a heavy tone. He was still quite displeased with her.

'Can you make Dick more cheerful?' he appealed to the company. 'Are you in a mood, Dick? What is the matter with you?'

'There is nothing the matter,' Dick retorted. 'How you keep on!'

'I do not like to see you so depressed—you had better have a drink—yet, I forget, there is no more whisky.'

'Dick is depressed because he has had a fruitless journey this morning,' Julia revealed. 'He rowed out to the island, and found no dome, no MacArtney.'

'I asked you not to tell anyone, Julia!'

'It is best that we should all know.'

'I am not in the least surprised,' Roderick declared. 'You must have dreamed the encounter.'

Dick was pink with anger; he wished to hit Julia, who was painting her nails as though nothing had happened. 'If I dreamed it all, where did I get this suit?' he cried.

'That is what we would all like to know; it is a disaster,' Roderick said.

Mrs Dolman silenced them. 'You searched the whole island?' she demanded of Dick.

He told her his story in a low tone; how the men, Donald Macrae and James Mackenzie, had been most unwilling to row him to the *eilean mallaichte*, which in their tongue means accursed island; and how he had searched each foot of the scorched and blasted rock, but found no trace of Mr MacArtney or his dwelling.

'I expect it was collapsible,' Mrs Dolman sensibly consoled him. 'Many buildings are nowadays. It would be easy enough to dismantle it in an hour, and carry it away by boat.'

Dick allowed himself to be comforted, and drawn away into the garden.

The thick mist was still hanging over Ebora; he confessed to her how it had made him choke, and left him so exhausted he had had to take an extra dose of elixir.

Only his belief in Mr MacArtney and the truth of his statements continued to sustain him; he had been told to be guarded in what he said; he had disobeyed—to be disbelieved and mocked must be his punishment.

'I get regularly fed up with it here,' Sylvia said to her husband. 'I mean, what is there to do? You just booze and lie about all day; now the whisky's nearly gone, you won't be able to do that even.'

'We might as well enjoy ourselves while we can,' the doctor replied. 'So for God's sake stop nagging.'

He stretched out a hand and caught her to him.

'I don't call it enjoyment.' Sylvia removed herself, and adjusted her tiara at a cracked mirror. 'You said we'd be moving into the house soon; that was days ago, and we're still in this dump. It's ever so miserable here!'

With a sniff, she refastened the diamond clip which held Julia's Chinese silk wrapper over her stomach. 'I should think they're all having the laugh on you, over there,' she said. 'They don't seem to be bothering their heads any more; they think you didn't mean what you said.'

'Oh yes?'

'They've even begun to clear up, this past day or so. I saw that Julia mopping the kitchen floor. The old lady came out and put some washing on the line; and there's smoke coming out of the kitchen chimney today; they must have a lovely fire going, and all hot baths. All those Highland men have gone back to the village, I saw them go. You've only got to go over and say: "*Right—this is it!*" They wouldn't lift a finger.'

'Wouldn't they?'

Sylvia filed her nails. 'All that funny business about poor little Lenny and Irene's bodies disappearing like that, and you taking it lying down!' she went on. 'I bet there was some hanky panky there—what you think they done with them, eh?'

'So long as they are disposed of, I could not care less.'

'Not even a proper funeral! It's not right. If they did put the corpses by the gate, like they said, someone must've come and taken them—— Go on, say something!'

'I have nothing to say,' Sydney replied, lazily embracing her.

Sylvia, making no effort to respond, watched the scene across in the garden of the house.

Mrs Dolman appeared to her view, walking slowly down the drive, giving an arm to Mr Mannifold.

'There,' Maggie encouraged him, unaware that they were observed. 'This sunshine, the first we have had for a week, will do you so much good! You will soon be on the road to recovery. How kind it was of you to help me peel all those potatoes! Who would have believed me, in the old days, if I had said to them: "*The Prime Minister peeled my potatoes for me this morning.*" To live as we do now, on the Edge of Disaster, has altered all our values. Great issues are reduced to the mere daily struggle for survival. Well, as I was telling you, this morning, dear Brother James has walked over, staff in hand, like the pilgrims of old, to carry to Strumph the message he received on Ebora. He will get no sort of a hearing, I warned him of that; yet he insisted on going. He said it was only fair they must know, as must everyone in the neighbourhood; as far as they are able to receive it, of course.'

There was no reply, nor had she expected any from William Mannifold, who, with staring eyes, shuffling walk and hanging arms, accompanied the actress wherever she chose to lead him. As they turned to enter the shrubbery, Maggie looked up, and saw Sylvia's face staring down at her from the window.

'That girl is wearing my Tanquery coronet,' she said. 'She has wrapped her vulgar little body in fine Eastern silk, and decked it with my precious jewels, but now I feel no rancour. Indeed, dear Mr Mannifold, a happiness and serenity I have not ever known, has come upon me. We have all lost everything; we have nothing material to hope for. Life has become a simple matter of hot potatoes and wood fires, of walks in the sunshine, and bathing the brows of the dying.'

So speaking, she drew her feeble charge by the hand through the shelter of wind-blown laurel and rhododendron bushes, out of the sight of spying eyes, and escorted him across the lawn to the summer house, where she had been accustomed, on the past few mornings, to spend an hour or so reciting to him from Shakespeare, Racine, Pope and Milton; with the New Testament as a *bonne bouche* to sweeten the literary feast.

This morning she was dismayed to find that two other nurses had brought their patients to this sunny place.

Julia had wheeled Nigel's chair into a sheltered position, and was now writing to his dictation, as she sat on the step, and Mrs Mottie (attended as usual by her faithful shadow Nyeri) had assisted Odysseus to a deck-chair within the shelter, where, a wreck, a mere grey outline of a man, he crouched, his head in his hands.

'There is room here for both of you.' Julia rose to her feet and came forward to forestall her aunt's displeasure. 'See, we have saved these chairs for you! We were in hopes you would recite for all of us; something really noble that would put us into an exalted state of mind.'

Mrs Dolman, who had been about to take Mr Mannifold to a seat at some distance, overlooking the bay, and as far as possible from the little conclave, was persuaded to remain.

'What, now what, shall I give you?' she murmured, putting on her spectacles, and laying down her pile of books, marked with white whiskers of paper.

'I like a nice bit out of the Bible,' Mrs Mottie said. 'You can't go wrong. Say a prayer, turn the Book endways, put in a 'airpin, and the Lord will Guide you.'

Nigel groaned in pain. His days had become a round of torture since Julia had adopted him as her life's work. In his weakness and isolation (since the doctor's defection) he had to submit to her ministrations; he was never alone. He was forced into day-light when he sought the dark. The oblivion he longed for, eluded him. He was becoming dependent on the person he most dreaded; and in this inflamed state of mind, the thought of Maggie's sonorous voice declaiming Holy Scripture was as knives and scorpions to him.

'Can we not have a passage from *Andromaque*, delivered in your own inimitable style?' he begged.

Mrs Dolman turned upon him her fine eyes of a deep river-brown, which held in their depths an appearance of irreversible tragedy.

'There are those here who are unable to understand French, Nigel dear,' she reproached him.

'There could be no misunderstanding your interpretation,' he affirmed. 'The flow of the beautiful language of the French master-dramatist, as you only are able to present it, would have the effect of inspiring all of us.'

'You are wrong,' the actress declared without hesitation. 'The artificial statements of even such a genius as Racine have no place for us, here and now. The Bible it shall be.'

'No, no!' came a dreadful cry. Odysseus raised his head at last, and gazed round, rolling his eyes. 'Not the Bible! Do not force me to listen to the Bible! How can I, a murderer by intention, support the hearing of the word of a God in Whom I do not believe, who has failed me, as I have failed Him?'

'Oh 'ow can you speak like that, Odysseus, when you 'ave little

Nyeri 'ere, saved by 'Is mercy and brought back to you?' Mrs Mottie reproached the Jamaican. 'God 'asn't failed you; it's you that's blasphemed against 'Im! Your life 'as been spared for some reason; so you sit quiet and listen!'

Odysseus rose from her restraining hands; he staggered a few steps, and would have fallen had it not been for assistance. The boy Nyeri remained quite indifferent to the episode. Sitting cross-legged on the ground, he traced a pattern with a pointed twig upon the sandy path.

'The hearing of the Bible will act as a cataplasm to your festering sore of guilt,' Mrs Dolman assured the negro, settling him into his chair with firm hands, and taking a long and shining pin from the coils of her dusty wig.

Raising it on high in one hand, whilst with the other she supported the upended bible, she smote blindly down into the pages.

The Book fell open, and, without further hesitation, in her most golden voice, she began to read:

' "Give no man anything but to love one another; for he that loveth another hath fulfilled the law." '

'We are not supposed to have any contact with Outside,' Miss Bulb whispered, through a chink in the main door of Strumph Hydro. 'It has been Given to Us to Keep Apart, you see. I am so sorry. Perhaps I could take a message, though?'

'Who is that you are speaking to, dear?'

'Oh, Mrs Boonyard, it is Mr Beek, who has come all the way from Achnabasalt with a message.'

'Then ask him what it is.'

Mrs Boonyard appeared at a nearby window, leaning down like the Blessed Damozel.

'I cannot shout it. I must write it, if I am not to be allowed to speak to you,' Mr Beek told her.

'Is it something of importance?' he was asked.

'It is of the gravest import, and concerns you.'

After a little consultation (during which Mr Beek, who was not offered a seat, sat down on the ground outside the door) Miss Bulb returned, and, keeping her distance, beckoned him through a back entry, through a number of kitchen passages and into a disused sun-parlour; where (once the windows were open to ward off contamination), a deputation, standing at a safe distance, agreed to hear his story.

When at last he had finished he was thanked courteously for his trouble in coming.

'We feel deeply for your little community,' Bernard Boonyard said. 'We realise that you are sincerely convinced that you have received a message telling you of a miraculous rescue to come; of the descent of Vehicles from Above, which will take certain people away, and of Physical Changes which are to take place in the near future. All this knowledge is ours already, from Higher Sources available to us; we are prepared. Our interpretation is not, however, the same as yours. We know that these things are to happen on the Inner Planes, and are entirely of the Mind. There will be no Physical cataclysm such as you envisage. By retreating on to the Higher Spiritual Planes, you yourself can avoid all injury; you will survive into a New and Splendid world.'

'There can be no rescue for Any on the Physical,' Stella Boonyard continued her husband's argument inexorably. She had a long thin neck, bounded by a purple velvet band. 'No Christ will appear to the eye in clouds of Glory. The way to salvation is open only upon the Inner Plains of Spiritual Realisation. Dear Mr Beek, we have known for some time that you are in truth One of Us. Will you not forsake these States of Illusion?'

'Once more, dear friend, I ask you—will you not fulfil your True Purpose, and come to us here to be purified for the Great Work to Come?' Bernard Boonyard intoned.

Mr Beek gazed at the Brethren in bewilderment. 'Do you mean you wish me to leave my friends at Achnabasalt? Now, when they need my help more than ever before, and when God has given me strength to be of service to them?'

'But they do not need you,' Stella hastened to assure him. 'They are, alas, incapable of progressing further. The terrible deeds (of which we will not, must not, speak, but bless them and pass on), those acts of horror which were perpetrated by them last week have surely proved their real nature to you? If you remain, you must go Down with them; there is no help for it. You are Too Great a Soul to allow such a Karma to overtake you through mistaken charity! Join us, and save yourself!'

Not for one minute did Brother James hesitate.

'Thank you,' he told them, 'but it is out of the question. I am weak, I am foolish, but my place is with them, up or down.' So saying, he made for the door, blindly tripping on the coco-nut matting, and catching his crook as he slammed it behind him.

16

> 'Michael, row the boat ashore,
>   Alle-lu-jah!
> Michael, row the boat ashore,
>   Alle-lu-u-jah!'

THE singing from the stableyard could be heard clearly by the group round the summerhouse on this fine, late August morning.

'If anyone had told me, even a week ago, that the campers would turn to negro spirituals I would not have believed him,' Roderick remarked.

He was busy writing; indeed the whole household had pens and paper before them. With a fury of application, or with groaning labour they were recording testimonials of their friends, at Roderick's suggestion.

'I like the singing; it is quite beautiful,' Julia sighed. 'I feel it must have some deep significance, although I cannot think what.'

'Go on with your writing, all of you!' was the order from their leader. 'I have just seen Sydney peering through the shrubbery at us. We must on no account encourage him.'

'I have finished,' Odysseus said. 'There is nothing more I can write.'

'You are drawn by the singing, I can see that,' Julia sat down beside the Jamaican. 'It is only natural; it is in your blood. You want to go over and join them, but you are held back by your guilt and grief. You feel an alien amongst us, especially since most of those poor young people in the drawing-room have died. You are young—so are those singers over in the yard. Join them, Odysseus, if you feel the call! You agree with me, Roderick, don't you? No loyalty you may feel towards us for our rescue of you and our care for you in your sickness should hold you back now you are almost well.'

'He is free to go if he wishes,' Roderick said.

'You'd be a fool to go,' Mrs Mottie said. 'And you don't take your boy back amongst those savages; that I will not 'ave. Nor would 'e want to go, bless 'is 'eart; he'll stop along of old Mottie. Like the Guides told us all last night at the sitting, the time is short. But please yourself.'

'I do not want to join them,' Odysseus said. 'I am not young any more; my youth went out of me by the funeral pyre. It was burned out of my flesh; it died with all who died because of me, with Glory and the others. I am older than all of you; do what you will with me!'

'Oh you should keep on with your singing, though,' Mrs Mottie insisted. 'The Chief was ever so pleased with that 'ymn last night. You 'ave ever such a lovely singing voice, 'asn't 'e, Mr Fernay?'

Sydney took the opportunity of their interest in this conversation to emerge on the lawn quite boldly, unarmed and unattended.

'Good morning!' he greeted them. 'A glorious day!'

Dick jumped up to confront him. 'What have you come here for? What do you want?'

His thirteen closely written pages were in danger of blowing away, had not Roderick secured them with a stone.

'Don't speak to him!' he ordered his secretary, writing busily, without a glance at the doctor.

'Childish, hn?' Sydney was unshaven, and wearing Nigel's new lovat tweed suit. 'Still bearing malice, eh? Your guilt, let me remind you, is as great, or greater, than ours. Your rabble killed and wounded eight of our people; only two of the sick have survived. It was only justice we should take what we did.'

'So you think that clothes and jewels make up for all those deaths? In the village a dozen perished!'

'Food was more important; but drink was most vital of all, of course; both to the murderers, amongst whom I distributed it (and who, because of it, forgot to be revenged), and to my poor followers in their loss. And you yourselves have benefited because of my deprivations. Come now, be honest, Roderick! Haven't you all become humbler, more unselfish, readier to learn from others? You owe this change to me!'

'How you have the effrontery to stand there and——'

'Leave this to me, Dick!' Roderick had made up his mind to speak, distasteful though it might be to him. 'If you think we shall hand over Achnabasalt to you without a fight because of the weak state to which you have reduced us, you are mistaken. We shall resist you to the death!'

'O-ho!'

'I am not impressed by your specious arguments; two wrongs do not make a right! You repaid my friendship and hospitality by treachery. I have nothing more to say to you!'

'Oh, you need not worry. I haven't come to take your house over, quite the contrary,' Sydney replied.

'He has come because he has no whisky left!' cried Dick excitedly. 'He thinks we may have some hidden here; he doesn't realise there is none left in the country!'

'I know that,' Sydney said calmly. 'I am here alone and un-armed. Can you not guess why?'

'It is a trick! Don't listen to him!'

'How wrong you are! Quite simply, I want to come back and live amongst you,' Sydney admitted. 'I can't stand the exuber-ance of youth any longer. The noise in the stables tires me; I find I have nothing in common with the beat generation.'

'You have the nerve to demand this, after all that has happened?'

'You take our breath away!'

'Why? It is only logical—I don't know what you are making such a fuss about! After all, I am one of you, and not one of them. You can't deny that.'

'You threw in your lot with them.'

Sydney shrugged his shoulders. 'A matter of expediency, my dear chap.'

'You have forfeited the right to our friendship by your conduct!'

'Not at all; you had it coming to you. Let's call a truce! At this late stage, we can't do otherwise; if you're sensible you'll see that. It wasn't good for your immortal souls to be in such a superior position to the rest of the community, now was it? How could it have benefited the spirituality upon which some of you set such store, if you hogged it while the rest of us starved, eh? It was plain silly for Roderick to set himself as leader, and expect everyone to obey him without question. What qualifications did he have, after all? You looked a prize idiot I don't mind telling you, Roddy; running about in that kilt, and leading your ragged band of gangsters on senseless expeditions up and down the country. It was a sheer waste of time and energy, now wasn't it? I've had one or two good laughs about it. But never mind that; that's all past history. I understand that things have now been taken out of your hands; the Government have sent a responsible agent at last to get us out of this. Relief will be sent any day; and I want to know where I can get in touch with this chap.'

'You have been misinformed,' Roderick returned coldly.

'Oh, come now! What's this story of the man on Ebora with the motor launch, who hands out bunny suits and dressing-gowns?'

'There is nobody on Ebora.'

'He had nothing to do with the Government!' burst from Dick, before he could stop himself. 'Nor with any world authority.'

Sydney folded his arms and looked about him with amusement. 'I suppose he was a messenger from Mars?'

Nobody troubled to answer him.

'I understand—— You have been told to expect a Day of Judgement any minute—that's why you're all so busy doing your homework!'

'You are deliberately offensive. We are not compelled to listen.' Roderick held his anger lightly and pleasurably. 'None of us wish you to return here. I have only one thing left to say to you—*get out*!'

Sydney looked from one to another. 'You agree with him?'

'I should not want your *wife* back under any circumstances,' Julia admitted. 'And I must say you are extraordinarily *rude*.'

'Sylvia has done with me,' Sydney said. 'I am still in love with her, but sexually she turned out to be frigid. Although she still enchants me, I find her lower-middle-class shibboleths tiring. Perhaps we're better apart for the time being.'

'I have asked you to go! Be good enough to leave this garden at once!' Roderick ordered.

'You can't force him to go, and he knows it,' Nigel pointed out. 'At the moment he is doing no harm; he is a welcome distraction. He acts as our guilty conscience. Let him stay; so long as he changes out of my suit.'

'Don't let me interrupt the flow of inspiration,' Sydney begged

Roderick uttered a cry of rage. He had to be restrained from. striking the doctor with his bare hands.

'You are not interrupting us. We have finished,' Nigel told Doctor Monro in a calm voice.

Maggie Dolman, who had taken no part so far in any of the argument, now rose from her chair, and went from one to another, collecting their papers like a schoolmistress, and placing them in a pile on the table before Roderick. She did not look in the doctor's direction.

Roderick picked up the topmost essay, and adjusted his spectacles.

'Aren't you going to read them aloud, and award the marks?' Sydney enquired.

As nobody answered, he relaxed, and lay back on his elbows on the lawn. 'So each one of you is making out a case for himself to present to the recording angel,' he thought aloud. 'In these papers are set forth the overwhelming reasons why you should be included in the flock of sheep to be raised to heavenly pastures. I can't think why you should bother! To my way of thinking it will be much more interesting to remain with the goats; at least they are individualists!'

'You are quite mistaken, we——'

'Dick! Don't argue with him!'

A new and clear voice spoke. 'They are writing about each other,' the boy Nyeri said. He was playing at his usual sand-divining, upon the ground; he had drawn up a small cone of earth and placed a marguerite upon it, as on a grave.

Sydney was overcome by laughter; he shook with it and could not speak; he rolled over on the grass. After a little, however, he was able to control himself and sit up, still grinning, and showing his strong, yellow teeth. With his scarred and pitted face, shining with sweat in the sun, Julia thought he resembled an animal; perhaps one of the goats of which he had just spoken.

She shivered deliciously; perhaps the ancient spirit of Pan. waiting a thousand years in these lonely coasts, had taken the opportunity to enter into the doctor; the idea excited and frightened her at the same moment.

'There is one thing certain,' the doctor grinned. 'No one has recommended *me*! I am quite safe.'

'Are you so sure of that?' asked Nigel.

'You have always been actuated by the highest principles of enlightened self-interest, Nigel; don't tell me you have lost your senses, or become a hypocrite in your extremity.'

'It is quite logical that I should choose to give you a testimonial,' Nigel explained. 'As you say, we have been taught a lesson. My sufferings of the past week have given me plenty of food for reflection—I realise that I treated you without consideration; I took away your self-respect. The least I can do is to attempt in this way to make amends.'

'You leave me speechless with gratitude,' the doctor replied. 'I can see that death-bed repentance is in order; although, as you don't believe in heaven or hell, I cannot see the point of it where you are concerned. But I was a free agent; it suited me to work for you, and I was well paid for my trouble. You had the worst of the bargain, for I was seldom sober; latterly, as you know, I lost interest in you completely.'

'Yes you are a lazy, drunken scoundrel,' Nigel agreed, with perfect good humour. 'But I shall receive high commendation with the Powers That Be for my defence of you.'

Nyeri spoke again: 'Brother James has gone to the village to tell the Minister and the people about the flying-boats that are coming to take all the good people away.' With a sudden swirling gesture he broke down his sand-castle, and broke the flower; in ever-widening, spiral movements he flattened the place where the shrine had been.

'Bully for Brother James,' the doctor said.

He was easier with them now; they would show him no violence. He plucked a plantain, and set the stalk between his teeth, with a savage smile.

'Let me guess whom our admired leader has recommended?' he began to muse. 'Not the most obvious choice—— No, no—— Why waste ammunition on one whose loyalty has been so constant? I am sure that Mr Bolton's place on the Heavenly Cattle Float has been booked from the beginning. I have it! It is Julia! Right?'

'Think what you like! I have nothing to say!'

'Julia it is then! And how does our Mr Fernay defend the beautiful and ineffectual lady?'

The doctor turned to study his subject, who sat quietly, in a conscious, Grecian pose, accentuated by the folds of the clean white sheet she wore; a green ribbon threaded through her silvery hair.

'Dear dear! How can he intercede with St Peter for a woman who has never done an honest day's work in her life, but who has been kept in luxury for the last ten years by a very rich man, whom she did not love?' Sydney asked himself aloud.

'You have no right to speak in this way of Julia! You are not fit to address her!'

'Julia did work, dear child,' Mrs Dolman was heard to say. 'She did modelling at first; then she danced in a very select club. She has had a training in judo, and can draw quite charmingly and make scrap-work screens. Several of her little water-colours were on view in a Bond Street Gallery only a year ago, and sold quite well. In her time she has given pleasure to a great number of people; that is by no means a negligible quality in a woman; nor is it true to say she was indifferent to Jack Bouncer; she was quite devoted to him, and he to her.'

'And what does the lady say?'

'I have no defence to enter,' smiled Julia sadly.

'Why should she defend herself to you?' shouted Roderick, letting go the leash of his strong anger at last. 'Enough of this farce! I order you to leave this minute!'

'Please, Roderick—I wish to hear what he has to say!' Julia laid a hand on Mr Fernay's arm to insist. She was greatly interested in this discussion of her own personality.

Roderick folded his arms. 'I shall take no further part in the argument.'

'So much for the lady—yet I wonder whom she has chosen?' laughed Sydney into her face. 'I wonder, I wonder!'

Julia put up her hands to her cheeks in a becoming gesture of embarrassment. 'Please, please—let's not go any further!' she was heard to mutter.

'Oh but she is enjoying herself,' Dick whispered.

With a smothered cry, Julia rose and fluttered to the far side of the lawn.

'She will come back; she's not out of earshot,' Dick pointed out.

'It is Nigel, Nigel, *Nigel*, of course,' Sydney raised his voice. 'But why should anyone be surprised? She could never love a whole man!'

'Why do you say that?'

'Because it would be too dangerous. A whole man might possess *her*; and that would never do!'

'Is this true, Julia?' Dick asked her, as she approached timidly towards them once more.

She neither denied nor confirmed it, merely drew her sheet more closely over her shoulder, with a pathetic drooping of her long, white neck.

'It is a shame to tease her! She is cursed with being more sensitive than the rest of us, aren't you, my poor love?' enquired Dick Bolton softly.

'And whom would you have recommended, Doctor?' asked Julia, daring to look directly at him at last.

'Why, my dear delicious, vulgar little Sylvia, of course,' laughed Sydney. 'My lovely, exasperating silly girl, whom I can't live with any more, yet can't live without! Whom did you suppose?'

Julia was confused by the beating of blood in her ears. 'It is easy to guess who has spoken for Roderick.' She changed the subject, a hand on her heart, and a little breathless. 'Although several of us may, Dick is certain to have done his job so thoroughly that no other commendation is necessary.'

'And who has spoken for me, eh?' clowned the secretary, making his hands into rabbit's ears, and hopping amongst them. 'Nobody, Nobody!' He looked into one face after another. 'Not one?'

'I will speak for you, Little Owl!' cried Julia, with generosity.

His pretended tears affected all of them; they masked a genuine disappointment.

'I will speak for you, poor creature!' Roderick stepped down from the summer house, and laid a hand on Dick's shoulder. 'You fool! I have already spoken—— Read, what I had to say!'

'You mean that you chose me, and not Julia?'

'Get up from that ridiculous position at once!'

'Had I been here, I would have recommended you, my dear friend,' Mr Beek, who had approached unobserved, spoke for the first time. 'Yet I could not have singled out one—I must have spoken for all!'

'Speaking for meself, I gave me word for them as needed me most,' Mrs Mottie announced.

There could be no mistaking the direction of her nod.

'You spoke for me?' asked Odysseus in amazement.

'And *he* pleaded for his little son,' Maggie Dolman said. The sound of her voice, coming as the summing up of their perorations, struck a final note, like a drum.

It had been '*Who spoke for me?—I spoke for you?—And who for him?*' The whispers, the pleading, had been so anxious that the game took on a significance beyond its worth; it was as if a real and final judgement had been pronounced.

Now, all on a moment, Maggie's words released the spell. She did not bother to ask who had testified for her, she did not sorrow that nobody had done so. She remained calm, and independent of their affection in her geranium-red blanket, to which adornment she had added a necklace of centimes and a corsage of fading, cabbage roses.

Everyone was a little uncomfortable.

'I must go and see if Mr Mannifold has awakened; it is time for our morning stroll. Don't forget, Dick, you and Julia are to prepare the luncheon today.'

She rose, swinging a fold of her blanket over her shoulder, like a Roman senator who is above common weakness.

'There goes a wonderful woman!' was drawn out of Mr Beek.

'She expected someone to say that!' Roderick replied.

Dick blew his nose. He had no wish to leave the sunny lawn for the dark and dirty kitchen, where Julia's domestic ineptitude would throw the whole burden of potato-peeling upon himself.

Mr Beek sat down and told the story of his mission to the village.

'A crowd awaited me on the steps of the Free Kirk. Mr Macalpine and his elders stood at the door. I tried to speak, but was shouted down. Then the minister raised his hand, and commanded silence; finally he addressed me.

'The evil which they had all witnessed during the past ten days, and which was still rife amongst them, he said, was the work of Satan's emissaries, chief amongst whom was their Laird. They had been right, he told them, to distrust you, Mr Fernay, in the first place, as you were not of true Highland descent, nor a Presbyterian. You had ensnared and deceived them; you had led them into the ways of destruction. (I am only repeating what was said, I deeply deplore having to tell you this, but you must know everything.)'

'It was only to be expected, I suppose.' Yet Roderick was hurt. 'They have turned completely against me, after all I tried to do for them! They blame me; I was a father to them once, so they said. I sent potatoes down to them, even when we were short of them ourselves.'

'I attempted once more to tell them of the message we received on Ebora, but Mr Macalpine cried to them, with a loud voice, to stop their ears. "*We abide by the Word of God, as given to us in the Bible,*" he said. "*Our strength is in the Gospel of Salvation through the Lord Jesus Christ; our damnation lies in listening to blasphemy and lies from this Papist.*"'

'Why should they think of you as a Papist?'

'I suppose it must be the cassock.'

'The village is very religious all of a sudden!'

'I tried several times to speak; it was no use. Indeed, some of the children threw mud and stones at me,' Mr Beek went on, showing a cut on his forehead, another on his foot. 'In the end, I went and sat on the shore, and asked God what I should do next? I feel so sorry for them; they are weak and starving and full of fear and hate, which is poisoning them quite quickly.'

'I don't know why they should hate *us*!'

'I could hear Mr Macalpine addressing his congregation in the churchyard. He has a carrying voice. Although I could not make out everything he was saying, I gather he is offended that the young people at the camp are singing hymns to pop music, and dancing to the guitars while they sing; it came near, he said, to sacrilege. He talked about their walking about half naked, and about our strange apparel, and stranger conduct; any contact with any of us would, he assured them, result in their eternal damnation.'

'Let them rot in their narrow-minded bigotry!'

'So you failed in the village,' Sydney summed it up. 'What about trying the stables now? You can't desert the campers, especially now they've got religion.'

'Leave them alone,' Odysseus spoke. 'They are accursed, as I am.'

'You healed them,' Nigel pointed out. 'You must help them.'

The Jamaican had been silent for so long that his intervention surprised everyone. 'I did not heal them; I used a very bad *obea*, a black magic,' he explained. 'It was like Voo-doo. My grand-mother came from Haiti; she taught it to my mother. I was mad that afternoon—a devil entered into me. I sacrificed a cock—I remember no more. Twice, I was possessed of the devil. I destroyed the woman I loved; I am accursed. I wish I had died then when she did.'

The news shocked, but did not surprise, them.

'You don't 'ave to tell *me*,' Mrs Mottie announced, to nobody in particular. 'That night, down by the bonfire, *what* I saw dancing round in the flames I will never describe to me dying day! But you 'ave paid for it, Odysseus dear; you are sorry. The Lord will 'elp you.'

So saying, she led the negro away. The group about the summer house dispersed in the summer silence, which was unbroken even by the twanging of a guitar.

Only the doctor continued lying on the yellow grass.

The bay, the island (misted only as by a veil of the thinnest gauze), hung in the golden air with a diaphanous appearance, as though the slightest tremor might disperse land and sea.

Into the watching, waiting calm, about noon, a sound came, an echo of a distant calamity.

'What was that? It sounded like thunder!'

'It came from underground, surely. The earth trembled.'

'Gunfire, perhaps?'

'It was a double echo; the explosion of a rocket.'

'Another bomb?'

'If it was, it hasn't affected us. The sea has hardly a ripple; there is no mushroom cloud.'

They discussed it over their mashed potato and cabbage; there was the feeling that it hardly concerned them.

Yet the day, which had been so fine and calm, began, about four o'clock, to be hazy. A dun phosphorescence clouded the face of the sun, and sent first a finger, then a widening, palm of darkness over the earth.

At six o'clock twilight descended and remained.

17

IT WAS unpleasant, thought Sylvia, to remain in the stables without Sydney's support, especially now the weather had turned so gloomy and unpleasant. Although his attentions had bored her, she never expected he would return to Achnabasalt without her; the house of her dreams, with two water-closets, and eight bedrooms, some supplied with spring-mattresses.

The airs she had adopted as the Leader's wife, had not made her popular with the others; now the girls began to smack and pinch her, to pull her long golden hair and take away her fine clothes.

She ran away, snivelling, into the furthest corner of the loft, and lay amongst the straw, peering over the edge of the floor into the space below, between the mangers, where the girls were dividing their spoils by candlelight.

'It's ever so dark! It must be midnight!'

'I canna see a thing—hold up the licht!'

'Och, it's jist a dark kin' o' a day.'

'Ah thocht I heerd thunder in the forenoon. Did you not hear it, Sandra?'

'Gie's yon blue nightie, Chrissie!'

'You don't suit blue, hen! Here, try this, Jeannie—— Gosh, here's the boys back. Put on your pants!'

Sylvia shut her eyes to avoid the sight of so many naked young men. It was not nice at all. It might be all right in a nudist colony, for there, Beattie had told her, clergymen and all went, and nobody thought of the flesh. They played handball together, and sex never crossed their minds; but here, with the end of the world so near, it was disgusting.

'You ought to be ashamed of yourselves!' she cried, silencing their squeals with her shrill tones (she, whose voice had once enchanted with its soft intonations). 'Behaving like that when you come from decent homes! I wonder what your mums and dads would think of you all now! It's no use going out and singing hymns after the way *you've* been going on!'

One of the younger girls began to sob. 'She's right! This darkness is'na natural—it's the day of judgement! I want me mam!'

'Och, shut up, Mrs Bloody Monro—ye're scaring the lassie! It's jist a storm coming up, wee Jessie!'

'That is no thunderstorm. Look out of the window!'

The campers jeered at her.

They ran out to their dancing ground on the cliff. Soon Sylvia heard the guitars spangling the leaden air. She came down the ladder, and a little way up the road; they had built yet another bonfire of drift wood; they were jigging round it with as much fervour as ever before. She returned and began to search amongst the torn fragments of garments on the cobble-stones, for something fit to wear; but a strange thing had begun to happen to those made of lawn, georgette, silk or nylon; like burned paper, they fell away to ashes at a touch—— No wonder the girls had rejected them.

She dusted the flakes from her fingers, shivering. 'After all, some of them were *new!*' she spoke aloud.

Now she had nothing to cover her but her petticoat, and the darkness.

'He can't expect me to stay here alone with *them!*' she sobbed. 'He must make them take me in too!'

She began running towards Achnabasalt House.

'It isn't only this confounded darkness—the air presses on my chest—I can scarcely—breathe,' panted Nigel.

'Ask Julia to breathe for you; I am sure she will oblige!' Roderick advised him.

'If you don't speak it will not put such a strain upon you,' Julia told him, without rising.

'This darkness is evil!' Roderick announced.

'Darkness of itself can't be evil,' the doctor pronounced. 'It's merely a physical phenomenon.'

'Someone's at the door,' Mrs Mottie announced.

'Go and see who it is, Dick!'

'I am not a slave; my time of subjection is over,' Dick replied.

'We will see about that.' In a softer tone: 'I ask you, please to go!'

The knocking came, more desperately than ever.

'I will go,' Odysseus offered. 'I will be the Keeper of the Door. It is the least I can do now. I will keep out those who have no right here.'

He shuffled from the room.

'Julia! Give me a sip of water! My mouth is so dry!' called Nigel. 'Please, I beg you!'

Julia did not answer. In the darkness, now that she could no longer see him clearly, she was more conscious of Sydney than ever.

'Julia! Nigel is speaking to you!' Roderick told her sharply. Julia rose with reluctance. She supported Nigel's head, as she gave him the water. His skin had become like wet clay; his stubbled face was that of a dead man.

'You will not leave me?' he whispered, holding fast to her hand.

Odysseus returned. 'It is your wife at the door,' he told Sydney.

'Oh no! Do not let her in!' Julia exclaimed.

But Sylvia had pushed past the negro, who had no strength to detain her. She rushed forward, and threw herself sobbing into the doctor's arms.

'They took my clothes, Syd! They were ever so nasty to me; they beat me up, soon's you went!' she whimpered. 'You can't let Mr Fernay turn me away—I can't ever go back there!'

'She 'as the strength all right,' Mrs Mottie was heard to remark. 'A week of good meals, chicken broth and tinned pork-meat, 'as gorn inside 'er. She can run; she can knock us all dahn, even the men; she can take our blankets off of us.'

'I don't trust her,' Mrs Dolman agreed.

'If you wish us to speak to you, you will order her to leave,' Roderick declared. 'Otherwise we shall continue to ignore you.'

'She is staying, whether you like it or not,' Sydney said. 'As Mrs Mottie so rightly reminded you, we are stronger than you are. If you choose to be unpleasant, we can make it very hot for you. We shall take over from now on. And you had better do as you are told without argument. What is more, we are moving into your bedroom, Roderick, old chum. The beds are comfortable, and there's a fire there. So, get your clobber cleared out now!'

'Our garments are falling to pieces before our eyes.'

'If it were not for the perpetual twilight we should be quite indecent.'

'Dick's Bunny suit is as good as new,' Julia whispered. 'I wish I had one, or a cassock like Mr Beek's! Neither of these show signs of disintegration! Dear Dick, can't you find your friend Mr MacArtney, and ask him for suits for all of us as well?' Her voice was so weak, so far away, he could scarcely hear it.

'I do not know where to find Mr MacArtney. I wish I did.'

'Rescue had better come soon,' Roderick murmured, 'or we shall be too weak to walk.'

'Perhaps there will be no rescue. It was all a dream of Dick's, an illusion.'

'No, no. I have assured you, many times, I——'

'Ssh! I thought I heard Sydney coming.'

'There is no need to whisper—they are still in bed. I have not seen them since last night.'

'Perhaps it is still night—one can scarcely tell night from day!'

'It is Maggie, coming downstairs, isn't it? Is it you, Mrs Dolman?'

'It is I,' the actress replied, coming into their midst, so that they could touch, if not see, her. 'I have sad news. Mr Mannifold must have died in his sleep, very peacefully. I found him just now; he is quite cold.'

'I will go up to him,' Mr Beek said, and almost immediately exclaimed: 'But, dear Mrs Dolman—you must be mistaken! I saw Mr Mannifold not half an hour ago, coming from his room! I spoke to him, even—I always speak to him, although he never answers. To have such a burden of responsibility for what has happened, upon his conscience, must weigh heavily with him—I cannot help feeling sorry for him! He looked at me, in a considering way, then went ahead of me down the stairs, and out through those windows into the garden.'

'*Those* windows?' Roderick rose and tried them. 'They are stuck. They have not opened since we arrived here!'

Mr Beek looked perplexed.

'You must have imagined you saw him, Mr Beek. In the darkness it is possible to mistake one person for another.'

'I am certain it was he! He has such a characteristic walk—besides, it is not too dark to see his face.'

'I have just remembered—I, too, saw Mr Mannifold today!' Dick announced. 'It was in the garden a quarter of an hour ago.'

'I think some of us should go upstairs and satisfy ourselves as to whether the Prime Minister is indeed dead.'

The men left the room. Julia yawned. She was not interested in Mr Mannifold. To think of Sydney, closeted for so many hours with Sylvia, was torture to her. 'I wish this awful fog would lift!' she screamed, in a little mewing voice. 'It makes me feel so listless and out of sorts!'

'You cannot surely imagine it is merely a sea-fog!' her aunt retorted, but Julia did not hear her.

The company at Achnabasalt now heard only what they wished to hear. Julia clutched her sheet rather suddenly to her, as she felt a draught; another length of it shredded away. The material was become as tenuous as an old banner hung in the aisles of a cathedral.

The deputation came downstairs from the Prime Minister's chamber.

'Mr Mannifold is indeed dead,' Roderick announced. 'We summoned Sydney; he confirmed it. We shall bury him this afternoon. There is no point in waiting longer. Mr Beek will take the funeral. I will give a small tribute. After all, he was a sincere man.'

'I hope he is not going to haunt us. It is very embarrassing to have the dead always with us,' Julia complained.

'He should haunt the House of Commons, the scene of his triumphs; not Achnabasalt, the token of his disgrace,' Dick said.

'There may be no more Houses of Parliament.'

'It is very inconsiderate of him to haunt us so soon after his passing,' Julia said. 'He should have waited.'

They were of the opinion that it must be something to do with the changed atmosphere. 'I hope everyone is not planning to annoy us in this manner, when their time comes,' Roderick remarked.

'I certainly shall not,' Nigel told him. 'I shall be in oblivion.'

'You cannot say where you will be.'

'I shall certainly not stop here,' was the retort.

'Mr Beek, please may I speak to you? ' Dick implored, later in the evening, after the funeral (a few ashes alone had remained of Mr Mannifold for burial). 'I mean—Brother James, may I have a quiet word with you, away from the others?'

They walked side by side on the cliffs, under a lowering sky.

'If I do not find Mr MacArtney soon, it will be too late to rescue our poor friends; I am almost out of my mind with worry! You see the terrible and rapid change in all of them? You realise they are dying before our very eyes?'

'I know, I know!' replied the clergyman. 'But, having promised, he will not fail us.'

'I have tried to send word to him by mental telepathy, even! He may understand such an extra-sensory means of communication. He must know the urgency of the situation—a few hours may make all the difference—indeed, a few hours may be all they have!'

'Surely you are mistaken!'

'I know I am not! Have you looked closely at Roderick? Or Julia? They are fading away before our eyes!'

'I will pray for them!'

'Dear Mr Beek, excellent though your prayers are, they can have no effect in this poisonous atmosphere! Even with our protective garments, even taking constant doses of the elixir, I feel as though I am choking! I confess, I have been tempted to give a dose or two to—well, to some of them—— Only the knowledge that they are in some way differently constituted, and that it would do no good, restrains me.'

'We must watch; we must pray constantly that help will be sent.'

'In the meantime, let us go back and be with them. They have no idea, fortunately, of the danger they are in.'

So saying, they turned, and walked back rapidly to the house.

'You seem very silent and depressed,' Roderick remarked to Dick. 'What is the matter with you?'

The hopelessness of an attempt at explanation overcame the secretary. 'Everything is covered in this white dust,' he hedged. 'It gets into one's lungs; one can scarcely breathe!'

'It doesn't worry *me*,' Roderick answered. 'I feel a little tired, that is all; but it is quite natural after all we have been through.'

'Don't you realise that it is your skin, which is drying up, flaking off and being blown away, little by little?' Dick demanded, trembling. 'It is so horrible, I cannot contemplate it!'

Roderick chose to ignore this hysterical outburst, if indeed he heard it, which was uncertain.

Julia uttered a little shriek. A figure was coming down the shadowy staircase; it was Mr Mannifold, dressed soberly in his Downing Street uniform, black jacket, clean white shirt, striped trousers. Looking neither to left nor right, he crossed the hall, and passed through the closed front door.

Dick hastened after him, calling his name; he opened the door and ran out into the garden. 'Mr Mannifold! Please don't go! There are questions we must ask you now!'

Yet there was no figure on the drive, on the lawns or in the shrubbery.

Dick came slowly back into the house.

'Did you see that?' he demanded of Sydney, who was coming from the kitchen.

'See what?'

'See Mr Mannifold, of course.'

'You must be mad! The fellow's dead. I saw nobody.'

'It was his ghost we saw.'

'There's no such animal.'

'How wrong you are—we are becoming a household of ghosts,' Dick murmured. He said in a louder tone to the doctor: 'Didn't it strike you as strange that his body had turned to ashes?'

'It's the effect of the radiation, no doubt.'

'Have you ever heard of such an effect before?'

'I haven't had personal experience of the effects of radiation,' the doctor said calmly. 'This may be a different kind.'

'It is. It is terribly different,' Dick assured him.

'Next time you see Mr Mannifold, Dick, tell him to stop haunting Achnabasalt,' Roderick said to his secretary. 'Let him return to the ruins of London, for which he is responsible. That would be far more suitable. It is untidy having a ghost, especially such a well-known one, cluttering up the house.'

.   .   .   .   .

'They are asleep,' one watcher whispered to the other. 'They are hardly breathing, though.'

Shielding the last remaining candles in their hands, they passed from room to room, never daring to relax.

'What a long night; it will never end!' Dick cried.

'Sit down, my poor friend. It can do no harm to rest ourselves a little! We do not neglect them by refreshing ourselves. There is nothing we can do but watch and wait.'

A clock struck two. 'Nothing? Nothing!'

They rose, and went about their vigil.

Mr Beek entered a room; he emerged immediately.

'Nigel has gone,' he said. 'In his sleep, quietly.'

'He was the weakest. It was expected. Come with me, dear Brother James—I have no courage left to go alone!'

They climbed the staircase.

'So we have been deceived; we alone are living!'

The terrible grief of the early morning had passed; a resigned and bitter stupor was all that was left. The cremated remains of the household had been consigned to the waves; a short service of commemoration held on the cliff's edge in the watery light. 'If I ever see Mr MacArtney again,' Dick cried, 'I shall tell him what I think of him—— A rescue indeed!'

Mr Beek laid a hand on his arm. 'The time has come to tell you,' he announced. He drew the distracted man into a cove below the rocks; they sat on the white sand. 'As you know, I was taken to the island before you,' he began. 'I knew from the beginning what must happen. Our task is still before us, as I will explain.'

18

FOR several days Dick and Mr Beek waited in the empty house for what must happen.

Not a whisper disturbed them; a blind flapped here in the listless silence, a shadow moved there, setting Dick's heart racing.

'I thought I heard whispering just now in the bathroom passage.' His lips were dry. 'Let's go out into the garden! I cannot stand it a minute longer!——I tell you, I would even be thankful to see Mr Mannifold!'

'Do not be afraid,' Mr Beek besought him. 'It is they who will need us; *they* who will have to be reassured!'

'It is so cruel! To think we must not tell them!'

'Not until they ask—not until they find out for themselves!'

'This afternoon I went down to the village; not a soul is left. The stables are deserted also. We are alone on the whole coast!' Dick declared.

'I understand that some of the Brethren survive.'

'I am not going to seek their help, if they were the last people on earth!'

'You are trembling. Take my hand!'

'How can you remain so calm? The dead are not ordinary!'

'Indeed they are; only a vibration separates us. We are lucky to have conditions so disturbed that the veil between us is severed at last.'

Dick looked disgusted. 'It is quite horrid. I dread it with all my heart!'

'Surely you do not dread seeing Mr Fernay again?'

'Of course I do!' wailed the unfortunate secretary. 'It will be highly unnatural! It is too much to ask. I feel thoroughly ill at the thought of it!'

'We will get used to it in a very short time, so I was told,' Mr Beek said.

'And what is to happen to us in the end, may I ask?' was the demand, which the clergyman, shaking his head, refused to answer, even if he knew the outcome.

It was on the third afternoon that the change began, for, on entering the house, after a lonely expedition to the shore, they could hear voices in the drawing-room. When they entered, it was as if they had been absent a few minutes only, and the gathering of people (who had a solid appearance) showed no surprise at seeing them.

'We are talking of the wretched state of our clothes,' Roderick began. 'Something certainly must be done about them; we are practically naked.'

'Oh, Roderick, Roderick!' Dick exclaimed, in a trembling tone.

'Whatever is the matter with you? Let us have no more hysteria!'

'You are quite pale—you must have walked too far,' came from Mrs Dolman, seated on the sofa. 'Make a little tea; there should be a spoonful or two left in the blue caddy.'

'This bright sunshine shows us up as a shoddy lot,' Roderick went on. 'Still, it is a relief, isn't it, that that gloomy fog has lifted.'

'But it is as dark as ev——' Dick began, but was silenced with a warning look from Mr Beek.

It seemed more than unfair that the visitants should be enjoying such heavenly weather.

He swallowed. 'Why don't you play a game?' he recited his lesson. 'What about *imagining* yourselves some wonderful clothes?' The words almost stuck in his mouth.

'I suppose it might pass the time; yet I don't see what good it will do.'

'It is the silliest game I ever heard of!' pouted Julia. 'It is for people who have nothing else to do. I refuse to take part in it.'

'We have nothing better to occupy ourselves with at the moment,' the actress insisted. She looked glowing, as she sat sideways, her white hand along the back of the seat. Indeed, she seemed to have shed a dozen years already. 'I have never believed in giving way to despair. Here we are, on the threshold of a new life—somewhere in Equador, Peru, who knows? Everything is changing hourly. The old is decaying before our eyes. May it not be true that astounding revelations await us? *A way will be found for us* in our weakness. Let us have faith. I have the most tremendous faith, I assure you!'

'That is obvious!'

'So, in the meantime, I am quite willing to play your little game, for who knows what may come of it. Hush! Let us have complete silence! I must concentrate!'

She breathed heavily, her bosom rose and fell, her eyes closed. 'At the moment, what I most fancy for myself is a beautiful grey jacket, of the warmest, softest woollen material, with silver frogging, and a double row of bright, metal buttons down the front. Oh, I can just see it! The cuffs are to be most military, with two rows of black braid, and, let me see, oh yes—there are epaulettes, with more black braid upon them!'

There was silence for the space of five minutes.

'How long is this farce to continue?' demanded Roderick.

'Ssh!' And then Julia uttered a cry. A nebulous, amorphous shapelessness embraced her aunt. It had the rough form of a jacket, yet it was a dirty white. Even as they watched in astonishment, however, it darkened a little; points of light gleamed where silver buttons began to show themselves; as her aunt breathed with the force of her concentration, they saw the garment become a reality.

Mrs Dolman opened her eyes wide, and sat up, gazing down at herself in astonishment. Then she rose, and stretched her arms.

'It works! It works, my dears!' she laughed in delight.

'Bravo!' cried Dick, clapping his hands.

'You have forgotten the braid on the right sleeve!'

A moment's further thought rectified the fault. She frowned. 'It isn't perfect,' she admitted. 'But it was a preliminary trial only. Now I know how, I will do much better. I will help you all to magnificent wardrobes of clothes!'

'There is nothing whatsoever at the back,' Dick pointed out.

'Oh, I forgot the back completely!' Mrs Dolman admitted. 'Let me have a minute more!'

'It is working,' Julia announced. 'You began a centre seam, then it faded away. It is better without it.'

'I thought so.'

'It fits perfectly. A beautiful skirt of matching material has appeared.'

Maggie stepped into the centre of the room to show herself without the slightest self-consciousness, but no little satisfaction. She made a charming figure, in a costume of the eighteen-nineties. Dick thought she looked twice as attractive as her niece.

'What if your costume melts away?' Roderick enquired.

'I don't think it will,' Maggie told him. 'I shall remind myself of it until it is part of me. Then when I tire of it, I shall make another.'

'Dear, dear Aunt Maggie; will you help me to make one, this minute?' her niece demanded.

'I don't see how it was done,' Roderick complained.

'Oh, the whole constitution of the atom must have changed,' Maggie told him, in an airy voice. 'You can all make yourselves clothes now, as quickly as possible. You have only to concentrate, and Have Faith.'

She drew Julia upstairs to their bedroom, and the others followed.

'So the first lesson is learned,' Dick said to Mr Beek, sadly. 'I had hoped it would take longer.'

'Not all of them will learn as quickly as Mrs Dolman,' the clergyman consoled him. 'And there are many more lessons.'

'They must come to an end before long.'

'They may not.'

For an hour or so, everyone was experimenting, with varying success. Julia, with her aunt's assistance, made herself a long pink robe; but its shapelessness depressed her. Roderick had a new plaid; but he had been too impatient—the tartan appeared only where it touched his breast and shoulder, the rest was cloudy. It had no particular form; merely it served to cover him and give him a sense of warmth.

'It will do, won't it?' he enquired.

'If you think so, chum,' was Dick's reply.

The doctor and his wife, roused by the excitement, came out on to the landing to see what was happening. They could make nothing at all of the game, and remained in their rags. Sylvia refused to try such a stupid experiment; soon they returned to their bedroom and everyone said they were thankful.

'Where is Nigel?' Roderick enquired.

'I am afraid he is dead,' Mr Beek told him.

'Poor fellow! It was only to be expected. I should have gone to his funeral; why did you not tell me before?'

'At any rate he will not haunt us,' Julia pointed out. 'He is in oblivion. It is sad, but inevitable.'

'By the way, have you seen Mannifold lately?'

'Not since—— Not for two or three days, Roderick.'

'You saw him yesterday. We all did!'

'But no—it was Mond—— Yes, yes of course.'

'Yesterday *was* Monday.—Are you mad?' As there was no reply to this pleasantry, Mr Fernay continued: 'I should think we have seen the last of him. After all, there was nothing for him here; I can't imagine why he appeared at all. I have a feeling he has cleared off elsewhere. I'll tell you one thing; if I die, *the last place you will find me will be Achnabasalt.* That surprises you?'

'Nothing you could ever do would surprise me,' replied Dick.

'If there is a personal survival after death (which I doubt) I can think of many more interesting places on the earth's surface to haunt, especially at this time. I think I should go first of all to London; then (if that is in ruins) to the present Headquarters of United Nations in South America. I should soon discover exactly what is going on. Oh no, you would not catch me remaining in this isolated and abandoned corner a moment longer than is necessary!'

'I am sure you would travel, *if you were allowed*,' was Dick's reply.

'Why don't you get rid of that ridiculous outfit, and make yourself a decent suit?' was the next enquiry.

'Because I can't; and that is that!'

'That is ridiculous; you can't have tried! You give in too easily, and always have done, that's your trouble.'

'Is that so? Then you should speak to Mr Beek too. He can't do it either.'

'It is a matter of concentration. Even Odysseus has made himself a pretty good striped blanket. If he can do it, so can you!'

'Yes, yes; take comfort, Little Owl, from Mrs Mottie's spotted blouse!' Julia urged him. 'If she can make clothes of air—— And my own stupid efforts!'

'Leave me alone, can't you!' Dick was goaded almost beyond

148

endurance by these taunts. He had quite forgotten any strangeness he might have felt at first; the dead had not changed in the slightest, except in their ability to provoke.

Roderick went away to practise, and soon became more adept at fashioning a careless grandeur for himself. In a purple robe (tartan proved too detailed, too finicky for an imagination used to the broader issues of life) and a black and gold cap, like a Florentine of the *Cinquecento*, he led an expedition to the village to teach his people how to clothe themselves.

For they had also returned; and in no time at all their Celtic genius was inflamed by his inspiration, their suspicions overcome. They began to create a melancholy splendour of soft plaids, in sunset and twilight colours, reproducing exactly the beauties of their own land (as they remembered it before their sorrow). As they folded themselves in clothes of heather mauve, bracken brown and hill blue; as they were decked out again in sand white, in machair green and sea-colours, their spirits and energies revived rapidly, almost as though they drew nourishment from their garments.

Everyone at Achnabasalt was so busy playing their new game that Mr Beek and Dick were able to be quite alone in the drawing-room.

'I found some raisins in a tin in the kitchen. Have some? I am quite hungry again.'

'Thank you. I found a tin of salted peanuts which had been overlooked. We need feel no guilt; there is nobody but the two of us to eat them.'

'Teaching the dead is very tiring. I am completely exhausted,' Dick confessed. 'I nearly *told* Roderick this evening.'

'Oh, but you must not! It would be fatal!'

Dick yawned. 'I suppose so. I wonder—do they sleep? I shall certainly go to bed early whatever happens. I could not keep my eyes open a minute longer.'

'Have you noticed how *light* we have become?' Roderick asked next day. 'I feel better than I have done for years! The destruction of the atom has not been such a bad thing after all!'

'You think so?'

Julia made an entrance. She had turned herself into a Watteau shepherdess for the morning; the dress, Dick saw, was much more skilful than her first attempt.

'If you are as light as you say, you should be able to jump quite a distance,' Dick suggested to his employer. 'If I see that, I may be prepared to believe you.'

'Let *Julia* jump,' Roderick urged.

'Jump? At my age? Why, I should look ridiculous!' she protested, with a coy glance.

'Jump! *Jump*, I tell you!' he thundered.

'Oh, very well!'

She gave a skipping step, rose into the air with a thin cry, and landed on the arm of a chair. Here she balanced for a moment, then floated, as gently as a feather, to the floor. She was overcome by the novelty of her experience. 'Oh how wonderful!' She murmured, in a swooning voice: 'It is the most divine feeling! How clever of you, Roderick dear, to discover it!'

'He did not,' from Dick, went unheard. He raised his voice: 'Now, Roderick, let us see you fly!'

'Yes yes! Fly down the stairs!' crooned Julia. 'My flying Roderick!'

'I do not know that I can.'

'Of course you can!' Julia encouraged him. 'It will be perfectly easy—you'll see! If you feel you are going to fall, you can always hold on to the banisters!'

Roderick looked a little uneasy; yet he would not be seen to hesitate. Slowly he walked up, turned, and launched himself into the air; in a slow motion, gliding movement he came to a safe landing on the mat.

'That was absolutely splendid!' Julia applauded. 'Now, let *me* try again. This time I will attempt something a *little* more ambitious.'

With a graceful arabesque, she rose into the air, seeming to be blown, rather than to direct her own movements; she perched on the top of the china cabinet, and struck a classical attitude, before jumping lightly down.

'Dick, you look positively cross!' she accused him. 'It is delightful, and so easy! Now you try it!'

'No thank you. I haven't the slightest desire to float through the air! The ground is good enough for me!'

'Are we to have the same nonsense again which we had on the

subject of clothes?' asked Roderick, in a warning voice. 'If so, I have had just about enough of it! You are merely jealous of my ability to fly, that is all!'

'God grant me patience!'

'What did you say? Give me your hand! If you are nervous, I will help you.'

Skilfully Dick avoided the touch which would have betrayed him.

'I promise I will not hurt you,' Roderick went on, in a calmer tone. 'There is nothing to be afraid of, I assure you. It is the most heavenly feeling—I could become quite *wedded* to it!'

Sydney Monro had entered during the discussion, and with a scowl of derision was watching their antics. On waking this morning he had discovered that Sylvia had left him. She had left a note beneath the clock, which said: *'You only think of one thing; you are no better than a animal. It's no use anyway. I'm going to find Mum and Barry. I shan't come back.'*

He had no desire, at the moment, to search for her; their relationship had taken a new, and most unsatisfactory, turn for the worse—her words were no less than the truth.

'Watch me once more!' Roderick exhorted Dick, and began to float away, up towards the ceiling. His billowing robe spread out, his legs threshed the air, he had become a purple balloon.

Sydney burst into a guffaw.

Julia, showing off, did an airy sarabande round the dado; she made a few sallies towards the doctor, and finally came to rest at his side, in order to challenge him.

'And how does your scientific mind explain all *this*?' she demanded, pointing upwards to where Roderick, having disengaged himself from a picture frame, was making a protracted landing.

'All what?'

'Why—our ability to fly in the air, of course!'

'I saw no flying in the air.'

'Then why did you laugh, if you weren't amused by Roderick's antics?'

'I laughed because our Mr Fernay was making a ludicrous exhibition of himself, stumbling about the room, that was all!'

'Take no notice,' Roderick ordered. 'He is lying as usual.'

'You saw me, didn't you?' Julia besought Dick. 'I flew, didn't I?'

'You flew very well indeed,' Dick answered her.

'You saw Roderick fly?'

'Most certainly I did, more than once.'

'Then why does he persist in saying he didn't see us?' demanded Julia, in a puzzled voice. 'Why does he deny it?'

'I saw nothing but two adult people, old enough to know better, who were making a childish exhibition of themselves hopping round the room,' Sydney declared. 'If you want to pretend you were flying, that is O.K. by me; unlike Dick I don't have to concur in your make-believe.'

'Leave him alone,' Dick advised them. 'Let him be; don't concern yourself about what he says.'

Something about the doctor, however, had unsettled Julia; she could not abandon her wish to persuade him to see. 'If you did not notice me flying, Sydney, surely you can admire my new clothes?' she coaxed him. 'What do you think of the shepherdess dress I created with such care this morning?'

'All I see you wearing is an old sheet, rather the worse for wear,' Sydney replied indifferently.

'I know it is a little dark in here—but surely you cannot be so blind—— Touch the silk—feel the lace and the ribbon rosettes! Come outside into the sunshine and——'

'Now listen, Julia, once and for all. I'm not in the mood for games! I see a torn and grubby sheet, that's all.'

'Dick, Dick!' cried Julia, running to him in terror. 'Am I mad? What do *you* see?'

'I see a pelisse of blue taffetas,' Dick replied, 'laced over a white shift of the finest lawn. It is drawn up at the sides in panniers over a quilted petticoat, embroidered in yellow and white daisies——'

'Yes yes! You are perfectly right!' she clapped her hands.

'The whole ornamented with clusters of green and white ribbons, and set off by a white fichu at the throat, and with lace ruffles upon the elbow-length sleeves.'

'I am in a nest of madmen,' the doctor remarked. 'That's plain. I could do with a drink, if I knew where to find one.'

He marched from the room.

'He grows hourly more disagreeable,' Roderick remarked. 'I refuse to speak to him.'

'Dick!' Julia persisted, coming so close to him that he was

afraid she would attempt to take his arm. 'Tell me—*did* Sydney lie to us! Was it true that he could not see my dress? That he did not see us floating in the air?'

'He saw what he wished to see,' Dick answered.

'And is it true, dear Dick, that you could not fly if you tried?'

'It is true—but why worry about it?' Dick changed the subject with the greatest celerity. 'Come, let us find the others, and teach them this wonderful game!'

The idea was enthusiastically received; Dick was presently able to leave the household to the 'nursery slopes' of landing and staircase, where with whoops of delight they precipitated themselves in airy sallies.

In the garden he met Mr Beek, reading his breviary.

'Lesson two is over,' he announced. 'It has been not without its pitfalls. Julia is suspicious, and Sydney unco-operative.'

'It is to be expected.'

'Now they have found their wings, they will fly further. They may not return.'

'They are bound to. They can play only within their limits.'

'The third lesson will be harder,' Dick cried. 'I am decidedly unhappy—— If I were to stop for one moment to think what it means, I——'

'Neither of us have time to think, which is a good thing,' Mr Beek replied. 'It is my turn to go on duty, whilst you rest; I will call you in four hours' time.'

19

'IF THE scientists of the world had envisaged that the final outcome of the splitting of the atom would be that the dead remained visibly with us, do you suppose they would have persisted in their experiments?' Dick asked Mr Beek, as they kindled a fire in the chilly drawing-room.

'I doubt it,' was Mr Beek's reply, as he plied the bellows. The prolonged absence of sunshine had brought an autumn temperature to late summer. 'How are the lessons progressing?'

'Some are learning much too fast,' Dick shivered, spreading his hands to the thin, yellow flames. 'They have outgrown the kindergarten exercises already. Flying and making new clothes no longer pleases them.'

'Then they are ready for lesson three.'

Dick put his hands to his face. 'I am afraid!' he muttered. 'I dare not begin it!'

'You dare not hold them back!' replied the clergyman, getting up from his knees.

'A fire? In this beautiful weather?' enquired Roderick, in astonishment, appearing behind them. 'There must be something wrong with both of you!'

Yet he did not require an explanation; some shock had disturbed him, so that his only thought was to confide in them.

'I have had an extraordinary experience,' he told them, striding up and down the room. 'I suppose it must have been a vivid dream; yet it was quite unlike any dream I have ever had before.'

He had been thinking, he said, of London; a strong wish had come into his mind to see what had happened to his favourite city.

'All at once, I was there!' he said. 'I was standing in Trafalgar Square! The place was completely deserted—everything was covered in a thick, grey dust. Nelson had fallen from his column; cracks had appeared in St Martin's Church—— The National Gallery, the Admiralty Arch, all the buildings, were crumbling into powder, before my eyes! It was horrible, horrible!'

He sat down, and covered his eyes.

'I expect you were dreaming!'

'No, no! It was not a dream! Why do you tell me it was?'

'You said yourself——'

'Never mind what I said! I was *there*, I tell you!' Roderick insisted. 'And, the next moment, having half expressed the thought that I would like to know the extent of this devastation, I was wafted into the air, to the height of St Paul's Cathedral, and drawn over the streets of the City, and up the course of the Thames. Not a sign of life anywhere! Not a boat, not a barge; not a wisp of smoke from a chimney! Not an electric train on any track from Acton to Earls Court—not a single Express deisel, or steam train on the lines to the West. And all those rows of bijou bungalows, those semi-detached scoriations on the face of England, each with their television aerial, empty, empty! Strangest of all, the Great West Road was innocent of a single car!'

'It sounds fascinating.'

'What do you mean? It was extremely disagreeable! I had a feeling of the utmost depression; I wished immediately that I was back here, and, to my astonishment, found myself in the garden at once. I don't know how you will attempt to explain that! If you tell me it is simply another example of the new conditions which have followed the atomic blast off, I shall not believe you!'

'My dear friend, please sit down!' Mr Beek begged. 'It is plain you have had a shock!'

'What shock?' enquired Mrs Dolman, entering from the garden, and furling a small, lace-edged parasol. Today she appeared younger and more charming than ever, in a morning-dress of sprigged print.

'Roderick has had a nightmare—he dreamed he was in London, and that all was devastated and deserted,' Dick began.

'It was not a dream!' Roderick protested. 'It was a reality.'

'I suppose you wished yourself there, Roderick?' Mrs

Dolman enquired. 'If so, you have only yourself to blame.'

'What do you mean?'

Maggie Dolman sat down, smelling a beautiful rose, which she brooched to her bosom. 'It has to do with your chemical constitution—your new constitution, of course,' she remarked. 'Although I must say, Mr Beek, that if you or Dick knew of this (since you appear to know all about everything) I think you should have warned us.' She spread wide her arms. 'You have only to *wish* to be somewhere, and you are *there*!' she told Mr Fernay. 'Of course, I suppose there must be limits. I do not imagine that one could wish oneself in the mountains of the Moon, or the plains of Mars; nor even at the Heavenly Gates. Apart from these restrictions, there are boundless possibilities. I have not attempted to explore them yet; it seemed to me, from what I had heard, that nearly all parts of our poor Earth must be equally repulsive at present.'

'How did you discover this?' asked Roderick, in some excitement.

'Oh, quite by accident! Fortunately, my desire was nothing more startling than to see how the Heavenly Brethren were faring. The next instant I found myself in the grounds of Strumph Hydro. Poor Miss Minim was coming towards me, dressed in what appeared to be *sackcloth*; yet, as she drew nearer I saw that it was merely a *feminine* version of your uniform, Dick. Poor dear, she was quite depressed, and most glad to see me. She feels herself to be somewhat of an outcast, as, like you, she is quite unable to make for herself the glorious robes which the others have created for themselves, in all the tints of the rainbow. These cannot fade, she told me, as ours are inclined to do; as they are the symbols of True Spiritual Status. Before I could say another word I saw Laetitia, swimming towards me in a dress of the clearest amythyst, pertaining to her advanced evolvement. She was followed, an instant later, by Mr Beveridge in the Emerald hue of a True Healer; and then the whole bevy were upon us——I had only one question to ask—where, I demanded, are your haloes?'

'Did they answer?'

'It was an uncomfortable question. Experiments had been made, I was given to understand—for some reason they had not

156

been entirely successful,' Mrs Dolman told them. 'They were anxious for me to go, and could not imagine how I had been let in. *I was not supposed to be there at all!'*

'I doubt if your thoughts were pure enough,' Roderick told her. 'Mine, I am sure, are not.'

'I was glad to wish myself back amongst you,' Mrs Dolman admitted. 'I begged poor Minim to come; she felt she must remain, however.'

They were interrupted by Julia, who floated in, in Grecian costume. 'I cannot find Sydney anywhere! I have not seen him since last night!' she cried. 'Have any of you come across him?'

'I expect he has gone after his wife,' Mrs Dolman said. 'And do not, for heaven's sake, wish you were with him; you would not be welcome, and goodness knows what shadowy, desolate spot you might find yourself in; it might be hard to return.'

'Mrs Mottie is searching for Nyeri, down on the shore,' Julia told them. 'I have never felt more alone! I wish——'

'Be very careful!' her aunt warned her. 'Remember what I told you!'

'I wish I were dead!' sobbed Julia, before anyone could stop her.

Nothing whatsoever happened.

'It is sinful wickedness,' the Reverend Murdo Macalpine was telling his congregation. 'No one in the village has done a stroke of work for a week! Whilst you were all stricken in body, there was some excuse; now that you are all filled with un-natural strength, there is none! The people are given over to gee-gaws; they have made themselves idols out of the finery they have created with help of the devil! All is vanity!'

'Where's the sense in working?' was the reply. 'In the old days, we worked in order to earn money; money is of no use any more. We needed money to buy food, and clothing. Now we no longer need to eat, and we can spin our clothes from the air, at a wish.'

'It is God's Will that man on Earth should labour, and earn his bread by the sweat of his brow. Do you deny the Scriptures? All day you lie about. You no longer come to the Lord's House to hear His Word and to pray for forgiveness, as you have much need to do! The Day of Judgement approaches; how are you to face the Risen Christ? Do you expect to be with His Chosen Flock, or cast out for ever?'

'I expect very little,' James Mackenzie answered the minister. 'I am well, and at peace; I have nothing more to lose.'

'Have none of you a fear of what is to come?' cried Mr Macalpine. 'Yet I see, I talk in vain to ears that are closed against me! I have seen how you occupy yourselves with trivial things; how you make yourselves little boats, and row for pleasure, round the bay! I have heard your singing. I have seen the dancing of your young people, by the light of torches, like the satanists in the camp at Rona. You should be down on your knees, crying to the Lord to save you from damnation; every man, woman and child of you!'

'I do not see that after all we have suffered it is wrong to be happy for a little space,' the postmistress was heard to protest.

'Happiness upon earth is no part of the Will of the Eternal for man born in sin. We are all here to be taught our lesson. There must be no pause in the strife with the devil; no, not for one minute! It is easy to see you are caught in the snares, Mistress Macrae!'

Padriac Macrae rose from the framework of the new salmon coble he was building. 'Then they are the same snares as your lady wife is caught in, Mr Macalpine, for she has made herself a curious little garden, has she not, all out of air? She has set in it all manner of flowers that grew up in a night; and blossoming trees, oranges, lemons, and such like fancy sub-tropical plants that have no place here, in the North. Does she wash and darn for you in the manse, like she used to do? Does she sit long evenings, by lamplight, turning sheets sides to middle for you? No, she is walking up and down, carrying a wee watering-pot, and what she is singing is neither a hymn nor a psalm.'

'Aaah! You dare to say such things to me!'

'And, Mr Macalpine,' James continued, unabashed, 'as an elder I would point out to you that you are subscribing to the very heresy of which we stand accused. You stand there in a new suit of black serge, of the very finest material, and in your vestry robing chest is a new gown, with new white bands. How did you come by them?'

'Why, I sent—why they came from Edin——'

'No, no, minister. You wished for them, and they appeared! Don't you remember?'

The tormented man fell upon his knees. 'Oh, Lord, deliver me from Satan's lures, even from the fog of heresy, and from the terrible temptations to which, unknowingly, I have succumbed!'

'Amen!' cried his elders, adjusting their beautiful new plaids, preparatory to embarking in their fishing boat for a trial sail round the islands. They were not distressed by their new world of palpable, trembling matter which could be moulded at will to their wish.

In a few minutes Mr Macalpine had wished his wicked suit away, and was as naked as the day he was born.

The Burniebank Bicyclists, or as many as were now left of them, deserted the stables, and returned to their camping site by the shore. Here they soon created a group of dwellings like white and yellow tents.

They existed without troubling any more about the other communities in the neighbourhood; when Mr Beek visited them they listened with indifference to what he had to say, or drifted away from his conversation.

At first they continued ragged, and nearly naked; yet, after a week, he saw that they had created for themselves a sort of uniform of tight trousers, and shapeless shirts, or jerseys; not to keep out the cold, for they could feel it no longer, but because these were their accustomed garments. He sensed that this uniform gave them a feeling of security, and of belonging together; they required to destroy their individuality and enter into a group consciousness, more and more. They cultivated it deliberately, until it protected them, and they could no longer act as single souls.

Mr Beek and Dick Bolton suffered much, as time went on, from cold and hunger, although the twilight seemed to have lifted a little; it was possible to distinguish noon-day from dawn, and to study the faces of friends.

Their state was not evident to the rest of the household, who lived in a perpetual summer's day, discovering new pleasures every hour.

As their strength and mastery of their new bodies increased, they would all, upon impulse, make off on some excursion. It was nothing to them to hover above the waves, or to drift over mountain ranges as high as the Andes; yet everywhere they found the same emptiness. Only once and again, in remote valleys, did they see signs of life; or encountered airy voyagers like themselves, to whom they called: 'Anything doing in the Alaskan regions? What news from the Antarctic?'

'I can gain no intelligence that any form of government remains,' Roderick said. 'Life as we know it seems to be extinct. It is a wonder that we survive.'

Each evening, he dictated to Dick a full account of his journeys.

'Tomorrow I will try the Caucasus,' he announced.

Mrs Mottie appeared, dressed for a journey, in an exact replica of her navy-blue coat, her white fabric gloves, her hat with the daisies, a small hold-all at her feet.

'Well, good-bye all,' she said. 'I'm off, then. See you later, I expect.'

'Why, where are you going?' Roderick demanded.

'I have to take little Nyeri to the island, see,' she announced.

'The gentleman told me yesterday—your friend, you know. I met him down on the shore. It's no place for a child, now is it, Mrs Mottie? he said to me. There's some other children over there, all waiting. You bring 'im tomorrow evening; we'll send the boat for you. So I got 'is things all washed an' ironed, see.'

There was a chorus of protesting voices. 'You shall not take my son!' came from Odysseus.

'Now, don't upset yourself, Odysseus dear.' Mrs Mottie took the boy's hand in hers. 'We've got to think of what's best for 'im, now 'aven't we? 'E'll be ever so 'appy with the other boys and girls, and it won't be long, so the gentleman says, before we all join 'im for the journey.'

She straightened Nyeri's straw hat. 'Say good-bye to your dad, there's a good boy!'

'Do you mean that you saw Mr MacArtney down by the shore? And he is to fetch you now?' cried Dick. 'Then I must come with you; there are things of the greatest importance I have to ask him——'

But Mrs Mottie and the boy had vanished.

With a cry, Dick ran down to the sullen, empty beach. He

thought he heard the thrumming of a motor; but he must have been mistaken; he was forced to turn back to the house, with a heavy heart.

'Do not be upset, Dick,' Julia had joined him. She wore a riding habit of blue velvet, and a tricorne hat. 'You cannot be more sad than I am!' He saw that she was leading a beautiful horse, furnished with a gilded, pommelled saddle. 'I am so alone!'

'We are *all* alone!' was torn from the secretary. 'From first to last!'

'Today I tried to kill myself,' Julia told him. 'I threw myself into the sea; I could not sink. I cast myself from that cliff—I floated down to the sands below. My body is immune, immortal; I cannot destroy it. The time has come to tell me the truth about us all.'

'I cannot tell you anything you do not discover for yourself,' Dick replied, still searching the sea for the blue boat.

'You can confirm my guesses?'

'Why won't you leave things as they are?' cried Dick. 'You have an ideal existence here, after all! You are never tired, or hungry, or cold—— The sun shines brightly for you, birds sing, flowers bloom!'

'Give me your hand!' she insisted, peeling off her long, green gloves.

'No, no!'

'I insist! You are still my friend, aren't you?'

Dick remained with his hands pressed to his sides.

'Am I contaminated, then, that you will not touch me?'

She advanced towards him.

'No, no! I beg you!' cried the unfortunate man.

He felt her touch on his neck, as though it had been an icicle; her deep shudder affected him as though it had been his own.

'My hand went through your shoulder, Dick!'

He did not turn; he was afraid to look at her.

There was a long sigh; unable to bear more, Julia had wished herself back at the house. 'I hope she will keep her knowledge to herself,' Dick said aloud. 'I never thought for one minute that *she* would be troublesome! If Nigel returned, dramatically recovered, what a powerful and welcome distraction that would prove! How I wish it would happen!'

20

'NO SOONER do we get rid of Mannifold, than Nigel returns to haunt us,' Roderick complained to Dick. 'It is inconsiderate of him, to say the least of it. If he has decided to do it, he should at least behave properly, instead of wavering in and out of vision, like the grin of the Cheshire Cat.'

'The poor soul's earthbound, dear,' Mrs Mottie remarked. 'Oh, the Chief and I 'ave 'elped a number of *them* in our time. It's being a athiest 'as done it. You should 'elp 'im with your prayers, and 'e'll be taken away to where 'e belongs.'

'You should make him your mission, Mrs Mottie,' Dick advised her. 'It will keep you from missing Nyeri so much.'

'Oh I know 'e's 'appy, with all them other kids,' Mrs Mottie replied. 'I don't want to be selfish; a *beautiful* garden they were playing in, white and black together.'

'On the scorched, deserted island?' Dick enquired. 'A garden?'

'—And it won't be long,' Mrs Mottie continued comfortably. 'The gentleman told me: "It won't be long now, Mrs Mottie. The first of the transports will be 'ere in a day or so." '

'Here he is again,' muttered Roderick. 'There—over in the corner, in his chair, where he always used to sit!'

'Do you mean Nigel?' Dick enquired, peering into the shadows.

'Yes, yes—whom else do you suppose I'd mean? Speak to him! Tell him to go!' cried Roderick. 'Tell him we don't want to be *haunted*! But wish him well, of course.'

'Why don't you speak to him yourself?'

'Because I've no wish to encourage him—can't you understand that? I am sorry for him; but ghosts make me feel uncomfortable.'

' 'E don't speak,' Mrs Mottie said, fashioning a new wreath for her hat. 'You don't answer, do you, dear?' she addressed the smoke-like spectre, whom Dick now observed for the first time in the corner.

'Ghosts don't speak,' Roderick said. 'You speak to them.'

'Can we 'elp you, dear?' Mrs Mottie asked. 'Is there something we can do, eh? You put up a prayer, dear, and so will we. You'll be fetched by your friends, never fear.'

'Perhaps we should send for Julia,' Roderick suggested. 'She was always able to deal with Nigel when nobody else could.'

Julia was out in the garden, searching for the doctor, yet, as ever, afraid to wish herself beside him, because of Sylvia. When she was told what was wanted of her, she entered with the greatest reluctance, and stood at some distance from her poor ghost.

'Well, Nigel,' she said. 'What have you come back for? I thought you were in limbo. It is very thoughtless and nasty of you to frighten us all by haunting us. Please go away!'

The effect of her presence now made Nigel appear more solid; yet he lacked the reality of the others. A thin echo of a voice came from the air: 'Help me!'

'Help you? You can help yourself! There's no need for you to sit there! If you are dead, you're not an invalid any more; you can get up and move about!'

'I can't, I can't!'

Mrs Mottie finished her millinery. 'It's 'is own selfishness as done it,' she said. 'Now 'e 'as to suffer. It's the law, see. But you must 'elp 'im, dear. You're the one as can!'

'She despises me!' Nigel whispered.

'You're a willing prisoner,' Julia told him. 'You have no real wish to be free!'

'Don't argue with 'im, dear; that never did no good with those that's passed on,' Mrs Mottie advised. 'Now, Mr Fidgeon dear, you're well and strong as ever you were; just step out of that chair, and stand up.'

'Don't speak to me as though I were a child! It is not easy. It is harder for me than for any of you!' Nigel exclaimed. 'I need help! Only Julia can help me, because she once loved me! Give me your hand, I beg of you; lend me a little of your strength, just this once!'

'Help him, ducky,' Mrs Mottie urged. 'They all need a bit of 'umouring!'

'I did try to help him,' Julia said. 'He rejected my love; he made use of me, that was all. I don't love him any longer. I have lost the one I truly love—I can never find him! All my life long I have been looking for him!'

'Let us have less of these histrionics,' Roderick commanded her. 'We do not wish to be given a detailed account of your sex life. All that you are asked to do, at this moment, is to give Nigel your hand. Do so, I beg, and let us get this over and done with!'

'You can't hold hands with the dead,' Mrs Dolman said, coming in through the french window.

'What shall I do, Dick?' Julia asked, giving him a look of significance.

'Help him, lovey. You will help yourself.'

'It is obvious the idea is repugnant to her,' Nigel said. 'I release her from it.'

Julia crossed the floor, and put her hand into Nigel's skeletal grasp; there was an immediate change in Mr Fidgeon; he appeared to take on a durable and material personality.

With an impatient tug, Julia pulled him from the chair, and to his feet.

'There!' she said, releasing her hold, and dusting her hands. He trembled, looking for his support, but it had gone.

'You took hold of a ghost!' Roderick exclaimed. 'That is quite horrible! Now that you are restored, Nigel, much as I like you, I must ask you to go. You will see yourself how impossible it is that you remain.'

'I have nowhere to go,' the baronet replied.

'Surely you have friends? One reads everywhere that they come and fetch you, if asked. Call upon them, now; I'm sure they'll respond.'

'There is no one!' Nigel repeated.

'Surely you had a mother?'

'I never knew her.'

'There must be a cousin, aunt, or old nurse, somewhere, who was fond of you. Sit down, if you must, and have a good think about it—but would you mind going into the dining-room?'

'I wish I had stayed in oblivion!' Mr Fidgeon exclaimed. 'It was what I longed for, but it has been denied me. I never expected to be rejected by all of you like this!'

'You could not expect to be welcomed if you haunted us,' Roderick replied reasonably. 'You would not like it if it happened to you.'

'I am sure he did not do it deliberately,' Mrs Dolman said. 'I expect it was a mistake. Let me help you to the dining-room, Nigel; you are walking remarkably well, already. You will be able to sit there in quiet, and think what is best to do. We do not mean to be unkind, but this is not the place for you. Yet, if we can help you in any way by putting out strong mental requests for somebody to fetch you, believe me we will do so.'

'I am most grateful, I am sure.'

'It would be awkward if you remained,' Roderick told him. 'Not only for us; but because we are to be rescued and taken from here by air, in a few days' time, and then you would be utterly alone.'

Nigel paused in the doorway. 'I promise to do my best to leave here as quickly as possible. I have no desire to remain where I am not wanted. Yet, before I go, there is one thing I would like to have explained to me. I would like to know why, although all of you appear as real and solid to me as though I were still alive and here in the room with you; although Julia's hand in mine was firm and warm to the touch, and so is Mrs Dolman's arm, Dick appears as shadowy as the ghost you say I am, and, just now, when I touched him, my hand went through his shoulder?'

'Don't worry about that!' Dick interrupted quickly. 'It is just a little matter of a difference in constitution—a chemical disparity, that's all!'

'No, it is not, Dick dear,' Julia contradicted him.

'It is, it is!' the secretary insisted. 'I told you days ago! You all accepted it then—what's the difference now?'

'We were occupied in making new clothes,' Julia reminded him. 'Presently we were flying in the air. Before we had time to wonder why you could not do the same, we had discovered how to span the world in the twinkling of an eyelash. You and Mr Beek kept us very busy, didn't you, Little Owl; but we aren't children any more.'

'I don't understand, Julia,' Mr Fernay said, in a hurt and puzzled voice. 'What is it that you are trying to tell us?'

'Come, Nigel,' Julia said. 'I will take you into the garden.

Amongst all the women you made love to before your accident there must be one who can save you; we will make a list of them. At least I will do that for you.'

'Dick, what is it that is so different about you?' Roderick persisted, after Julia and Nigel had left the room. 'Why is it you cannot fly, or make new clothes?'

Instead of replying, Mr Bolton was, as usual, overcome with emotion, and had to leave the house and walk in the garden until he had recovered.

It was during a stroll upon the shore, a day or so later, that Mr Beek and Dick Bolton had their second encounter with Mr MacArtney.

The secretary was in the utmost state of depression; nothing Mr Beek could say consoled him.

'As soon as they realise what has happened to them, they will all go, and leave us in this deserted place!' he lamented. 'For I am sure you have come to the same conclusion as I have; *we are not to go with them.* Oh yes, it's no use denying it; perhaps *you* knew it all along, but *I* feel I have been thoroughly misled! I believed you when you told me that nonsense about helping and teaching them how to accustom themselves to their new conditions, and having to be different for that purpose—yet, it wasn't long before I began to have my doubts about it! If I could have five minutes with that scoundrel MacArtney——'

'Good gracious—surely that is he, over there, talking to those two nuns!'

The light was so uncertain that they were almost upon the group as soon as they saw them.

Mr MacArtney hailed them, with the utmost good humour, and seemed heartily glad to see them.

'I was just coming to find you, but this saves me a journey,' he told them. 'May I introduce Sister Margaret, and Miss Ethel Minim?'

'Miss Minim is known to us already.'

'Sister Margaret you do not know. She comes from a convent at a little distance from here, where she was in charge of the kitchens.'

'How do you do?' Mr Beek said. 'I did not recognise you, Miss Minim, in your religious habit.'

'It is no more a religious habit than your own, Mr Beek.'

Miss Minim, who seemed in a state of distress, pressed Brother James's hand; she and the Sister, who was a fat and jolly nun, took their leave and made off in a southward direction, quite the opposite to Strumph Hydro.

'She is upset,' Mr MacArtney explained. 'She finds herself in the same position as yourselves; in spite of my efforts to show her how matters stand, she feels that in some way she has failed to come up to the standards of the Brethren.'

'I suppose they turned her out?'

'Oh no, she was treated with every consideration and forbearance,' Mr MacArtney replied. 'Yet she felt increasingly that she was a castaway. Of her own free will, she left the Hydro, rather than contaminate her friends. Fortunately I was able to contact her, and put her in touch with Sister Margaret, a most sensible woman. They are sharing a coastguard's cottage at the moment, and I am in hopes that the Sister may bring Miss Minim to a more settled frame of mind.'

'I have every sympathy with Ethel Minim,' Dick said, in a bitter voice.

'Certain people would be most envious of you, if they knew the truth,' Mr MacArtney fell into step beside them. 'Well now, it is time to talk of the future. Things have been going to plan, but perhaps a little faster than anticipated. We did not look for that final two hundred megaton explosion, which has darkened the earth so disagreeably; it interfered with the world's balance, being on such a large and destructive scale. Yet, in one way, it has simplified matters. It has destroyed those who perpetrated it, and who were working against us. Yes, and of course it fulfilled some outstanding prophecies in your Bible, and other important sacred writings, especially those dealing with the time being shortened for the sake of the elect. The entire operation should soon be completed.'

Dick felt he could keep silent no longer.

'Things may be going according to plan, but it is a very ill-conceived one, in my opinion!' he spoke up. 'Why have the two of us, and those unfortunate women, been left out of it? What does the future hold for us? Nothing that I can see!'

'You will know very shortly.' Mr MacArtney was quite calm. 'I am sorry that this has upset you. Things will seem a little awkward and strange at the moment; but they will sort themselves out, I assure you.'

'Our friends are dead; we have taught them the lessons concerning their new state, just as you prescribed. We have not let them know they are dead; yet they are learning fast, it can't be kept from them much longer! In spite of the inhuman situation we found ourselves in, and the torture, to say the least of it, which it has been to us to be in daily contact with people already in another dimension, we have kept faith with you!' Dick cried. 'But you have deceived us, in the most dastardly manner!'

'I do not think so! How is that?'

'You led us to imagine that our present situation was a necessary but temporary one!' Dick said in a trembling voice. 'We thought we should be released from it when the rescuing airships came; but that is not to be; now is it?'

'I did not tell him,' Mr Beek interceded, in a low voice. 'I could not!'

Mr MacArtney remained silent.

'I feel there must be some reconsideration of my poor friend's case,' Mr Beek pleaded. 'Some mistake has been made; that is clear to me, and has been for some time.'

'It is impossible; mistakes are never made on such a level,' was the reply.

'So I am to be left behind!' came a terrible cry from Mr Bolton. Until that instant he had not truly known it; the shock unnerved him.

'It is all right for me, you see,' Mr Beek was continuing, but was interrupted by a moan from the ground, where Dick had cast himself:

'Yes, you are accustomed to be in a state of humiliation and martyrdom! I believe you enjoy it!'

Brother James paid no attention to the outburst, but continued his pleading: 'I beg you, Mr MacArtney—if you have any influence with the Powers that Be; get them to change their minds about Dick! It really would be best if he went with them all!'

'I shall kill myself, if I am left behind, I warn you!' came from Dick, in a muffled tone.

'It would be no use; you would have to return and do this all over again,' Mr MacArtney replied regretfully. 'I am sorry I cannot alter your particular destiny. It was predetermined, you see, both by your nature and your conduct. It is in the records; it is irrevocably laid down; the meek and the pure in heart shall inherit the earth.'

Dick uttered a cry of the utmost anguish. 'You are mistaken! I am very impure in heart, and not in the least meek! I am filled with anger and rebellion to the brim!'

Mr Beek knelt down beside him, both in order to comfort him and to be in a more suitable position to plead for him.

'I do not know your true identity, sir; time alone may, or may not, reveal it to us. I do not know on whose authority you speak. But I believe you to be good. If you are so, and if you come from God, I say that He in His Mercy would never order such a punishment as is meted out to this unfortunate soul, whose only sin is that he has loved too well.'

'My dear Mr Beek,' Mr MacArtney addressed the clergyman. 'I must ask you to rise from your knees, and persuade your friend to get up also. You are confusing the issue. Mercy is the prerogative of the Great Creator of the Universe. I am not He. I am here merely as an instrument to carry out certain orders, pertaining to this Region. The judgement on Mr Bolton is not an arbitrary, nor a cruel, one. Your Bible tells you, "*As ye sow, so shall ye reap.*" '

Between sobs Dick was heard to wonder what sin he had sown to reap such damnation.

'Damnation?' cried Mr MacArtney in astonishment. 'I am amazed! What is in store for both of you is an unparalleled honour—one that religious bodies and persons have fought to secure for themselves since the beginning of the Christian era. You are to be of the Remnant, left on this unfortunate earth, who will help to found a new order of things, once the debris of the old world is cleared away. Only a few very hundred individuals have been chosen from the entire population of the planet!'

'Then there has been a most dreadful mistake!'

Dick crawled until he could embrace his avenging angel about the knees, and stare into the calm and bearded face. 'I am quite unworthy of the honour—it is mine under false pretences! The records must be mixed up——'

'They are never at fault; it is out of the question!'

'Oh but they must be—they must! Have another look at

them! Someone else, with a similar name, is meant—give the honour to another—what about one of the Heavenly Brethren?'

Mr MacArtney was quite undisturbed. 'They are all accounted for, I assure you; only Miss Minim is chosen to remain. In two hours' time they will step aboard the vessel which has come to fetch them, and which is, even now, approaching the island of Ebora. They have been contacted, and are fully assured they are being removed to a sphere where their unique qualities will be of most value.'

'And are they right in supposing so?'

'Certainly. They will find themselves in a state of being where nothing is on a material plane. There they can wander in perennial light, instruct those below them, and commune with the Highest.'

'This—this aerial boat—it will not take anyone from Achnabasalt?' Dick faltered.

'No, my friend, not yet. Their destination is entirely different. It will be a day or so before transport can be arranged for them; indeed they may be the last to leave the district. There's the matter of evacuating the people from the village, and then the young campers. They are a very interesting group indeed, destined to found the population of a new planet in the region of Sirius. I think they will make a good job of it; they have the qualities that are needed—singleness of purpose and a good sense of rhythm. Besides, they will have a reliable leader.'

'Whoever can that be?'

'Odysseus Jackson. It is an obvious choice. He feels himself bound to them.'

There was a pause, while they considered the information. Then Dick sprang up. 'I still have a little time—— If I were to be exceedingly wicked and subversive in the next few days; if I were to tear off my protective suit, and fail to take my daily dose of elixir——' he pleaded.

Mr MacArtney shook his head. 'You would find you could not do it. You cannot go against nature. Well, time is getting short. I will give you your final instructions, as it may be impossible for me to contact you directly again. As soon as the last ship (which will be the one to take your friends) has departed, go down to the shore. There you will find my little blue boat. Make all haste to the islands, where friends await you. On no account must you delay, even for a few minutes. Conditions will become exceedingly unpleasant, almost at once. When you reach the island you will be taken to the deep shelters, which are well stocked with all you require; there you are to remain, and on no account must you come out until I send to fetch you.

'For a week or so there will be electric storms on the earth, of such intensity as have never been seen before in this civilisation, there will be gales and tornadoes and earthquakes, but they will not affect you if you stay where you are. It will all be part of the process of universal vacuum-cleaning, as you would term it; there is nothing for you to be afraid of. As you will all take a triple dose of elixir, on entering the shelter, you will sleep soundly for several days, and know little about it. It is necessary, in order to remove the dust of contamination, and the signs of destruction, and enable us to reshape the land. However, once it is all over, things will be better than they have been for an age. You will see the sun clearly once more, and it will be quite pleasantly warm. Everything will look new, tidy and clean as at the Beginning, and it will not be long before you are sent for.'

'Sent for?' cried Dick hopefully. 'You mean, to join the others?'

'If you mean, to join your old friends from Achnabasalt, I am afraid not. No, to link up with the new colony where you are to learn your duties for the Golden Age to come.' Mr MacArtney took a gold, half-hunter from the waistcoat pocket of his excellent knicker-bocker suit and consulted it. 'I must be going. I promised to be on Ebora to say good-bye to the Brethren, and wish them God Speed.'

He entered his whirlyboat, with the utmost expedition; next minute he was with them no more.

The faint hum of the engine retreated over the dark water.

'Do not despair!' Mr Beek put an arm about Dick's shoulder. 'We can take your petition to a Higher Authority. I shall not cease to pray that God will have mercy on you!'

'It is practically useless; but I appreciate your kind thought for me.'

Dick spoke in a voice from which all hope had departed; yet he clung to Mr Beek's arm, and took some slight strength from the clergyman's promise.

21

'I CANNOT understand why the Heavenly Brethren were given priority over us,' Roderick protested.

'I could scarcely endure the self-satisfied smirk your friend Laetitia gave us as she embarked in her mauve night-gown,' Julia told her aunt, as they returned from the shore.

'I am neither surprised nor disappointed,' Mrs Dolman answered. 'If I had to share life in some remote part of the globe with any set of people, the last companions I should choose now would be the residents from Strumph Hydro. I am glad our destinations are different.'

'Oh, none of us wanted to go with *that* lot,' Mrs Mottie agreed. 'There would be no fun in it. No, no, ducks, we're off to a far cheerier spot, if Chief Bubandu has the rights of it; and I trust the old Chief,' e's never told me wrong yet. Sort of like a seaside, 'e said, with all lovely palms, like Torquay, and a sandy beach with umbrellas and all. And there'll be little Neeri and the other children, all larking about.'

'I do hope you are wrong, dear Mrs Mottie,' Roderick remarked. 'It sounds like a holiday camp.'

'I hope you will spare the time to drop me a postcard,' Dick said. 'Mark the window of your room with a cross, and wish I were with you.'

'*Write* to you? But you will be there!' exclaimed Mr Fernay. 'Why do you say "*Write me a postcard*"—— What ridiculous nonsense is this?'

'I shall not be going with you, Roderick. I have told you this several times, but you will not listen.'

'You will be there! What could prevent it? *I wish you to come!*'

'In this case your wish is no longer law.'

Roderick was astounded. 'You mean that you don't *want* to come with us, Dick?'

'I mean that I am not allowed to come,' was the secretary's reply.

'What are you blethering about?' cried his employer, in the greatest irritation. '*Not allowed!* Who, or what, is to prevent you, tell me that!'

'The difference between our states prevents it,' Dick was beginning, but:

'Take no notice of 'im, Mr Fernay dear. 'E's just 'aving one of 'is turns,' Mrs Mottie assured Roderick. Already the argument was forgotten in the excitement of preparing for departure.

'If we are to be fetched within the next forty-eight hours, I must design a comprehensive wardrobe,' could be heard from Mrs Dolman. 'A seaside resort, with palms, recalls the French Riviera; yet I suppose it must be somewhere on the Pacific seaboard of South America—Colombia? Panama? I have forgotten so much geography. White shall be the basic colour; piqué was always satisfactory; and for an evening at the Tables, an electric blue taffetas would have its moments. Do they gamble on the Pacific? I do not suppose, at this crisis, they would. On second thoughts, a simple princess gown establishes a mood of calm acceptance of one's fate, yet allows for any eventuality.'

'Does it never alarm you that you have grown at least thirty years younger in the past ten days?' Dick enquired of her, with desperation. 'Do you never question why that should be?'

'My dear boy, as you say yourself: "*It is chemistry. It is the effect of radiation,*" ' Mrs Dolman replied calmly.

In the throes of composition, she and her niece retired to their bedroom.

'Julia has become a perfect ninny in the last week or so,' Roderick said, in a tone of disgust. 'Since the change in our circumstances, although she looks younger and prettier, her intelligence has completely deserted her. I told her to get rid of Nigel; he is still hovering about the place, craving attention. I take no notice, and I advise you to do the same. If he finds himself ignored, he will have to go elsewhere.'

'Perhaps he has nowhere to go.'

'Of course he has! The dead have plenty of space to live in; they have the whole Universe, if one believes all one hears. I don't know why he has to crawl after us. It is unnerving, to say the least of it. You ought to speak to him.'

'I haven't seen him since yesterday.'

'You know, Dick, I will tell you something that will surprise you. As you know, I disliked Mrs Dolman; now, I have to admit, she has more wit in her little toe than her niece has in the whole of her voluptuous carcass.'

'Surely you are a little unfair!'

'She apes the attitude of a young woman. I never had any use for girls, especially silly ones.'

'She is still the same Julia, underneath.'

'Then I have been mistaken in her from the beginning.'

'You are mistaken in thinking she is merely silly,' a voice came from a dark corner. 'She is cruel, as well.'

Dick glanced in the direction of the sound, but could see nothing. Roderick, however, gave an exclamation of disgust, and strode out of the room.

'Is that you, Nigel?' Dick enquired. 'You really must stop this haunting; it is getting on everyone's nerves. I can't see you, but the rest of them can. If you had any consideration for Roderick, you'd go elsewhere.'

'I have tried to leave this place, but I can't,' was the whispered reply. 'Something prevents it. I have to return. Julia alone could help me, but she has ceased to care.'

'I would help you, if I could,' Dick relented to say. 'But I have enough problems on my hands. I will ask Mr Beek to pray for you, when he comes back from the village.'

'He cannot help me!'

The tone of absolute helplessness in which this was said, and the feeling that Nigel expected everything to be done for him without the slightest effort on his own part, exasperated Dick in the highest degree. 'We have done what we can for you! It is up to you to help yourself!' he told the darkened corner where Nigel waited. 'And for goodness' sake keep out of the drawing-room in future. We must at least keep one room to ourselves!'

'You seem rather scared of what I might do or say, if I remained!'

'That's nonsense!'

'Are you frightened I might tell them that they are all ghosts, like me?'

'They would not believe you, Nigel,' Dick said stoutly.

'We shall see!'

'If you dare to upset Roderick any more, I shall—— Nigel, where are you?'

There was a faint, and mocking, laugh; then silence and emptiness in Nigel's corner of the drawing-room.

'If Sydney does not return soon he will miss the airship,' Julia sighed. 'I hate to think of him wandering the wastes of England, in search of that soppy little Sylvia. When he finds that she has run after her former boy friend, or her dreadful relations, it will be a great shock to him. She will have nothing to do with him, and he will have had his journey for nothing.'

'Why do you worry about Sydney?' Roderick asked. 'He does not spare a thought for you, I am sure of that! If Sylvia wandered far from here, she will be dead by now; certainly her friends and relations will all have perished.'

'Perhaps he will come back here when he finds it is no use!' Julia whispered.

'How can he come back? Are you completely witless? He must be dead himself by now!' thundered Roderick.

'*As you all are!*' came a distinct voice from the staircase. There was a stunned silence.

'Who said that?' Roderick demanded.

'It was Nigel. He is upstairs,' Julia told them.

'I cannot see him!'

'I can see him. He is there, looking down at us!'

Nobody spoke; there was not the expected protest. No voice, not even Roderick's, was raised in order to tell Mr Fidgeon to go away. In the silence, the grandfather clock in the hall measured off momentous minutes of realisation.

At last: 'Ask him please to explain himself,' Roderick told Dick Bolton.

It was a plea, not an order; there was apprehension in Mr Fernay's request. It was as though, until that voice had spoken, a great disturbance had prevented hearing; now, everybody was forced to stop and listen.

'Nigel is coming down,' Julia announced, to those that could not see. 'He is standing on the hearthrug.'

'So we are dead,' Roderick said. 'That is the explanation, is it?'

'You are as dead as I am,' was the equivocal reply.

'I do not believe it. I feel very much alive.'

'You do believe it, Roderick,' Julia said. 'Really you have known it in your inmost heart for some time; yet you refused to admit it, as I did.'

There was no use in denying the truth. Even Mrs Mottie was satisfied ('All that flying wasn't *natural*.') and Mrs Dolman was ashamed that death had not found her Aspiring to Higher Things than taffetas gowns.

It was necessary now to readmit Nigel to the household, and cease to treat him as an outcast. There had to be a complete re-appraisal of their whole situation in the light of this fresh knowledge.

Mr Beek's position, and that of Dick Bolton, was made clear; it caused grief, at the prospect of parting, and a refusal by Mr Fernay to accept the judgement.

'I shall intercede for you,' he promised. 'They shall not do this to you! You will not be left behind!'

In the midst of this emotionally heightened atmosphere, and all the excitements that accompanied it, Julia entered the house, leading Sydney Monro.

The doctor's return, in a dirty, dishevelled and dispirited condition, amazed nobody; nor was it particularly welcome; especially when it was found that Sydney refused to believe himself dead.

'I sent out my thoughts continually to him!' Julia announced in triumph. 'So he found his way back to us, and can't think how he came here!'

She drew him from the unsympathetic company of the rest of the household, out to the steps of the summer house, where Dick, walking at a little distance, could observe her in the twilight darkness, ministering to him with a simulated glass of whisky, and soothing him with words and caresses: 'I know how worried you are about Sylvia; but she is safe with her own people, and I'm sure you'll find her at the end of our journey! Drink some of this, it will do you good!'

'No thanks, Julia! I don't know where you got that whisky from; it may taste like the real thing, but it has no more effect than ginger ale! I've been sober far too long!' was the embittered and ungrateful reply.

With a rumbling crash, a part of the verandah outside the drawing-room windows collapsed in a shower of glass and rubble; the company inside and outside the house paid not the slightest attention, but Dick started violently. The whole house was rapidly becoming ruinous; a chimney in the kitchen premises had fallen through the roof the night before, plaster fell from ceilings at regular intervals; it was no longer safe to go upstairs.

'Darling Sydney, do not look so unhappy!' Julia was begging. 'Let us try and cheer you, and make you well again; you have had so many disappointments lately, you poor boy!'

Sydney must have disengaged himself, for he appeared standing beside her in the doorway of the summer house. (Dick had not the slightest compunction about eavesdropping upon them.)

'You are quite a charmer, Julia, but you are just not my type. Sylvia is the woman I'm crazy for and always will be. We mayn't be able to live together, but I'm damned sure I can't exist without her, *and* I'm married to her, which you seem to forget. My silly, pretty little Sylvia; now God knows where she's gone; but I shall find her, if it's the last thing I do! You can't keep me here, dear girl, thanks all the same, so it's no use trying!'

'You are both dead, Sydney! We all are!' came from Julia, in despairing tones. 'Wait a few more hours, and we are to be fetched away to heaven!'

'You're crazy!' was the contemptuous answer, followed by such hopeless weeping from the other poor ghost that Dick felt bound to show himself.

'Touch me, Sydney!' he ordered.

'Whatever for?'

'Punch me, as hard as you like, here on the chest!'

'Watch it, chum! I could knock you over!'

'Try it!'

The lunging fist felt cold as it penetrated his breast bone; the doctor made an instant recoil.

'What happened?' he demanded, trying to clutch Dick by the shoulders, and failing. 'Am I mad, or drunk?'

'How did you get here?' Dick persisted. 'You can't remember? When last did you eat? Sleep? Excrete? You have no need of any of these things. You are free of the body that chains me still. Just as Sylvia is free. If you wish hard enough, you can be with her in an instant, wherever she may be; you are right, we cannot hold you here.'

'I can, can I?' asked the doctor.

'Why, oh why, did you tell him that?' sobbed Julia.

'Say her name! Call to her! Tell her you are coming!' Mr Bolton was carried away by his own eloquence. 'Imagine yourself flying to her side!'

'You had better warn Sydney that if he finds himself disappointed, he will have to return immediately in case he misses the airship!' Julia sniffed. 'Otherwise he may wander in limbo for simply ages; and things are going to be most unpleasant here on earth!'

It was doubtful if the doctor heard her. 'Sylvia!' came a strong shout. 'Sylvia!'

'Good-bye, then, Sydney!' Dick called, as the doctor vanished.

'Thank you for absolutely nothing!' Julia turned to Dick, in a voice trembling with anger.

'Don't be angry, lovey; after all, as you say yourself, he may come back!'

'I don't know that I want him to! He has turned very coarse!'

'Dick!' called Mr Fernay, from the house. 'Where are you? We must get ready to go down and say good-bye to the villagers; word has come that they are to be evacuated at seven this evening.'

Roderick led his household down to the shore, splendid in the kilt and plaid his people had made for him. Dick followed, with Brother James, carrying his crook before him. The ladies, in costume of clan tartan, with little baskets of heather and rowan berries, came a little behind them, together with Odysseus in splendid melancholy and a striped blanket.

A small, pathetic group of Highlanders had gathered on the quay, seated on boxes which contained the last of their belongings.

'It is like the Clearances all over again,' whispered Roderick. 'They seem to imagine their going is a tragedy, not a cause for rejoicing.'

Now that the moment had come for them to leave their beloved shore the pipes, playing a lament, the wailing of women and children, made a properly dramatic setting for the departure. Anchored out in the bay, to the leeward side of the island, a great white sailing ship could dimly be seen.

Roderick mounted upon the harbour wall.

'My friends—no, my people—for now I may (I hope) after all we have suffered together, venture to call you my people,' he began, swaying a little in the light breeze which, Dick perceived, caused the twilight conditions to fluctuate as though veils were drawn across the sea. 'There is no need to fear the future. I have had assurances that the place you are going to will be as much like this as possible. You will not be separated from one another; indeed, you may find some of your kith and kin, whom you believed lost, at your destination already. A delightful life is promised you. I see flashing signals from your ship; time is short, you must embark immediately. So it only remains for me to say *Beannachd Leibh*, God go with you!' His voice broke, there was a feeble burst of cheering. The ladies of Achnabasalt burst into tears, as, like sheep, the people were ushered into the boats they had built themselves, and to the wail of the pipes were rowed with uncanny rapidity across the oily sea.

The last sight was of Mr Murdo Macalpine, clothed decently once more, in the deepest mourning, standing at the prow of the foremost coble, his hands clasped in prayer.

'Well, that is that,' Roderick was assisted to descend. 'I cannot help having a feeling of foreboding. I hope those poor souls will have a happy outcome; I hope so indeed. They went like cattle to the slaughter; I feel a sense of responsibility.'

'Let us wait and see the ship leave, Roderick!'

'No, no! I don't wish to do so! I suppose you blame me for that?'

Nobody answered; for the incident had depressed them unaccountably. Indeed, it had changed the mood of the company from a happy anticipation to a dread of the unknown. The excitements of preparation, the delight they had experienced in using the miraculous new powers of their revitalised bodies, gave way to an itching melancholy nothing could dispel.

'We have behaved in a most trivial way,' Maggie Dolman sighed. 'It is bound to be held against us.'

She expressed the general fear.

22

'I HAVE not been good,' Roderick said. 'How could I alter now? It would be the sheerest hypocrisy.'

'There is no absolute standard of goodness!' Mrs Dolman reminded him.

'I know what goodness is; you do not have to tell me!' was the reply. 'So it will be Purgatory for me; it will be an eternal holiday camp; Mrs Mottie is right. Because I have despised the Great British Public, who worshipped me, my punishment will be to have them always with me. There will be mass entertainment, mass dining, mass living, for ever and ever. There will be canned music and canned voices, blaring platitudes from loudspeakers; there will be no more silence—I shall never be alone again!'

'I shall be alone,' Julia said. 'I see myself—I shall wander up and down an esplanade at a British seaside resort on a dull summer Sunday; there will not be a single soul in sight—the houses will have their blinds drawn down in permanent Sunday rest. I will sit in a rectangular shelter of ornamented ironwork, looking out upon a steel-grey sea. Nobody will see me. I shall search for friends, from end to end of Gothic piers, with leaning slot-machines; I shall knock on the doors of haunted boarding houses, and a curtain will flap in the wind, that is all. I will run after shadows on endless asphalt promenades.'

'I also will be alone,' Nigel whispered. 'In the midst of crowds. Gay people will pass, I will recognise friends, but I will be invisible to them, as I was to all of you. I shall call to them for help but they will not hear me; I shall touch their arms; my hand will melt into their flesh. I will cry "Love me! Love me!" But I have not loved, so they cannot respond.'

'—Like Torquay,' Mrs Mottie, without having heard these

conversations, continued one of her own. 'I like a nice band. The sandy beach is nice for children; I never did care for Brighton— too many stones. Of course, I wouldn't like to stay there, not permanent. A 'oliday, a fortnight or so, then back to dear old London.'

'In *Heaven*?' Dick asked, a little surprised.

'There are replicas of cities,' Mrs Dolman recited, fanning herself with an Egyptian fan of coloured straw, on a long handle. 'Budapest, Rio, Warsaw, Paris—London, if you wish. They satisfy a need, until the soul outgrows them.'

'Have you no curiosity to know where you will be sent?' Roderick asked her sternly.

'I have been a great traveller,' Maggie Dolman replied. 'I can settle almost anywhere, and be content. My heaven is within.'

Dick and Mr Beek found themselves overwhelmed, at this time, with their labour of consolation and encouragement. Their difference imposed it; this difference, at long last, was accepted by the others; it was paramount.

They were referred to as though they were not present.

'It is quite true that they cannot fly.'

'They still need to eat, and sleep! It's true, I tell you!'

'I tried to force Dick through the dining-room door. He could not do it. I hurt him.'

' 'Is legs is solid—'e weighs 'eavy.'

'They feel the cold—they are always lighting fires!'

'They complain of the dark, even in sunlight!'

These and a hundred other comments pursued them, as the true situation took shape in the minds of those who prepared for their journey. As each new fragment of information was digested, the whole appeared more unpalatable; it was not possible, any longer, however, to reject or ignore the truth that they were dead.

By evening, nobody spoke, but sat in silence in the great drawing-room, until the weight of their combined depression caused Dick to cry out: 'This is ridiculous! I can't stand it any longer! You are going to a delightful place, so I understand. Why *you* should be depressed, I can't think! You cannot stay here! Everything is falling into decay around you; in a matter of days, the world, as you know it, will be gone completely!'

'I was fond of this world,' Roderick said. 'After all, I was born in it. Although I have enjoyed travel, I always liked to come *home* at the end of a trip. Home to London, or here to Scotland, it did not matter. To know that one will never come home any more, that there is no chance of doing so ever again, is unbearable to me. That may surprise you.'

'Don't think of it as the end!' Dick begged. 'When everything has been cleaned up, and made anew, I don't doubt that they will send for you. They will need men like you; people who are capable of broadcasting a new, a confident image! Oh yes, I am quite certain that——'

'I do not wish to return to a sterilised desert!' shouted Mr Fernay. 'I could have nothing to do with a virgin territory, unwritten on with the etching of man's blood, tears and triumph! No, no—if this world, as I know it, is to be utterly destroyed, if all its wonderful history is to be wiped out, it is the end for me! I want nothing to do with it again, ever!'

The next morning everyone appeared in a similitude of the costume in which they had arrived at Achnabasalt.

Julia was once more pensive in blue; Mrs Dolman regal in lovat tweed, and Roderick in a dove-grey worsted. As though these constumes were an extension of their mood, they had become again (as well as they could remember) the persons they had been on that distant July day.

Upon this nostalgic appearance they had laid (a buttonhole— an embellishment?) a gentle film of resignation towards events to come.

Roderick began to follow Dick from place to place, like a large, worrying dog, growling for attention. He began several complaints with the words: 'As you are so soon to be rid of me——' and was dissatisfied with any reply.

Dick was glad when Mr Beek waylaid him, and begged him to come down to the camp.

'If it were not for Odysseus' influence, I don't know what I should do,' the clergyman confided, as they scrambled over the rocks towards Rona Bay. 'The young people will listen to him, when they will pay no attention to me at all. I have tried, but they tell me to get lost.'

'What is the matter, then?'

'They refuse to go!'

'But they must! There is no alternative!'

'That is what we have been telling them. I am hoping to hear Odysseus has been successful at last!'

'Is he going with them?'

'I believe so.'

'Mrs Mottie will miss him.'

They were approaching the tents. The noise of guitars was silent in the sullen morning.

'Odysseus still feels himself to be a murderer and an outcast,' Mr Beek told Dick. 'He feels responsible for the change in these young people. He says he has betrayed his education and his friends.'

'Hush! Here he comes!' Dick warned the priest. 'How tall he is grown!'

'It is the effect of the fog, which makes him seem taller.'

'No, I don't think so. You yourself are taller; you hold your head higher. I have shrunken,' Dick announced, as the Jamaican approached, wrapped in his striped robe.

'I have explained once more to them that they must go,' Odysseus said at once. 'But they are determined to remain here. They just say to me, Man, we don't want to move; this is like Peaceville. I say to them oh yeah, brothers, but you can't stay here; a big hurricane is coming—— But they just look at me and say this we got to see.'

'What are they doing now? They are very quiet!'

'Perhaps they are discussing it amongst themselves?' Mr Beek suggested.

'No, they're doing no talking, Mr Beek. They haven't got out of bed yet. For them, there's nothing to discuss. They just wait, that is all there is to it.'

'I will make one last effort to speak to them!'

'Pardon me, Mr Beek, sir, but they would not listen. They don't trust any of you, but they accept me. And I've tried all the ways I know to get them to co-operate.'

'If only I could find Mr MacArtney; he would know what to do!' Dick exclaimed.

Mr Beek stood apart, his head bowed, his hands clasped.

Dick looked about him uneasily; the silence from the tents was hostile. He heard Roderick shouting his name from the rocky path, and knew that Mr Fernay had followed him, disliking him to be out of sight for even a quarter of an hour.

He turned to meet his employer.

'Oh there you are! What on earth have you been playing at! I have been searching the place for you! You've no business to run off like that, without letting me know where you were going! I have papers to clear up; I need you more particularly now that you are soon to leave me.'

'It is not my choice. You are leaving me!'

'Never mind that! Where is Mr Beek?'

'He is saying his prayers, he——'

'There's no need to wait for him, then! Come *on*!'

For a few minutes, Roderick glided ahead, until he remembered the secretary puffing behind him. He waited with as much patience as he could muster.

'What was Mr Beek praying about?' he asked, and when Dick had told him, remarked: 'I wonder why really good people often appear weak and ineffectual? It is the *weakness* of the idea of the Christian Jesus which makes an appeal to people, not His Strength; how strange that is. You and Brother Beeky seem to me sometimes to be the most ineffectual and negative of characters; yet you have been chosen to remain and colonise a New Earth. It is extraordinary, to say the least of it. Can it be that God's strength lies in His weakness? It is a contradiction in terms. If the New World is to be populated by Dicks and Beekys, then I thank whatever Powers there Be that I shall soon be out of it—— I cannot imagine a duller place.'

Dick was unable to retort, as Roderick, forgetting as usual, had risen into the air and flown ahead of him over the dyke, above the fir coppice and into the hall at Achnabasalt, which now presented a tattered and forlorn appearance. A stag's head, ripped from the wall, was lying upon the hearth; since breakfast time, part of the staircase had collapsed, and the ceiling had fallen down, revealing a ragged lake of sky; for the roof also was collapsing, hourly.

Roderick did not remark upon the recent damage; he had become accustomed to an increasing ruin about him.

'I shall not go down and bid good-bye to the bicyclists,' he told Dick. 'They dislike me, and I have nothing to say to them. They have made trouble from the beginning.'

'Oh, but Mr Fernay, dear; you will say Good Luck to Odysseus, now won't you?' Mrs Mottie had come in from the kitchen, wearing, like a crown, the hat with the green daisies. ''E'd be ever so disappointed if you weren't there to see 'im off!'

'I did not realise he had decided to go with them.'

'Oh yes! 'E told me last night. "I feel I 'ave a duty towards them campers," 'e said to me. "If you feel like that, Odysseus," I told 'im, "then God will bless you. You don't want to worry about little Neeri," I said. "'E's coming with us, and 'is old Aunty Mottie'll look after 'im till you come 'ome."'

'How splendid of Odysseus!' cried Julia, floating down the broken banisters. 'He is truly unselfish; he puts us to shame!'

'I shall be sorry to lose poor Odysseus, mind you. 'E 'as sinned, but 'e 'as suffered for it.'

'You can tell him so, if you hurry. Here comes Mr Beek, with news.' Mrs Dolman came forward to greet Brother James. 'I hope you have made those foolish children see sense. In all probability they will be fetched this afternoon.'

'We have failed,' Mr Beek confessed. 'Odysseus and I have used every argument.'

'Then it is up to the authorities, it is no longer our responsibility,' Roderick said. 'They must stay and be blasted.'

'They cannot be blasted; they are dead.'

'Then why worry?'

'Dick should contact Those in Authority,' Mrs Dolman said. She sat, a neat wickerwork luncheon basket on her lap, like a rich lady in an airport lounge, waiting for deliverance.

'I am sorry, but I don't know where Authority is,' Dick said.

'Then you should know! You should have made arrangements as to a means to contact them in an emergency; that never occurred to you?'

'It occurred to me, but I was never given a chance to——'

'Then it will be your fault if these obstinate, ignorant young people are assigned to limbo,' Roderick asserted. 'I suppose you realise this. I have no love for them, but I can't allow it to happen. Some of us must fly over to Ebora and try to contact your Mr MacArtney.'

'It is no fault of Mr Bolton's,' came Odysseus' rich sonorous voice from the doorway. 'The failure is mine.'

'I have prayed,' Mr Beek reminded them.

Nobody paid attention to this contribution, which could, they felt, have little practical value.

'The Authorities may have means of knowing what is happening, and ways of dealing with it without our interference,' Dick suggested, but Roderick's voice rose above his remark, blotting it out.

'There is nothing for it but to go down and speak to them myself. I have no wish to go; but I would have it on my conscience if I stayed away. Dick, will you forgive me, and accompany me? You were not to blame—I see that now.'

'I will come if Odysseus comes too,' Dick agreed.

'We will all come,' Mrs Dolman said, putting on her cloak.

There was a noise of thunder, as yet another wall of the house gave way, but the procession pressed bravely forward without a glance behind, down the rocky steps and over the sands. They would have flown; yet they suited their pace to the feeble earthly steps of Dick and Mr Beek.

'It is strange—I don't hear any music!' Roderick remarked, as they paused for the clergyman to regain his breath.

'No singing either!'

Odysseus approached the white bells of the tents. He put his rounded hands to his mouth shouting, 'Jock! Al-lan!' Not an answering echo was heard. 'Frank-ie! Chris-sie!' Names with no faces, no personalities to round them, unknown, friendless names floated upon the air. 'Ree-nie! Sandra! Hee-igh! All of you!'

Not a movement, not a sound. They ran towards the flower-like tents, toppling and blowzy already; they looked within. Here lay a pile of records, there a red woollen sock.

From tent to tent Odysseus ran.

Then he led them down to the water's edge.

'Hey! Campers! He-ey!' his call went over the sightless sea.

Far off, from the direction of the island, they heard the plucking of the guitars; from Ebora came flashing signals.

> *'We will overcome,*
> *We will overcome—some day.*
> *O deep in my heart—I believe*
> *We will overcome some day.'*

The voices ebbed, were amplified; they were distorted by distance; all at once they seemed loud, near and cheerful, a stone's throw away from shore.

'I must go,' Odysseus told them. 'It is a clear call.'

They said farewell to him.

'Wait for me!' his hail went over the sea. 'Don't leave without me!'

He skimmed the waves; one moment his striped cloak, like the wings of a tropical bird, shadowed the sea's surface; next he was lost to them.

'They must have sent a powerful group to Ebora since this morning,' Dick remarked. 'Only that could have moved them.'

'They're off! See the green and orange flashing lights! Hear the humming of the great ship, as it rises!'

The knot of people on the shore waited until nothing was to be seen any longer, then, reluctantly, turned towards the house.

23

PERHAPS it was the magnetic storms caused by the power-ful space craft, as it passed overhead with its burden of so much vital youth (even if on a higher vibration?), which was the direct cause of the end of Achnabasalt House.

The rush of wind caused the stunted trees to bend over; it felled Mr Beek to the ground; a hum, like a million bees filled, the ears of the watchers. This sound was followed almost im-mediately by a dull '*Th-lump, th-lump*', a double echo such as accompanied the landing of a rocket, in far off nineteen-forty-five, in London.

When they mounted at last to the cliff top, even in the dark-ness they perceived the heap of ruins.

'Well, it was not an old house; it had no historic associations,' Julia consoled Roderick. 'I did not think it had a friendly atmo-sphere, even. It never made us welcome.'

'You were glad of its shelter,' Mr Fernay reminded her. 'It was my home. It was full of childhood memories; now I have nothing left.'

'With its fall has gone the last memento of our past selves,' Maggie Dolman said. 'That is symbolic; all that we were is now destroyed. We have no past to cling to; therefore we must face the future with more courage.'

As she spoke, she walked away from them to examine the remains.

'That's all very well,' Dick said, 'but where are we to sleep tonight?'

'Why spend it anywhere but here in the garden?' asked Roderick. 'Our last night on earth—why waste it in sleeping? I am full of anticipation and excitement. You do not look pleased, Dick!'

'I am very tired, strange as it may seem to you, and so is Beeky. We find it cold out here.'

'I am sorry. We must search for some place for you to sleep, then.' Roderick was disappointed.

'Oh, don't bother. I shall find somewhere; perhaps the summer house—it is still standing.'

'I cannot understand why you should wish to sleep on our last night here,' Mr Fernay went on. 'We shall be gone tomorrow; it may be some time before you can join us.'

'For the last time, Roderick—*I shall never be permitted to join you!*'

'Oh, fiddle!' his employer remarked. 'We will find some way. Yet on my last night here, your only thought is how to get some *sleep!*'

'Oh very well—I will stay awake!'

'No, no—you must sleep if you need to; I shall not prevent it.' It was at this moment that Dick became conscious of the change in his friend; he cried out before he could stop himself: 'I can see through you! Oh, Roderick, you are transparent!'

'O Bottom, thou art translated!' Nigel echoed him.

Dick trembled; he could hardly stand, so frightened had he become. 'Nigel, let me see you,' he begged. 'Do not play hide and seek with me, I beg you! I could not stand it!'

'What is the matter, Little Owl?' Julia enquired. 'Why are you crying?'

'I can't see you!' was the anguished reply. 'I see shadows only, wisps like mist before my eyes. Even your voices come and go!'

'I have found your family Bible amongst the ruins,' came Mrs Dolman's calm announcement. 'Look!'

'So Holy Writ is indestructible,' Nigel said.

'If we look within it, we may find guidance for the new life we are entering upon,' was her next pronouncement.

Dick strained his eyes; the voice came from above his head; for an instant he saw her, comfortably settled in the fork of a lone Caledonian pine tree, which fringed the lawn, and survived in a blighted condition.

'I have always wanted to sit up here,' her voice floated down to them. 'One has a magnificent view.'

'Oh give up all this nonsense do!' Roderick told her, in the greatest irritation. 'Why can't you come down and behave like a human being!'

'I am not certain any more of being human,' Mrs Dolman replied. 'I will be your watchman. At the first sign of activity on the island, I will give warning.'

Roderick ignored her, and the next Dick heard was: 'I wish you would tickle my feet, Julia; you do it better than anyone I know! ——Why are you wandering about in that restless fashion, Dick! If you are too cold to sit down, you must find some wood and light a fire.'

'I can no longer see you!' cried the unfortunate secretary. 'You are gone already—I hear your voice by fits and starts! How can I settle, knowing you are all to leave me?'

'Oh go to sleep do; perhaps you'll feel better when you wake —you are no use as you are!' Mr Fernay told him. 'Aah! Aarh! That touched the spot, Julia—— Do it again! Eeeh! No, no, not any more! That was exquisite torture! How odd that I can still enjoy being tickled, though other sensations have disappeared for good, more's the pity!'

'How can I sleep?'

Dick's question passed unnoticed.

'Shall I read to you all?' came Mrs Dolman's voice from the tree.

'How can you see to read?' asked Mr Beek.

'How? The pages seem quite plain to me. I do not even need my spectacles!'

'Nobody is to read!' Roderick pronounced. 'If Odysseus had still been with us, he could have sung one of his C.N.D. spirituals about the brotherhood of man; that would have been appropriate, and soothing.'

In spite of what he had said, sleep was overcoming Dick. He sat down, his back to the tree-trunk, peering up through the branches to where the actress perched, like a great bird. Beside him, in the darkness, he could just make out Julia's white hand, poised above Roderick's foot, holding a long brown feather.

'. . . *it is written, I will destroy the wisdom of the wise and bring to nothing the understanding of the present.*'

'Julia . . . pretty singing voice—sing, Julia!'

'I would rather listen.'

'. . . *Because the foolishness of God is wiser than man, and the weakness of God is stronger than man.*'

'Say that again!' Roderick ordered.

'I wonder, Mrs Dolman, that you would quote the Apostle Paul,' Nigel said. 'His attitude to women was retrogressive. He would not allow them to hear the Word of God with their heads uncovered, you know; they were mere chattels to him.'

'I never did 'old with Paul,' came from Mrs Mottie.

'The weakness of God is a contradiction in terms,' Dick quoted, in his sleep, but the voices went on with their discussion, and did without his unspoken contribution.

'. . . such a time blasting at the sin of fornication . . . wasn't it Paul who said it was a sin for a man to touch a woman? . . .' (That, surely, was Julia's voice) 'A nasty old man, that's what *I* say . . . don't let's waste time on 'im.'

For a few minutes Dick floated away in dream; he heard, without taking in the sense of what was said, but was shot into wakefulness by a phrase:

'I have to search for my silver coin, even amongst the rubble!' spoken like a clarion call by Maggie Dolman.

Mr Beek was expostulating; his murmuring tones were a *basso continuo* barely distinguishable in the general vehemence.

'. . . the gifts of the spirit, you know—the interdependence of each member with the other, and to the whole—I think it very valuable.'

'. . . two different writers, different altogether.' Now Mrs Dolman sounded far away; perhaps she had flown to the topmost tuft of the pine, and swayed there. 'Obviously, Paul borrowed whole passages from Christ's own sayings—— After all he never knew Jesus on earth. He distorted them, gave them his own Jewish, Pharisaical angle——'

'Pure Spirit? I don't think so!'

Dick opened his weighted eyes for a moment; a drugged inertia pressed him down.

'*How are the dead raised up? And with what body do they come?*'

Mrs Dolman must have descended into the garden; they were reading, it seemed, over one another's shoulders, with great urgency of purpose.

'Let *me* see!' came from Roderick; then he announced: '*There are celestial bodies, and bodies terrestial.*'

Try as he would, Dick could not open his eyes again.

'*There's a natural body, and a spiritual body,*' Julia read next.

'*The first man is of the earth earthy.*' It was Mrs Mottie, and they burst out laughing. 'Go on,' she told them amiably. 'I don't see nothink to laugh at!'

'*Behold, I show you a mystery. We shall not all sleep, but we shall all be changed——*'

'*. . . In a moment, in the twinkling of an eye . . .*'

Dick could no longer distinguish one voice from another; yet as he was sucked over the weir of sleep, someone proclaimed loudly and heartily: '*O death where is thy sting, O grave thy victory!*'

Mr Beek was the first to awake in the unpleasant yellow light of dawn; Dick still slept in the lee of the leaning summer house. The clergyman did not disturb him from his death-like pose, but went to collect some crumbling laths, and other timber from the ruins, and kindled a fire. When it was lit he boiled water, and made some weak coffee, with yesterday's grounds, and with the last of the oatmeal cooked a thin gruel.

A few flickering flashes of lightning and tumbles of thunder disturbed him at his task.

He looked up, to find himself watched by the boy Nyeri, who, together with a small girl, stood at a little distance in silence.

'Where did you spring from?' he asked. 'Who brought you here?'

To this question neither child vouchsafed an answer; the girl took what appeared to be an apple from her tunic pocket (both children wore the uniform protective garments), and having rubbed it on her sleeve, set her teeth in it. He thought she had a slavish or Chinese appearance.

'Where are the others?' Mr Beek asked the boy. 'Mr Fernay, and the ladies? Have you seen them?'

'They've gone,' was the nonchalant answer.

'Where? Down to the shore?'

'No. The boat that brought us, took them to the island; then they went away in a big air-ship, just before day.'

'Oh no! Without a good-bye! What will poor Dick do?' Mr Beek exclaimed. 'They should have woken us! He will never get over it!'

'They tried to wake you,' Nyeri said. 'Mr Fernay shook you and shook you; then he said: "It's no use, we can't wait any longer!"'

A more vivid flash of lightning flapped overhead. Mr Beek stooped to pick up the Bible, revealed in its glare. It had suffered since being thrown down in the haste of departure; like an injured bird with a broken back, it lay spread-eagled on the path.

'They could not have gone without a word!' was Dick's constant iteration when he awoke at last.

He stood in the stream of rain which fell unmercifully out of the tattered sky.

'I beg you to hurry! You remember the warning!'

The dinghy, which Mr MacArtney had so thoughtfully provided for them, was waiting; already the wind was rising, the waters, with their white horses tossing.

'How can I go? They may be hiding somewhere from the storm! They may have left a message for me, under some stone—I must search for it! Go without me!'

'I saw Mr Fernay shake you!' the shrill voice of the boy asserted. 'But you went on snoring; you did not budge!'

He and the girl stepped aboard the dinghy. 'We can't wait for you,' the boy said. 'Here's a rubber boat you blow up; we'll leave you that!'

He started the propeller, and the blue boat departed, while Dick still ran about the shore.

'Come back!' cried Mr Beek, but his words were blown away; they were drowned by an unwonted cannonade of thunder. Dick proved to be of no help whatsoever in inflating the frail craft; only with the greatest difficulty was he persuaded to embark. A squall of wind drove it immediately upon the crest of a giant wave, which threatened to dash them back upon the shore. Not the strength, but the prayer, of Mr Beek retrieved it; miraculously they survived, and were set once more upon their course.

'Let me drown!' cried the unfortunate secretary.

'Dick, you must help me with all your strength! Another buffet like the last, and we shall not survive!'

'Let us perish! What is the use of going on!'

'We—are not meant to—die!' gasped Mr Beek, straining at the paddles. 'I—am on the—point—of collapse!'

The boat, so ineffectually manned, began to turn about like a top in the trough of the waters.

'I can do no more! May the Lord help us in our extremity!' The old man fell across his oars.

The response to his prayer was immediate; a current took the craft in its grip; they were swept with the utmost velocity towards the shore of the island, and thrown upon the gritty shelf of a cove.

Mr Beek fell upon the sharp shingle, to thank his Maker, while Dick lay prone, and allowed the waves to sting and slap him into senselessness, and the wind, like a beast unleashed, to begin to drag him back into the ocean.

However, help was near, for they were not, evidently, alone on Ebora. A party had arrived in advance from the mainland, and two watchers had seen their arrival from the cliff top, and ran down to assist them to the deep shelters.

Miss Ethel Minim and jolly Sister Margaret seemed to be in charge of the arrangements, and a change of clothing was given to the voyagers. The nun had to be called to quieten Dick Bolton, who laid hold of Nyeri and questioned him ceaselessly.

'Did Mr Fernay leave no message with you for me?'

'No, he didn't, I tell you!'

'Then I know you are lying!'

'He didn't see me!'

'Why didn't they see you? You were hiding? Why were you hiding, wretched boy! Answer me!'

'I was afraid,' the boy sobbed. 'The great voice from the island, which called to them, frightened me. I thought it was God.'

'Now, now, Mr Bolton, you are upsetting the boy,' the Sister told him, in her comfortable voice. 'You must leave him be; everything will be explained in God's good time. You must not distress yourself.'

As if he accepted her word as the final dictum of Mother Church, Dick Bolton became suddenly as silent as a stone. His large eyes looked from one to another of the company, like those of an orphan child. He watched the ritual by which all was made secure; when his turn came, with an infant's obedience, he took his triple dose of elixir, and climbed into his sleeping bag. The members of the various denominations now said their offices each to a different aspect of the Eternal, and Mr Beek was particular to lay his hands in blessing on Dick.

Even as the lamps were extinguished, and the score or more of survivors lay in a blue and drowsy darkness, they could hear above them the fury of the Celestial Cleaners, rising to attack upon a crumbling world.

EPILOGUE

THE shelter was filled with light.

As patients, awakening after an anaesthetic, the survivors were not at first certain where they were. One by one they sat up, shielding their eyes from the brilliance.

Mr MacArtney had arrived, as promised, with two strange young men as helpers. These were talking quietly, but cheerfully, to the recumbent figures on the bunks, encouraging them to rise and stretch themselves.

They were given cooling and astringent drinks to moisten their parched mouths, and so, as in hospital, leaning on friendly arms, tottered their first steps up into the open air.

Dick met Mr Beek at the foot of the steep ladder which led to the upper world.

Murmuring in subdued excitement, the few who were left came to the surface to see the new earth they had inherited.

The sun shone brightly; there was a light breeze; no cloud stained the sky. They breathed deeply of the unpolluted air. The sea was a clear blue; small, regulated waves broke tidily upon an undamaged shore. The island, on which they stood, had been smoothed, as though by the giant hand of an order-loving God. New grass, of a tender, piercing green, grew already upon its rounded contours; strange sheep with curling horns and golden fleece browsed upon it. In the crevices of polished rocks, which appeared as ornaments, violets, as large as pansies, opened their flowers with an aspiring fragrance.

As their view extended itself, as they ventured to look up, and further afield, flocks of birds could be seen, making for land; single gulls, appointed each to an outcrop, gave out a musical, un-gull-like call.

On the shore of the mainland the same green undulations

were repeated, leading upwards to a building with pillars, not unlike a Grecian Temple. The shape of the land was unfamiliar to them; no one could say with certainty where the village had stood, the Hydro, or the house of Achnabasalt.

'I think we have managed to make a tolerably good job of it in the short time available,' Mr MacArtney decided. 'Of course, the design isn't final; one or two alterations will have to be made; we are open to suggestion. What do you think of it, eh?'

'It will seem strange to you at first to have everything so ideal and perfect,' one of the helpers remarked. 'It will take time to accustom yourselves to the change.'

'Is all the world like this?' Ethel Minim asked.

'No, not necessarily so at all. We kept to the idea of Britain as a garden. The Garden of the Hesperides, you know. Anciently it is what Britain was; now it must be so once more. The old land which sank at the time of the deluge, has risen again from the sea; the kingdom of Lyonesse has reappeared between Land's End and the Scillies; a delightful spot. Of course, other parts of the country have sunk. A great deal of South-East England was too badly contaminated by civilisation, even before the bombs fell, to be worth preserving.'

'Do you mean that London is drowned?'

'I am afraid so, and Paris too.' MacArtney told them, with regret, and, before there could be recriminations: 'We have tried to provide you with an equable climate here, not unlike that of the Mediterranean, but without its disadvantages. It should be most pleasant. You can grow oranges, grape-fruit, and so on, and of course vines and olives.'

'It is not Scotland,' declared a young man, who had been a Nationalist. 'Where are our moors of heather, our rugged mountains and rushing rivers? Where are our people, strengthened and nourished on the strong and vital climate of ours with its winds, snow and frost?'

'To tell you the truth, we have had to do away with Nationalism,' Mr MacArtney replied. 'It had such dangerous potentialities. And that must be said also for the racial and geographical peculiarities which produced it. We must strive for a feeling of Brotherhood between men of all races (keeping of course our own individualities) and I am sure you will all agree this is highly desirable in the interests of progress.'

'What then do you expect of us?'

'Nothing at first, but to become accustomed to your new surroundings. Then, in a little while, it will be necessary for you all to undergo instruction in order to be able to colonise this New World, and to be able to teach the new souls who will be born here. That building on the hill is one of our schools, and from there you will be taken and shown as much of the world as possible.'

'Is it a large school? Will many people attend it?'

'About two hundred perhaps. We have quite a few of these centres, scattered over the earth, to accommodate the one hundred and forty-four thousand survivors, of which your Bible has told you. One of the more famous, where the advanced students will attend, is in Tibet. There are two on the restored Pacific Island of Mu, and one in Atlantis.'

'So Atlantis has arisen once more?'

'In a reformed, cleansed condition, I assure you.'

Mr Beek was anxious. 'What kind of people will be attending our school?'

'Oh, very pleasant people, wouldn't you say so, Smith?' MacArtney appealed to his helper.

'Yes indeed. One of the Instructors is an Ammonite; there are two or three Hopi Indians: they have always led a Christian life, in the truest sense. We have a few from the orthodox religious orders of the old world, of course, but not many.'

'What about politicians?'

'The only political leaders of your world who would have qualified to govern here have, alas, either been assassinated or died of a broken heart.'

'What have we to learn?'

'It is a natural question, but one which would take too long to answer here and now. The course will appeal to you all; it includes all you need to fit you for your life here.'

These words, while they appeared to inspire and satisfy most of the Remnant, had a depressing effect upon Dick Bolton, inciting him to a last, desperate appeal.

'If on the completion of the course anyone were to feel that he no longer wished to remain, or take up his duties here in the New World, would he be allowed to go?' he asked.

His temerity astonished the others, sitting upon the jewelled lawns; and his words fell into a silence which seemed to last for several minutes.

'It's no use blinking the fact that a mistake has been made in my case,' Dick continued bravely. 'Last time I spoke to you, you told me it was impossible for the records to be wrong; yet in my inmost being *I know that I should not be here!*'

He received no present answer, but was made bolder by observing that MacArtney, while grave, was still giving him his closest attention.

'I should be utterly miserable helping to colonise this antiseptic paradise!' Dick cried. 'I would not have the slightest interest in doing so, oranges or no oranges! I am sorry, but I must speak! I loved this place as it was before, with all its shortcomings! And as far as going to school is concerned, I don't want to learn anything from Ammonites, Mennonites, or any other ites; nor Hopi Indians, nor any of the really good, kind, noble people there! They would soon find me out! I am not in the least meek or humble. I am a rebel, and my heart is far from this wonderful new world of yours!'

The echo of this speech rebounded amongst the sculptured rocks, and sent the harmonious birds into the air; it caused waves to rise in the calm sea, and dismay in the bosoms of the faithful.

Mr MacArtney rose, and descended to his private room.

'Dick, my dear boy—I had no idea you felt as strongly as this!' Mr Beek exclaimed. 'Won't you reconsider your opinion? You may feel very differently in a little, when you have had a day or two to get accustomed to the change. It is so beautiful here, like a dream of Paradise, and everyone is so kind!'

'It is completely empty. I shall not change!' was the inexorable reply.

'I have been in touch with the Director of this Region,' Mr MacArtney told Dick. 'It is most unusual—quite unparalleled, in fact, but he is prepared to reconsider your case. It appears that someone has gone over our heads, and petitioned the Mercy Seat, so it is beyond our jurisdiction. Orders have come through that you are to be released very soon.'

'To rejoin my friends?'

'If that is what you wish. You realise what it means?'

Dick skipped in the air. He clasped MacArtney's hand in both of his. 'Even if I have to die——' he began.

'Of course you will have to die! And, because you have refused this honour, you will have to return to earth again—how very tiresome you human beings can be! However, you have free will; you have decided.'

In a few days Dick had departed; Mr Beek mourned for him as he went about his new tasks.

'The only consolation I have, is that my poor friend will be so happy with the others,' he sighed.

'I should not be too sure of that,' Mr MacArtney replied. 'God is not mocked. Although Mrs Dolman is doing useful work, our friend has found himself in just such a situation as made him unhappy before on earth; his companions are not angels. At this moment they are seated in a replica of the drawing-room at the old house of Achnabasalt, arguing and trying on new finery; Dick has been reproached for forgetfulness, and Julia is making love to the doctor, whose Sylvia has rejected him once more. They are free to remain turning in this squirrel's cage as long as they like.'

'Yet if they choose to leave it?' Mr Beek besought Mr Mac-Artney.

'We will gladly help them to break away,' was the cheerful reply, as they walked towards the blue boat.

Speedily the rotor turned; they stepped on board; the light craft rose and skimmed the waves. So clear was the water that, looking down, Mr Beek saw a thousand coralline fish darting from their wake. Birds accompanied them, without fear, circling overhead, and a group of laughing children ran into the warm waves, and swam to greet them.